So few books rattle me to the core yet lift my hopes to the heavens in the same breath. Tosca ~~~~~~~~~~~~~~~~~~~ ind that must be read.

—**Ted Dekker**, *New Y~~~~~*
The Bride Collector and ~~~~~~~~~

Imaginative, compelling, deep, memorable. If you want a novel that has you compulsively turning pages and makes you think at the same time, you'll love *Demon: A Memoir*.

—**James Scott Bell**, best-selling author of *Deceived* and *Try Fear*

Wise, imaginative, funny, and poetic, this is a book that lingers in memory after you've turned the last page.

—**Sophy Burnham**, *New York Times* best-selling author of *A Book of Angels*

Even readers who don't believe in the biblical elements of this tale will have a difficult time not being coaxed into this struggle of intellects.

—**Eric Wilson**, *New York Times* best-selling author of *Fireproof* and *Field of Blood*

The story—the writing—is mesmerizing . . . It has jumped high onto the list of my all-time favorite novels.

—**Frank Redman**, FictionAddict.com

Riveting, graceful and razor sharp.

—**Claudia Mair Burney**, Christy Award Finalist and author of *Wounded*

I will not read the Creation story or the story of Lucifer's fall again without picturing the scenes described in *Demon*.

    —Brandilyn Collins, author of the Kremer Lake Series

Demon: A Memoir isn't a mere work of fiction. *Demon* is an experience.

    —Tracey Bateman, Christy Award-winning author of *Thirsty*

Compulsively readable and subtly convicting, *Demon* will forever recast your understanding of redemption.

    —Nicole Baart, Christy Award Finalist and author of *The Moment Between*

This book is a masterpiece of fiction. It's hard to put down and impossible to forget.

    —Nancy Mehl, author of *Malevolence* and *Graven Images*

This is one of the most sensational, thought-provoking books I have ever read. It is a masterpiece and will sit alongside C. S. Lewis and other such luminaries from now on.

    —Kristine Smith, author of *Purposeful Christianity*

Lee's prose is powerful and beautiful. Her imagery of Eden, of Paradise and angels and Elohim filled me with awe.

    —Novel Reviews

An excellent novel that will hold your attention and stretch your perspective on life.

    —Jake Chism, Armchair Interviews

Lee is really proving to be a leader in the art of speculative fiction.

—Inside Corner Book Reviews

Demon took me totally by surprise. Tosca Lee has crafted a story that snatched my attention from the first and compelled me to turn the pages.

—Mike Parker, LifeWay

A magnificently entertaining story.

—Inspire Monthly

One of the most captivating books I've read.

—Sara Mills, author of *Miss Match*

Demon is supposed to be fiction . . . but is it? Tosca Lee has created a stunning work of pure genius.

—Wanda Winters-Gutierrez, author of *The Search for Peace*

Highly Recommended.

—ChristianFictionReviews.com

You will find many well-known Bible accounts unfolding vividly before your eyes in a way you never imagined.

—Virginia Smith, author of *Stuck in the Middle*

An intellectual and spiritual thriller that begs to be read.

—Crosswayz

A must-have that'll haunt the reader long after the last page
   —**Press & Sun-Bulletin**, Greater Binghamton, NY

This book simultaneously chills and awes.
   —**Eternity Happens**

A riveting look at one demon's reflection on his fall from grace, and the shuddering implications for each of us. This story is about YOU; it will change the way you look at life.
   —**Austin Boyd**, author of the Mars Hill Classified series

A powerful, discerning tale that will have fans pondering their own deals with the demons.
   —**Midwest Book Review**

Demon: A Memoir may well be the most creative, mind-twisting novel of this summer.
   —**Kevin Lucia**, author of *Hiram Grange* and *The Chosen One*

One of the best books I've read yet this year.
   —**Camy Tang**, author of *Sushi for One?*

I adore Tosca Lee's ingenious use of soul-deep first person point of view writing. This is one of those books I couldn't put down until I crossed the finish line—what a ride.
   —**Julie Garmon**, Guideposts

The Bible and urban fantasy combine to create an intelligent and thought provoking multilayered tale.
   —**Harriett Klausner**, Amazon.com #1 Reviewer

TOSCA LEE

DEMON

A MEMOIR

B&H
PUBLISHING GROUP
Nashville, Tennessee

ISBN: 978-1-4336-6880-7

Published by B&H Publishing Group
Nashville, Tennessee

Dewey Decimal Classification: F
Subject Heading: DEMONOLOGY—FICTION \
SPIRITUAL WARFARE—FICTION \
GRACE (THEOLOGY)—FICTION

Scripture quotations are from the Holy Bible, New
International Version, copyright © 1973, 1978, 1984 by
International Bible Society.

1 2 3 4 5 6 7 8 • 14 13 12 11 10

For Amy.

I

It was raining the night he found me. Traffic had slowed on Massachusetts Avenue, and the wan light of street lamps reflected off the pavement. I was hurrying on without an umbrella, distracted by the chirp of a text message on my phone, trying to shield its illuminated face from rain and the drizzle off storefront awnings. There had been a mistake in my schedule, an appointment I didn't recognize and I had stayed late at the office for—until six forty-five—just in case. Our office manager was texting me from home now to say she had no idea who it was with, that the appointment must have belonged on Phil's calendar, that she was sorry for the mistake, and to have a good night.

I flipped the phone shut, shoved it in my bag. I was worn out by this week already, and it was only Tuesday. The days were getting shorter, the sun setting by six o'clock. It put me on edge, gnawed at me, as though I had better get somewhere warm and cheerful or, barring all else, home before it got any darker. But I was unwilling to face the empty apartment, the dirty dishes, the unopened mail on the counter. So I lowered my head against the rain and walked another two blocks past my

turnoff until I came to the Bosnian Café. A strap of bells on the
door announced my entrance with a ringing slap.

I liked the worn appeal of the Bosnian Café with its olfac-
tory embrace of grilled chicken and gyro meat that enveloped
me upon every arrival and clung to me long after leaving. That
night, in the premature darkness and rain, the café seemed
especially homey with its yellowing countertops, chipped mirrors, and grimy ketchup bottles. Cardboard shamrocks, remnants of a forgotten Saint Patrick's Day, draped the pass-through
into the kitchen, faded around their die-cut edges. A string of
Christmas lights lined the front window, every third bulb out.
On the wall above the register, a framed photo of the café's
owner with a local pageant queen and another with a retired
Red Sox player had never been dusted. But no one, including
me, seemed to mind.

I stood in the entry waiting for Esad, the owner, to notice
me. But it was not the bald man who welcomed me.

It was the dark-haired stranger.

I was surveying the other tables, looking for inspiration—
chicken or steak, gyro or salad—when he beckoned. I hesitated.
Was I supposed to recognize him, this man sitting by himself?
But no, I did not know him. He waved again, impatient now,
and I glanced over my shoulder. There was no one standing in
the entryway but me. And then the man at the table stood up
and strode directly to me.

"You're late." He clasped my shoulder and smiled. He was
tall, tanned, with curling hair and a slightly hooked nose that
did nothing to detract from his enviable Mediterranean looks.
His eyes glittered beneath well-formed brows. His teeth were
very white.

"I'm sorry. I think you have the wrong person," I said.

He chuckled. "Not at all! I've been waiting for you for quite some time. An eternity, you might say. Please, come sit down. I took the liberty of ordering for you."

His voice reminded me of fine cognac, the Hors d'Age men drink aboard their yachts as they cut their Cohíbas.

"You have the wrong person. I don't know you," I insisted, even as he steered me toward the table. I didn't want to embarrass him; he already seemed elegantly out of place here in what, for all practical purposes, was a joint. But he would feel like an elegant fool in another minute, especially if his real appointment—interview, date, whatever—walked in and saw him sitting here with me.

"But I know *you*, Clay."

I started at the sound of my name, spoken by him with a mixture of familiarity and strange interest. I studied him more closely—the squareness of his jaw, the smoothness of his cheek, his utter self-possession. *Had* I met him before? No, I was certain I hadn't.

One of Esad's nephews arrived with a chicken sandwich and two cups of coffee.

"Please." The stranger motioned to a vinyl-covered chair. Numbly, stupidly, I sat.

"You work down the street at Brooks and Hanover," he said when the younger man had gone. He seated himself adjacent to me, his chair angled toward mine. He crossed his legs, plucked invisible lint off the fine wool of his trousers. "You're an editor."

Several thoughts went through my head in that moment, none of them savory: first, that this was some finance or insurance rep who—just like the pile of loan offers on my counter at home—was trying to capitalize on my recent divorce. Or, that this was some aggressive literary agent trying to play suave.

Most likely, though, he was a writer.

Every editor has stories to tell: zealous writers pushing manuscripts on them during their kid's softball game, passing sheaves of italicized print across pews at church or trying to pick them up in bars, casually mentioning between lubricated flirtations that they write stories on the side and just happen to have a manuscript in the car. I had lost count of the dry cleaners, dental hygienists, and plumbers who, upon hearing what I did for a living, had felt compelled to gift me with their short stories and children's books, their novels-in-progress and rhyming poetry.

"Look, whoever you are—"

"Lucian."

I meant to tell him that I was sure we didn't publish what-ever it was he wanted me to read, that there were industry-accepted ways to get his work to us if we did, that he could visit the Web site and check out the guidelines. I also meant to get up and walk away, to look for Esad or his nephew and put an order in. To go. But I didn't say or do any of these things because what he said next stopped me cold.

"I know you're searching, Clay. I know you're wondering what these late, dark nights are for. You have that seasonal disease, that modern ailment, don't you? SAD, they call it. But it isn't the disorder—you should know that. It isn't even your divorce. That's not what's bothering you. Not really."

I was no longer hungry. I pushed away the chicken sand-wich he had ordered and said with quiet warning. "I don't know who you are, but this isn't funny."

He went on as though he hadn't heard me, saying with what seemed great feeling, "It's that you don't know what it's all for. The hours and days, working on the weekends, the belief that you'll eventually get caught up, and on that ultimate day *something* will happen. That everything will make sense or you'll at least have time to figure it out. You're a good man, Clay, but what has that won you? You're alone, growing no younger, drifting toward some unknown but inevitable end in this life. And where is the meaning in that?"

I sat very still. I felt exposed, laid open, as though I had emptied my mind onto the table like the contents of a pocket. I couldn't meet his gaze. Nearby, a couple—both of their heads dripping dirty blond dreadlocks—mulled over menus as the woman dandled an infant on her lap. Beyond them, a thickset woman paged through *People*, and a young man in scrubs plodded in a sleep-deprived daze through an anemic salad. Had any of them noticed my uncanny situation, the strange hijacking taking place here? But they were mired in their menus, distractions, and stupor. At the back counter a student tapped at the keypad of his phone, sending messages into the ether.

"I realize how this feels, and I apologize." Lucian folded long fingers together on his knee. His nails were smooth and neatly manicured. He wore an expensive-looking watch, the second hand of which seemed to hesitate before hiccupping on, as though time had somehow slowed in the sallow light of the diner. "I could have done this differently, but I don't think I would have had your attention."

"What are you, some kind of Jehovah's Witness?" It was the only thing that made sense. His spiel could have hit close to anyone. I felt conned, angry, but most of all embarrassed by my emotional response.

His laughter was abrupt and, I thought, slightly manic.

"Oh my." He wiped the corners of his eyes.

I pushed back my chair.

His merriment died so suddenly that, were it not for the sound of it still echoing in my ears, I might have thought I had imagined it. "I'm going to tell you everything." He leaned toward me, so close I could see the tiny furrows around the corners of his mouth, the creases beneath his narrowed eyes. A strange glow emanated from the edge of his irises like the halo of a solar eclipse. "I'm going to tell you my story. I've great hope for you, in whom I will create the repository of my tale—my memoir, if you will. I believe it will be of great interest to you. And you're going to write it down and publish it."

Now I barked a stunted laugh. "No, I'm not. I don't care if you're J. D. Salinger."

Again he went on as though I'd said nothing. "I understand they're all the rage these days, memoirs. Publishing houses pay huge sums for the ghostwritten, self-revelatory accounts of celebrities all the time. But trust me; they've never acquired a story like mine."

"Look," I said, a new edge in my voice, "You're no celebrity I recognize, and I'm no ghostwriter. So I'm going to get myself some dinner and be nice enough to forget this ever happened." But as I started to rise, he grabbed me by the arm. His fingers, biting through the sleeve of my coat, were exceedingly strong, unnaturally warm, and far too intimate.

"But you *won't* forget." The strange light of fanaticism burned in his eyes. The curve of his mouth seemed divorced of their stare, as though it came from another face altogether. "You will recall everything—every word I say. Long after you have forgotten, in fact, the name of this café, the way I summoned you to this table, the first prick of your mortal curiosity about me. Long after you have forgotten, in fact, the most basic details of your life. You will remember, and you will curse or bless this day."

I felt ill. Something about the way he said *mortal*. . . . In that instant, reality, strung out like an elastic band, snapped.

This was no writer.

"Yes. You see," he said quietly. "You know. We can share now, between us, the secret of what I am."

And the words came, unbidden, to my mind: *Fallen. Dark Spirit.*

Demon.

The trembling that began in my stomach threatened to seize up my diaphragm. But then he released me and sat back. "Now. Here is Mr. Esad, wondering why you haven't touched your sandwich."

And indeed, here came the bald man, coffeepot in hand, smiling at the stranger as though he were more of a regular than I. I stared between them as they made their pleasantries, the sound of their banter at sick odds with what my visceral sense told me was true, what no one else seemed to notice: I was sitting here with something incomprehensively evil.

When Esad left, Lucian took a thin napkin from the dispenser and set it beside my coffee cup. The gesture struck me as aberrantly mundane.

He sighed. "I feel your trepidation, that sense that you ought to get up and leave immediately. And under normal circumstances I would say that you are right. But listen to me now when I tell you that you are safe. Be at ease. Here. I'll lean forward like this, in your human way. When that couple over there sees my little smile, this conspiratorial look, they'll think we're sharing a succulent bit of gossip."

I wasn't at ease. Not at all. My heart had become a pounding liability in my chest.

"Why?" I managed, wishing I were even now in the emptiness of my apartment, staring at the world through the bleak window of my TV.

Lucian leaned even closer, his hand splayed across the top of the table so that I could see the blue veins along the back of it. His voice dropped below a whisper, but I had no difficulty hearing him. "Because my story is very closely connected to yours. We're not so different after all, you and I. We both want purpose, meaning, to see the bigger picture. I can give you that."

"You don't even know me!"

"On the contrary"—he slid the napkin dispenser away, as though it were a barrier between us—"I know everything about you. Your childhood house on Ridgeview Drive. The tackle box you kept your football cards in. The night you tried to sneak out after homecoming to meet Carrie Kraus. You broke your wrist climbing out of the window."

I stared.

"I know of your father's passing—you were fifteen. About the merlot you miss since giving up drinking, the way you dip your hamburgers in blue cheese dressing—your friend Piotr taught you that in college. That you've been telling yourself you ought to get away somewhere—Mexico, perhaps. That you think it's the seasonal disorder bothering you, though it's not—"

"Stop!" I threw up my hands, wanting him to leave at once, equally afraid that he might and that I would be stuck knowing that there was this person—this *thing*—watching me. Knowing everything.

His voice gentled. "Let me assure you that you are not the only one. I could list myriad facts about anyone. Name someone. How about Sheila?" He smirked. "Let's just say she didn't return your message from home, and her husband thinks she's working

late. Esad? Living in war-torn Bosnia was no small feat. He—"
He cocked his head, and there came now a faint buzzing like an
invisible swarm of mosquitoes. I instinctively jerked away.

"What was that?" I demanded, unable to pinpoint where the
sound had come from.

"Ah. A concentration camp!" He looked surprised. "I didn't
know that. Did you know that? And as for your ex—" He tilted
his head again.

"No! Please, don't." I lowered my head into my hand, dug
my fingers into my scalp. Five months after the divorce, the
wound still split open at the mere mention of her.

"You see?" he whispered, his head ducked down so that he
stared intently up into my face. "I can tell you everything."

"I don't understand."

"I've made a pastime of studying case histories, of following them through from beginning to end. You fascinate me in
the same way that beetles with their uncanny instinct for dung
rolling used to fascinate you. I know more about you than your
family. Than your ex. Than you know about yourself, I dare-
say."

Something—some by-product of fear—rose up within me as
anger at last. "If you are what you say, aren't you here to make
some kind of deal for my soul? To tempt me? Why did you order
me coffee, then? Why not a glass of merlot or a Crown and Coke?"
My voice had risen, but I didn't care. I felt my anger with relief.

Lucian regarded me. "Please. How trite. Besides, they don't
serve liquor here." But then his calm fell away, and he was
staring—not at me but past me, toward the clock on the wall.
"But there"— he pointed, and his finger seemed exceedingly
long—"see how the hour advances without us!" He leapt to his
feet, and I realized he meant to leave.

"What? You can't just go now that you've—"

"I've come to you at great risk," he hissed, the sound sibilant, as if he had whispered in my ear though he stood three feet away. And then he strode to the glass door and pushed out into the darkness, disappearing beyond the reflected interior of the café like a shadow into a mirror. The strap of bells fell against the door with a flat metal clink, and my own stunned reflection stared back.

Rain pelted my eyes, slipped in wet tracks through my hair against my scalp, ran in rivulets down my nape to mingle with the sweat against my back. It had gotten colder, almost freezing, but I was sweating inside the sodden collar of my shirt as I hurried down Norfolk, my bag slapping against my thigh, my legs cramped and wooden, nightmare slow.

The abrupt warmth inside my apartment building threatened to suffocate me as I stumbled up the stairs. My ears pin-tingled to painful life as I fumbled with my keys. Inside my apartment at last, I fell back against the door, head throbbing and lungs heaving in the still air. I stayed like that, my coat dripping onto the carpet, for several long moments. Then a mad whim struck me.

With numb fingers I retrieved the laptop from my bag and set it up on the kitchen table. With my coat still on, I dropped down onto a wooden chair, staring at the screen as it yawned to life. I logged into the company server, opened my calendar.

There—my six-thirty appointment. It was simply noted: *L.*

For the next two days, I kept to my office and home. I stared at my monitor by day and at my ceiling at night in bed, trying to dissect how someone with enough research, a talent for suggestion, and a few lucky guesses might pretend to be a demon with seeming credibility to the point where I might actually believe I was in the presence of evil. And while I decided it was possible, the one thing I could not answer was why.

Of course my mind went first to Aubrey. But to think that she would direct so much energy my way—even out of cruelty—seemed pure vanity on my part. I had given her no cause for vendetta toward me, having stepped aside with near silence once her resolve to leave was clear.

I briefly considered Sheila, who was not only our office manager but the wife of my college roommate. I owed her much, I supposed; it was through her that I first met Aubrey. She had also been the one to alert me to the position at Brooks and Hanover when my predecessor left to join Random House. And she was the only one in the office with ready access to my calendar. But while our conversation had been stilted, if polite, since the divorce, such a scheme was so far beyond and beneath her that I rejected the idea immediately.

That left three options. The first was Richard, but I could think of no reason for him to take the trouble. He already had what he wanted. Still, he had the resources and access to a storehouse of information about my history via Aubrey.

The second was, again, that Lucian was a writer. And while I had heard stories of writers tracking editors like crazed fans stalking movie stars, I had to wonder why anyone would direct so much interest my way when editors for the Six Titans, as I called them, were a train ride away in New York City.

The third was that Lucian had targeted me for more mysterious reasons of his own. This was the most disturbing possibility of all.

On Thursday afternoon I put in a call to Esad to ask if he remembered the man I had been sitting with two nights past. "Yes!" He raised his voice over the sear of the grill in the background. I could practically smell cooking onions. "Very nice!"

"Do you know him?" I asked, feeling foolish.

"No, no, it's the first time to meet him. Bring him back! I'll make something special."

I had no intention of doing that. Further, I determined that if this Lucian pursued me again, I would go to the police.

NEW YORK LITERARY AGENT Katrina Dunn Lampe was a polished, vivacious woman who sapped my energy. But because she represented talented clients, I tried to meet her for lunch whenever she came to town. And so I was shifting time blocks in my schedule like square pieces in a puzzle box, trying to find that doable—preferably short— lunch slot during the two days she would be in town, when the appointment materialized in the corner of my screen.

6:00 p.m.: L.

Tonight.

I got up, hardly able to take my eyes off it, not trusting that it wouldn't disappear the minute I blinked. Forcing myself away, I strode out of my office and down the hallway. Sheila was missing from her desk. I sat down in her chair and tapped her keypad, bringing her screen to life. I closed an open e-mail, but not before catching the subject line: *"have to see you."* I noted it wasn't from her husband, Dan. Opening the group schedules, I found my own, scrolled through it.

It wasn't there.

I went back to my office and stared at my monitor.

L.

What did it mean? Did he just expect me to show up at Esad's again? Or did he plan to follow me when I left work? Was he waiting, watching for me even now?

I sat like a ghost through a last-minute titling meeting. Stared at the sandwich I had brought from home without eating it. Shifted manuscript pages on my desk without reading them. Watched the clock.

I distracted myself by thinking of Sheila's mysterious e-mail. A part of me wished I had noted the sender, a part of me wished I hadn't seen it at all. I couldn't help but remember Lucian's insinuation. I hoped for Dan's sake it wasn't true.

By five o'clock I was useless. I shut down my laptop, shoved it along with a stack of proposals into my bag, grabbed my coat, and left.

Outside on the street, I realized I had no idea where I was going. But one thing I did know: I was *not* going to Esad's.

Neither did I want to risk anyone following me home. For a moment I actually considered going to Carmichael's, a small restaurant with a decent wine list, once my favorite watering hole. I quickly discarded the idea—not for my three months on the wagon so much as the thought that my supposedly preternatural acquaintance might find it pathetic.

Which just made me mad.

If he was what he claimed to be, the last thing he should want was for me to stay sober. And the last thing I should want was to care what he thought. But here I was, a flustered wreck, having doubted my experience and second-guessed myself a thousand times since Tuesday.

I descended into Kendall Station. I normally hated the claustrophobic press of rush hour, but today there was something comforting about the electric lights, the subterranean warmth, the flow of bodies to and from the T.

On the train I did something I rarely do: I studied the faces around me. I took note of clothing, skin color, and watches but saw no one resembling the Mediterranean stranger. Packed in the Red Line car, I considered the distant dullness of the commuters' eyes, even of those playing games on their phones or jacked into iPods, of the book readers who had all but escaped their bodies for the ride.

How long had I been one of them?

I filed out and up onto Park Street, one in a milling flotsam of bodies. I often felt lost in this current, everyone around me having places to be and going there with a purposeful intent I envied.

But not tonight.

Tonight I meant to end these three days of anxiety—days during which I had somehow forgotten that I was a rational and intelligent person. I meant to remember that, despite how I had felt in the past, I was not at the complete whim of circumstance—or of any other phenomena either.

I walked down School Street in the brisk cold of pre-twilight and entered the bookstore.

There was a time when this sheer volume of books—shiny in their crisp dust jackets, stacked along the new arrivals section or, better yet, orphaned on the bargain table—was as intoxicating to me as any wine. That was before I entered the business. Now I couldn't remember the last time I had been here—only that it had been with Aubrey.

I took the stairs up a half level toward the back of the store. I wasn't sure where I was going; I just wanted to get out of the entry. Passing between shelves like labyrinth corridors, I veered off between Women's Studies and Sexuality and found myself, ironically, in Spirituality. There I sequestered myself at the end of a row housing books on guides, angels, and psychics.

Demons, too.

5:40. I felt a spike of anxiety but reminded myself that tucked away here, I was the colloquial needle in the haystack. Six o'clock would come and go, and here I'd be, my nose in a book on psychic healers. By seven o'clock I'd be taking dinner at a restaurant in Chinatown, perhaps contemplating writing an essay about the lengths desperate writers will go to get published, or at least requesting that our technical team put up a better firewall.

I had a second reason for coming here—one that had more to do with the exorcism of Aubrey than disproving the authenticity of demons. Sometime last summer I realized that in moving to Cambridge, I had penned myself in to a little safe-cage and that the city I first loved for its culture, for its civic and intellectual history, had become a connect-the-dots of locations infused with painful memories. So I had started the slow, deliberate process of reclaiming those places I had frequented with Aubrey and of putting new pins in my map that were solely my own.

It was difficult. Even today, walking in through the oversized double doors and passing the coffee bar, I remembered the soy lattes that Aubrey used to drink, the way she drifted up that stair to wander the travel section, there to pick up books on Africa, Italy, and Mongolia, to point out the exotic locations where one could hike to the summit of Kilimanjaro, walk through ruined Pompeii, or overnight in felt yurts—all trips I agreed should go on our list of future places to see. All places I knew I could not afford to take her.

Walking up that half flight of steps tonight, I recalled the collection of *Eyewitness Guides* she had kept on our bookshelf— a constant reminder of unfulfilled hopes and my own shortfalls as a provider. A detail I had forgotten until now. But it came upon me, reflexively and fully formed, the way the smell of a hospital room could conjure my dying father.

It was always like that. I might open a box—there were several in my apartment I had not unpacked yet—and find one of her long, dark hairs still clinging to a spare set of towels or even one of my sweaters. They used to stick to our pillows and sheets, adhering in tangled twists to the lint collector in the dryer. I still expected to see them there sometimes, still smoothed their phantom presence off the pillow before I lay down, just as I still got out of bed in the morning without pulling back the covers.

I slid three books from the shelf and then—on a whim—set up camp in the middle of the aisle as I had done as a college student in the Amherst library. As I folded my legs, I noticed that the hem of my pants was fraying. That surprised me as I considered these pants relatively new, but then I realized that they were simply among the last pieces of clothing Aubrey had chosen for me.

The thought summoned a small surge of panic. As much as I was on a mission to mark the corners of all our old haunts, I did not like the idea of her presence disappearing from my life altogether. The long hairs clinging to the sheets were gone. Soon the clothes she had chosen for me would be pawned off to a charity and worn by another man.

I forced my attention to the book in my hands.

I was camped there, well into the first chapter of *Unseen Hands: Discovering Your Guardian Angels*, when a woman tried to sidle past my makeshift roadblock.

I apologized, tried to scoot to the side, and then gave up and got to my feet.

"Sorry." I nudged my bag out of the way. But instead of passing, she bent down and retrieved two of the books I had left on the floor. Long curly hair the color of new pennies fell over her shoulder. When she straightened, I saw that she was pert-featured and curve-lipped, her skin devoid of the freckles I expected. A tiny diamond winked from the side of her nose as she tilted her head one way and then the other to read the titles in her hands. No wedding ring.

"What do we have here? *Unleashing the God Within* and *Angelic Voices*. Well, it's official"—she returned them to me— "you're a seeker." She smiled, the bow of her lips stretching in a generous curve. She was wearing a burgundy coat—velvet— and a low-cut top beneath it. A silver ankh hung in the open neckline against a smooth expanse of skin. She would have stood out anywhere, but she did so especially here, where the local dress code seemed to be anything black.

She was possibly the most beautiful woman I had seen in years.

"Actually, I'm a Republican," I said stupidly.

"In this town?" She arched a sleek brow at me. "Then you'll need all the guardian angels you can get."

Was she flirting? "Are you volunteering? Because I make a good charity case. Obviously."

Was I flirting?

She fingered the thin chain at her neck, the ankh dancing like a body on a hangman's noose. Her hands were slender, almost girlish, and I found myself wondering if she were a pianist. "Well, as fate would have it, I just happen to be between appointments."

I looked around. Not a well-groomed Mediterranean in sight. I glanced at my watch—it was just past six o'clock. "Would you be willing to discuss terms over coffee?"

"It's a deal," she said, laughing. The sound was warm, like sun against my chest.

Downstairs, I ordered coffee and scones—just a snack to tide me until dinner. Who knew, maybe I wouldn't be dining alone.

Now that was an odd thought. It occurred to me that such an event would constitute my first real date since my divorce, frayed pant hems and all.

At the table I watched with some curiosity as she emptied no fewer than three sugars into her mug, the ankh drawing my attention back to the skin beneath it every time it swayed on its silvery chain.

"So, how is the guardian angel business these days?"

She traced the handle of her mug with a fingertip. "Well, for one, the pay is horrible."

"Sounds like editing." I chuckled. "My name is Clayton, by the way."

"I know," she said, her hazel gaze leveled upon me.

"Guardian angel intuition?"

"No, Clay, because I know everything about you."

I hesitated. "You didn't tell me your name," I said, slowly.

"Yes, I did." She was no longer smiling.

"You did?" But I knew she hadn't. Then I saw it: the dark intelligence behind her eyes. Every capillary under my skin bloomed to startled life. She glanced at her wrist; an expensive-looking watch peeked out from beneath her sleeve. "You were early today."

My heart beat at my ribs like a cudgel. I flashed back to the office I had left an hour ago, to my hesitation on the street—and the fact that even as I entered the *T* station I had not known for certain where I was headed. Had she been following me? I didn't recognize her from the myriad faces I had studied on the train.

I found myself staring at the copper-haired woman, trying to reconcile what I heard and saw, what I knew to be possible and had formerly thought impossible. I felt fear like a pickax in my gut. "This can't be real. How can this be real?"

"This is real. So calm down and listen to me."

"I can't calm down! This can't be real. No! I refuse to accept it. Who put you up to this? Was it Richard? He has my wife—what more does he want?" I was trembling, my mind splattered in too many directions at once: Richard, Aubrey, the Mediterranean stranger, the dark presence—and now I felt it, as

I had in the café—cloaked in the flawless skin before me. "Tell me why you're doing this!"

She muttered in a language I didn't recognize. Suddenly she lunged forward, copper coils splayed over her shoulder, the color at odds with the burgundy of her coat. The effect struck me for an insane moment as one of fire.

She grabbed my hand. "I told you," she said, as though I were unintelligent or a child, or both. "To tell you my story."

Warmth spread like something injected directly into my bloodstream, creeping up my arm to my shoulder. I tried to pull away, but as in the café three nights ago, the demon's grip brooked no argument. The warmth spread into my chest. My heart rate slackened. It was still too fast—I don't think any power could have quelled it in that moment—but even as I thought this, I felt my anxiety, the alarm, the intensity of my fear, smooth out into something more placid. As alert as ever, but at least within my control.

"I don't have time for your breakdown, Clay. There are things I need you to know, and at the rate you're going, you're going to give yourself a heart attack, and then you won't be any good to either one of us." Her voice was as smooth as a hypnotist's, and I thought again of my theory that this was, in fact, a hoax, that it was merely the power of suggestion working its way through my muscles and veins that even now had relaxed back into the chair.

Then I remembered that for suggestion to work, the subject had to be willing.

My gaze dropped to the table, to her hand, holding mine. Ten minutes ago I had considered the possibility of this very circumstance. Now that it had come to pass, though not in any way I might have imagined, something inside me splintered.

With the same kind of spontaneous recall with which I had remembered Aubrey and the travel guides, I returned to that night in our apartment when, long after she was asleep, I crept out of bed, careful not to uncover her. And I saw again the e-mail on her account from Richard, a man I didn't know, saying that he loved her, that he would be thinking of her tomorrow as she told me she was leaving, and that he would be waiting up for her with warm arms afterward. And I knew that night that nothing would ever be the same again.

I knew the same thing now.

Were it not for the unnatural tranquility that had probably saved me a public scene here in the bookstore coffee bar, I might have been overcome by the uncontrollable urge to shout like a madman, to lash out at her with a fist, or even to bury my head in my arms and weep.

But I did none of these things. And the woman—the demon—nodded as though satisfied and let go of my fingers. The calm ebbed, but only slightly, when our contact was broken.

"Your body simply needs some time to adjust to what your mind now knows. Meanwhile, no, Richard did not send me. He could no sooner send me than he could call down rocks from heaven. I am here of my own volition, and I have much to tell you."

"Am I going to hell?" I asked, ashamed at the smallness of my voice. "Is that why you're here?"

She sighed and rubbed the back of her neck, rolling her head slightly, in an all-too-human way. "I don't know the answer to that right now."

No comfort there. And while my visceral self had returned to seminormalcy, my mind was as frenetic as before, in ways that would have been impossible had my calm been the result of any conventional means like a drug. I was desperately trying to remember what, if anything, I had learned about demons in eighth-grade confirmation class.

Something, like a shiny bit of pottery mired in the mud of a shipwreck, caught the eye of memory: *Father of Lies.*

"If you're a demon, why should I believe anything you say?"

She nodded, making no apparent effort to pass it off. "You raise a very good point. So let's get this issue of credibility out of the way right now. I won't waste my time telling you I'm not a liar because that, in itself, would be a lie. But I tell you, lying to you now will not serve my purpose."

"What purpose is that? And why should I care or listen to anything you say?"

"*Finally* an interesting question!" the demon said with what nearly sounded like relief. "The first answer is that I want to set the record straight. To shatter a few myths about my kind. The second answer is this: because it is a story unlike any other. I believe you'll find it to be of personal interest."

"Why, because I'm a seeker?" I didn't hold back the bitterness.

"Because my story is ultimately about you."

Something in me recoiled. "I don't see how that's possible."

She folded her arms on the edge of the table. "When you were growing up, you honestly believed in the morals of stories, in the integrity of comic-book heroes, of Batman on television, didn't you? And it had a greater impact on you than having morality drummed into your psyche by a church telling you to please an angry and distant god. You were good on principle. And yet here you are, without a wife or kids, or the success that being good was supposed to win you. Am I right? I know I am. And so you're on a quest for new meaning because the alternative is only this: that goodness has won you nothing but pain. And you're not willing to accept that."

"No."

"You need a sense of context, that larger picture. As I said before, I can give you that. But you have to hear me out."

As she said all of this, I found myself drawn to her in a wholly different way than I had before, against judgment, against instinct. And perhaps this was the grandest seduction of it all: that she was right.

"Don't worry about anything else. Simply write down what I tell you. Each word. Everything. And then you'll know it is real and you are sane."

"I can't remember each word. My mind is shattered, can't you tell?" But even as I said this, I knew I could recite that first conversation verbatim if I wanted to. Even now the full flow of that conversation came over me, as though summoned by the mere act of thinking of it, our exchanges of that night and this one intertwining and overlapping like competing melodies in my mind.

"You'll remember."

She glanced at her watch and frowned. The ankh swung in the window of her neckline as she gathered her coat. I had been transfixed by that view before, but found I could hardly look at it now.

She . . . he . . . it left, as it had before, without preamble. *I come to you at great risk,* Lucian said the first night. What, exactly, had the demon meant by that?

İ SPENT THE NEXT two weeks going through the motions of a job that seemed suddenly meaningless. I checked the time, the date, my calendar, with a regularity that bordered on obsession. I wrote down and read—and then reread—my accounts of both encounters, though I didn't need to. As promised, I hadn't forgotten one word of either. I began to think that this was the real demonic trick: to trap me in this limbo—less dead than before, not quite alive.

And then the mysterious L appeared again.

Trying to get away from my home before the appointed time, I noticed the church down the street with new eyes, saw it for perhaps the first time as more than scenery on the way elsewhere. A moment later I was checking the doors—it was Saturday, after all. But they admitted me easily, and I found myself loitering in the narthex until, with great hesitation, I entered the sanctuary.

I chose a creaky pew toward the back.

I immediately felt out of place. I hadn't been to church in years, and then only for holidays or weddings. I was conscious of every sound, of the still postures of those few sitting or kneeling in the pews ahead of me. I wondered if, having been in the presence of a demon, I would conversely better notice the presence of God.

But I felt nothing.

In the last week I'd been tempted to search through the boxes remaining in my spare room for my old confirmation certificate. But I couldn't bear the idea of discovering something of Aubrey's, of even seeing her writing on the side of the box from the first time it had been used when we moved in together.

Ultimately, I decided a weathered certificate would shed light on nothing. Nothing could have prepared me for this. I couldn't remember Pastor Feagan ever teaching about demons, or even the devil, except in the vaguest terms.

Not that God had been a specific notion to me, either. God was as real as the gravity on Jupiter or the expansion of the universe. Conceptually significant, yes—especially if one studied astronomy or lived on Jupiter—but nothing I expected to know much about, firsthand, in this world. I had always subscribed to the more modern belief that religion was fraught with contradictions, the product of an overgrown oral tradition that only the fanatical tried to package neatly as one tries to tame kudzu.

And, as Lucian had aptly observed, I'd never needed religion to be a good person. My father brought that out in me on his own. Never a perfect man, his temper would lie dormant for weeks at a time, waiting to erupt at the first sign of any misdeed or bad grade. Silence was a good sign, no news always the good kind. With an upbringing like that, there had been no need for God

A stretch of afternoon light angled across several pews as the church door opened. A moment later a black man in a denim jacket entered my pew from the other side and sat down next to me. He smelled like sandalwood and soap. My gaze slid to my watch.

4:15 p.m.

"I wondered if you'd be able to walk through the door." I kept my eyes fixed on the altar, on the cross atop it.

"Lucifer himself has access to the throne room of God. Do you think a church is any problem for me?" His voice was a warm baritone that did not need whispers to be kept between us.

"How can that be?"

"Why would it not be? Neither of us is evil by design."

DEMON: A MEMOIR   27

"Because you were angels, you mean."

"I was. Lucifer is a cherub."

With some confusion I conjured chubby-winged children in diapers and practically heard his answering scowl. "It isn't what you're thinking," he said, more loudly than before. "The cherubim are the highest of our order, the most powerful of us all. Know that on Lucifer's creation, El called him perfect."

I turned toward him, openly studying him now. He had a broad forehead and long, high cheekbones. The angular lines of a short moustache exactly delineated the curve of his upper lip, which was perfectly matched to the lower one. A hint of stubble smattered his chin and neck, like lichen growing on a great, smooth stone.

"He called him perfect with good reason. Lucifer was his masterwork. He was powerful, anointed by God, and so very beautiful."

I thought I heard him sigh.

"Then what about seraphim?" I asked, not because of any spectacular knowledge of my own, but according to literary lore, CHERUBIM and SERAPHIM had once been the license plates on Anne Rice's two limousines.

"The seraphim are fearsome fighters, but the cherubim out-rank them. And then there are the archangels. You've heard of Gabriel and Michael—"

There was a slight, just-perceptible intonation to his words when he spoke these names, as well as the name of Lucifer, and even his own name. Not quite an accent, it was more an elongation on the tongue, as though the pure names in another language might be unpronounceable in ours. Hearing it now, I remembered it in the speech of the woman in the bookstore and of the man in the café.

"I won't go into detail about all the various kinds of cherubim and seraphim. It may be best that I not describe them, lest, with all those faces and wings, you think us a spiritual freak show."

Beyond his profile, a stained-glass saint stared out upon us both with hollow, fractured eyes. "And you? What about you?"

"Ah, me." He spread his hands on his lap. They were lighter colored on the inside, the creases in them dark. The calluses on his palms struck me as aberrant. A stainless-steel watch peered beneath the edge of his cuff. "I was a member of the Host. A shining light, mere and marvelous."

"How did it happen then—your change, I mean?" The question tasted surreal on my lips.

Lucian reached up to rub the back of his neck. I had seen Sheila do the same at the onset of her migraines. "I should tell that story from the beginning. But this place isn't conducive to talking."

"Because of the crosses?"

"No, because the praying of those people is giving me a headache."

"The crosses don't bother you?"

"They should bother you a great deal more. They were used to kill humans."

I had not thought of that.

"Stay if you like, but I'm going." He rose and moved down the length of the pew to the side aisle where he'd entered. Two weeks ago I would have gladly let him go. I would have camped out, in fact, in the front pew and inquired about moving in. But now I needed to know what this, any of this, had to do with me.

This, the question that had niggled at me these last two weeks, was helped not at all by his cryptic answers.

We stepped out, blinking, into the cold afternoon light. Now I could see the wiry gray hairs above his ears, the dark spots dotting his cheeks, betraying his age. He had a presence about him, an unflappability that I found slightly unsettling. He was casually dressed, his pants not dissimilar to mine that day in the bookstore, albeit softer around the knees. To any other eye he might have been a local academic out for a casual weekend. An accountant on his day off. A tourist.

"So you popped up from hell to meet me in church." I shoved my hands into my pockets.

"I've never been there."

"To church?"

"To hell."

I squinted at him.

"You've got so much of this wrong, Clay. Your conventional wisdom lacks one thing: wisdom. None of us have been to hell."

"So it doesn't really exist."

"Not now, no."

"So you mean you haven't been to hell *yet*."

He flashed me such a baleful glance that my heart tripped in my chest. I started down the street, stiffly, my shoulders having risen toward my ears in the chill. A moment later, the demon fell into step beside me.

"To begin my story I should say that my beginning predates yours by a brief infinity."

"You're not making sense." I didn't look at him.

"The beginning of the world is only the beginning of time. Your Scriptures, being written for your benefit, begin at the point where you enter history. But my beginning came long before."

"In heaven, I suppose."

"No, Eden."

"What, the garden of Eden?"

"Yes. That garden, the green one, was in Eden. And Eden is here. This." He spread his hands out toward the expanse of sidewalk in front of us. "Eden preexisted that garden and the first of your kind. It was Lucifer's—and my—home first."

I raised my brows.

"What—you thought the world was full of nothingness before your creation?" He gave a short laugh. "Rather ethnocentric of you, isn't it? Do you believe the earth is flat, too? Listen to me: Elohim created Eden. He also created us. And that includes Lucifer—which is important because no creation is equal to the creator. What that means for you is that, contrary to popular myth, Lucifer is no evil opposite of God."

"I thought Lucifer was God's nemesis."

He stopped. "Clay, for this to work you have to let go of that. This is not your so-called classic human tale of the struggle between good and evil. Hades, but you humans always have a way of distorting the truth into something utterly simplistic and banal—not to mention trite."

We walked again, and for several moments there was nothing but the steady sound of our heels on the sidewalk and the occasional brittle leaf that skittered across it, joined from time to time by the orphaned bits of conversations from passing pedestrians and the cars on Massachusetts Avenue. In the distance a church bell chimed the half hour.

At length he said, "Elohim was my god before you ever existed. We called him that—'Mighty God and Creator'— though the name implies so much more. I say this for you because the fearful names we have known since those first days cannot be formed by human tongues."

I thought again of the barely perceptible lilt of his words that I had noticed earlier.

"El made a garden in Eden and lavished Lucifer with everything—all government, total power. He lived there like a favorite first son, the hawk to our sparrows, the jewel to our quartz."

"So why did he make you? Especially if he knew you would turn out . . . like this."

"I could ask you the same thing." But he didn't. "Why El made us, I've never known. One could surmise that El was lonely, but the fact is that he didn't really need us. You, created in his image, might actually have more insight into that question than I do. We're not so privileged as you in that way. As for me, my purpose for living, my role in this great scheme was clear to me from the first: to fall down, to worship, to praise, to wait upon the word of El."

"That sounds really boring."

"Really? Imagine the bliss of fulfilling one's created purpose."

I couldn't. "Why do you sometimes call him *El*—irreverence?"

"Here is where your language fails you utterly. *El* means 'Mighty God', though that does the meaning no justice. *Elohim* implies more, including plurality—'the God of gods,' you might say. Regardless of what you call him, he was all things to us then, which is very different from what he may be to you. Not a father—no, never that for us—but the reason for our very existence. The Great Initiator. Ever Enduring. Alpha and Omega." The demon sighed. "As for us, we were a sight to behold, glorious, unequivocal, each of us distinctly individual but of one purpose. Shining, more than brilliant; we had spent a brief infinity reflecting Shekinah glory like so many polished mirrors. How radiant we were! It was my happiest, most glorious moment. For a small eternity—if you can fathom such a thing—I was happy."

There was poignancy in the rich timbre of his voice. Walking with me like this, he might have been any man retelling the tale of a happy, thirty-year marriage before his wife died. For a moment I almost felt sorry for him. "So why did you turn your back on it?"

He tilted his head skyward, narrowed his eyes. "I was promised more."

We were on Brattle Street and had come to a drugstore advertising a post-Halloween sale. Masks hung in the window, a motley assortment of orcs, Klingons, zombies, and former presidents—the presidents looking too much like the zombies for any zombie's comfort. In the corner a red-faced Satan peered out between Yoda and Spider-Man. The sight of it startled me, as though Lucifer himself, having heard his name, had come to eavesdrop on us.

Lucian stopped before the red face, the stubby, polyurethane horns that protruded from the forehead. He studied it so thoughtfully I wondered if it were possible he hadn't ever seen one like it before.

"I remember the first time I ever saw a rendering of one of my kind," he said, finally, seeming to gaze beyond the glass, beyond even the store. "Belial took me to see it with such passion and insistence that I expected a wonder, a thing of marvel—anything but the hideous vision before me with the man's body and bird's taloned feet. It was covered with fur like a mangy goat and had dark and hideous wings. I was stupefied and not a little offended. 'What kind of abomination was that supposed to be?' I demanded. Belial, finding this uproariously funny, bowed and pointed. 'Behold, the fearsome Belial!' he said, which was ridiculous, as he has always been beautiful."

He turned a baffled look on me. "I thought your mad and genius artists were supposed to succumb to higher visions beyond the corporeal world. But there you are, still painting your devils red with horns, making Lucifer, our shining star, into a grotesque goat-man. And these are the images that remain to this day: ugly, marred, toppling from heaven, herded toward hell by the swords of shining blond men with stoic faces and bleached togas—Michael and Gabriel, I presume." He turned away.

"Just think," I said, in a moment of facetiousness, "you can dress up as a devil on Halloween and no one will recognize you." I regretted my recklessness the moment I said it.

"Just think," he said, too lightly, "you might pass me in the street and never know it. If I wished, you might even feel lust for me."

He glanced sidelong at me, and I shrank back at the memory of copper hair, of a silver ankh swinging against smooth skin, pointing at the breasts beneath.

"Why do you show up like this, in these different guises?" I hated the feeling of being caught always unawares.

"I like the feel of trying them out," he said, as though they were nothing more than new shoes or a bicycle.

I thought of the calluses on his hands, the telltale record of a history not his own. I wondered if they belonged to someone, or once had.

I shook the thought away. I might be a seeker, but there were some things I did not want to know.

ONE BLOCK FARTHER, LUCIAN stopped in front of a tea shop. "They have a good oolong here. Didn't you take a fancy to oolong in China?" He pushed through the glass-paned door of the shop.

I knew I had never mentioned the trip I had taken nearly twenty years ago. I had fallen in love with the country, and, at one point in our marriage, even suggested adopting a baby from China.

Of course, that was all moot now.

In a show of defiance, I did not order oolong but decaffeinated Earl Grey. The demon, for his part, preferred jasmine.

The wall at the back of the shop was plastered with academic, activist, and personal notices, ads seeking dog-sitters and lesbian roommates and advertisements for Pilates instruction and colonic irrigation. Lucian was silent as he plucked the tea ball from his cup and set it aside on the saucer. It occurred to me then, with a sense of strange intuition and even stranger incredulity, that he was procrastinating.

"You were promised more?"

He'd been right that first night in the café: I hadn't forgotten a phrase, a detail. While I'd never had an eidetic memory, his words came back to me with such repetitive insistence that the only way I could exorcise them from my consciousness was to write them down. Even now his last words on the street echoed in my mind and, I suspected, would continue to do so until I was at my desk.

He ignored me, and I thought about prompting him again,

but just then he did something so subtle as to wring at reason: He pursed his lips, the chapped skin creasing reluctantly, dry as a newly fallen leaf. And I marveled at the mundane aspects of his humanity, against which I must remember the truth of what he was: *Demon*. All around me life hummed along like a machine, oblivious to any sound but its own, as unaware of the interloper among its cogs and wheels as the diners in the café had been that first night, deafened by the drone of the everyday.

"With the clock on the wall over there ticking so loudly," he said, "I've just realized I can't tell you how long it went on like that—my life before. Isn't that funny? I just can't say. You can point to the calendar and say you were born on such-and-such a date and married for five years. But as for me, I could not begin to guess. Eons must have passed. Millennia. Ages. Or maybe it was really only a moment. I don't know. When one pre-exists time, an epoch can pass like a day, and who would know it? It's so cliché, a trite line from novels about lovers: 'Time had no meaning.' But that's how we were: enrapt, enthralled with our very situation, with every aspect of our circumstances, our whole purpose for being. It was the golden age of ages—of which every age since has been only the palest shadow."

He took the tea ball from the saucer, squeezed the hinges together just enough to crack the sphere open but not enough to let the mass of sodden leaves fall out. "It all ended with a glance."

"What do you mean, 'a glance'?"

"How does anything new begin? How does an extramarital affair begin?"

"I wouldn't know."

He looked up at me. "Then I'll tell you. With a glance. A thought. And the possibility of that thought acted upon. Even your Narcissus of legend, who might most resemble my master in this account, started his own infatuation with a glance into a pool where he found . . . himself."

He dropped the tea ball into his cup. He was silent for a moment, stirring the tea that had gone, so far, unsampled. "Clay, I want to tell you something. I'm going to tell you a secret. One I hardly dare whisper. When you write down this conversation and append it to the others, this is the page I would condemn to molder first were it not so central to everything."

I had a sudden vision of a demonic Pied Piper luring me not with music but with words and story to some unknown end.

"I was swept up in the ecstasy of worship, of praising Elohim for all that he was and had been and was yet to be. And I had lifted my arm to shield my eyes—the Shekinah glory is too great even for us. And I had wept with it, with the fervency of it, until my tears nearly choked me. My awareness of God was, in that moment, so great that I was overwhelmed. It was always that way." He didn't so much look at me as through me. "But this time, as I lowered my arm, the tears hung like prisms in my eyes, like crystals held up to the brilliance of the sun. And I gaped at the beauty of the garden, at the refracted beauty of my own kind filling it. Suddenly, one thing stood out to me as more brilliant than all the rest of that dazzling host, blinding me through the lens of my tears so that I wiped them from my eyes like scales."

"Lucifer," I whispered.

"Yes. Our prince and governor come down to walk among us like so much wheat in an open field. I was dazzled! So help me, I stared and thought myself blinded. Can you fathom it? Can you possibly understand? His head was more brilliant than your sun. His wings, like a metal so pure that your quicksilver is a pathetic comparison, glimmered like so much pavé jewelry, crystals set so closely together as to appear like one winking eye of a diamond. Even his hands and feet were as perfect as unclouded ice, smooth as alabaster. But it was the *power*, the power and the glamour that overwhelmed me. I knew then, in a way I had not known before, that I stood in the presence of the greatest being under God. I staggered at the sight. Light. Glory. My beautiful one!" He closed his eyes as he spoke, each word falling like a boulder between us.

Lucian leaned his cheek into his hand. "And Lucifer, my prince, heard my heart and turned his eyes to me. It was almost more than I could bear, the direct brunt of that gaze—such a long and considering glance. As for me, I was rapt, seared by the stars, scorched by perfection. I fell down on my face, as I had before El a million times before, but this time to Lucifer. And my heart praised him—not for the work of the Creator in him, or even his office under God, but simply for the sake of his own magnificence. And Lucifer knew it."

"And that made you a demon?"

"No. The sin isn't in the temptation."

I could not help but think of Aubrey. I never knew when she crossed that line. I had tortured myself with trying to pinpoint exactly when she betrayed me—in spirit, if not yet in deed—and at what moment I lost her. Even after she was gone, I scoured phone receipts, credit card statements, the caller ID log. I reconstructed the entire schedule of her off-site meetings and business trips during our last month together, mad with it, obsessed despite the futility.

The demon curled his fingers around his teacup as though to warm his hands—another human gesture I found somehow grotesque—and said, "I sometimes wonder what he must have seen at that moment: a lowly angel, prostrate before him—a being beautiful in its own right but so dull by comparison? Or maybe a reflection of himself, cast back as though from the watery and unworthy mirror of Narcissus. I don't know. I don't know why he even looked at me. I suppose he felt my adulation and was pleased by it. In fact, I know he was."

"How do you know that?"

"I felt it. Keep in mind we aren't like you. When we share the same purpose, we are a legion of one accord. The perfect army. So I felt it, too, when he looked away from Elohim, and then at me . . . and finally, at himself. And among our perfect awareness, the ripple it caused spread through us like the falling of dominoes, one against the other. But unlike your ivory pieces with their neat and shuffling clinks, the momentum of that disturbance was a roar—thunder—in my ears. You can't comprehend what it is for an angelic being to hear the fabric of perfection rent." He rubbed his forehead, pinched the bridge of his nose. "It's deafening . . . deafening. And Lucifer rose up, inspired by that mayhem, his eyes terrible, his bearing resolute. How beautiful, how awful, was the look on his face! I believe the sight of it will be with me forever, burned into the retina of my mind, the sentence of perfect recollection."

He dropped his hand and abruptly stood up. "More hot water?"

As he rounded the bend of the front counter, I fully expected that he might not return. To my surprise, though, he came back a moment later with a small pot of water. He refilled my cup before pouring a drop into his own—all the cup would allow, as he had never drunk any of it.

I looked at my teacup.

"Go on—" he gestured at it—"I want to watch you enjoy it."

"As though you haven't seen people doing this for centuries."

"Millennia. But I'll never tire of it. I like to wonder what it must be to take pleasure in something so short-lived."

I took a sip. "Let me ask you something."

"Of course." He reseated himself with a magnanimous tilt of his head.

"It's obvious you haven't liked telling me this part of your"— I fumbled for a moment—"background. So why do it?"

I had a strange sense then—the same one I used to have as a boy when I ran up the basement steps, chased by shadows— that coalesced into this thought: *Were his compatriots here? Did they know, and would they approve of his coming to me like this?*

"Are you with him now?" I added, on impulse.

"What, this minute?"

I nodded.

He gave me a queer look. "Are you serious? Oh, you are. No, of course not. Like you—and like him—I can be in only one place at a time. Really, you watch too much television." He glanced at his watch, seeming to weigh the time.

A surge of anxiety streaked toward my heart. But the demon, normally so well tuned to my discomfort, seemed to be in conference with his own thoughts. Finally, he crossed his arms. "When people talk about this story, they make it so idiotic: 'Lucifer was proud, he wanted to be like God. When he rebelled, a third of the angels followed him.' I've heard all the stories— yes, even in your churches. But you have to understand: We were *all* proud. And Lucifer—he was the governor of the mount of God. So how natural and right it seemed that when he held out his hands like a liege accepting fealty, we would give it.

"For a moment—whatever that can be without the boundaries of time—we forgot El. And I heard Lucifer's thoughts then as clearly as if he had exercised his voice, raised up his fist, and shouted. *And why shouldn't you praise me? Why not bow down? Am I not your perfect prince, with strength a thousand times a thousand of you, with beauty a thousand times greater, with power beyond measure? Watch now! I will go up to heaven. I will raise my throne beyond the stars of El. I will sit upon the sacred mountain. I will ascend above the clouds of glory. I will make myself like the Most High!*"

His gaze had left me again, and I knew that a part of him was back in that place, in Eden *then*. There was a curl to his lips, but the smile was not congenial.

"A moment, an eternity earlier, I would have *known* it for blasphemy, for damning ambition, independent of Heaven. I would have known! But in that instant his logic was perfect.

How could anything less come from such a creature? In the shadow of Elohim, he seemed worthy to do it. He seemed like a god. His glamour was so great; I wanted him to *be* God."

Lucian picked up the tea ball and stabbed it into his cup, sloshing water into the saucer.

"Did he know it?"

"How could he not? The assumption was—unspoken, of course, but put forth in suggestive and sultry thought—that those of us who followed him would be something greater as well. He would be a god, and we would become like him.

"The bulk of the Host stood stunned at the discordant thunder of this break. Still, I bowed to him, as did many others like me. And with that, the fate of a legion was set in motion. Time, not yet created, had begun its phantom tick for us alone. Not that we knew it then; we were caught up. We rushed the throne of Lucifer in all its shining estate there in Eden. It was the seat of a government outgrown, and we rose up, ready for our new order. And we seized the throne, determined to move it. I can remember the feel of it in my hands still. Can you understand, Clay? No, of course you can't!"

Before I realized what he meant to do, he grabbed my hand, his skin tingling against my palm. I started, but as in the bookstore, his grip tightened. I couldn't pull away.

"The gold of it was hot, burning glory—the glory of Lucifer. It branded me the moment I touched it"— he squeezed my hand tighter—"melding flesh with metal like skin melting on an iron. But instead of letting go, I clasped it tighter, reveling in the white-hot burning of my flesh, the happy cost of my metamorphosis."

The tingling in my hands turned to pain. His palms seemed inhumanly hot. And then I felt it: a rush of power, thudding through my veins like adrenaline. The drum of my heart roared in my ears, faster—faster. In another minute I was sure I would have a heart attack.

Or that I could run a marathon.

I heard the demon from a distance now: "I, too, would become something more than the mere angel I was. And *this* would be my transfiguration. This searing was not pain but *alchemy!*"

The track lighting, the fliers on the wall, the bins full of exotic teas faded into my periphery. Once, back in college, when I had torn a groin muscle while running hurdles, simple shock and the rush of blood to the injury had caused me to nearly black out. I felt the same way now, except that I was not nauseous, and my vision had not narrowed to a tunnel. In fact, it had expanded, pushing reality to the fringes of my consciousness like curtains sliding into the wings of a stage.

Now came a distant rustle. It grew in volume into the beating of a thousand wings, as though I had entered an aviary ten miles wide, crowded with giant, winged creatures, the bodies too dense above and around me to see anything but intermittent shards of light. Voices deafened my ears, galvanized my heart.

Lucian's voice came to me: "Our fervor intoxicated me. We would have another god, one who walked among us, granted favors—one of our spirit kind risen to the third heaven where he was permitted but never resided. And we, the interlopers, would rise up with him and set up his throne there. We would come into the presence of our new god, walk upright and proud at his side."

With demon-induced vision I felt, more than saw, a singular form, his span gigantic over the din. He did not blot out the light as he should have but against all logic seemed to intensify it. And now I realized that the giant form radiated its own brilliance down onto the horde like mirrors reflecting the sun.

Lo, the light of Lucifer!

I was elated, high on a rush different from any recreational substance I had ever dabbled in at college. No designer drug, no hit of pure cocaine could begin to compete with it.

And then the hand clasping mine let go. I snapped like a retracting cord—back to the table, to myself—with a jolt that made me gasp. I sucked air into my lungs like a swimmer surfacing from near-fatal depths. The electric lights in the tea shop seemed as severe as surgical lights in an operating room, and I felt pinned by an abnormal gravity to the hard chair beneath me, my limbs as stiff as they would have been after days in traction. I felt the inexplicable urge to weep; I was too aware of my human shell, the conflated emotions—human and otherworldly—roiling in my gut.

Across from me, Lucian dredged the tea ball through his cup.

"What—what was that?" I demanded when I knew I wouldn't vomit on the table.

"A memory. History. What once was," he said, waving his hand.

In the frame of my pathetic human shell, I could still feel the elation, see the body emanating light like spots in my eyes after a flash. I was out of sorts. Dismantled. The urge to weep became contempt. I felt toyed with. As though I had been slipped a drug without my permission—one that had taken me to a state that my human condition could never support or ever hope to reach again except through him.

"I do apologize. I needed you to understand, to know, to feel what my kinship with him meant."

That's what it was, that intoxication. I shuddered. If what he said was true, I had just vicariously experienced communion with the devil. I pushed up from the table, sturdier on my legs than I expected.

Lucian spread his hands. "Oh, come now."

But I picked up my jacket and walked resolutely out the door.

Out on the street I wondered if I was being foolish—if, like a lover ending an argument in a huff, I should turn around and go back. What if this was the end? Maybe I would be rid of him, of this entire thing.

That thought brought me no relief. In fact, it conjured panic. If this was the end, it would close the portal to *something*, some greater context, containing answers to questions I had not known to ask. Worst of all, I would never know what this had to do with me—a question that had begun to eat at me. Would I wander around half-cooked after this, knowing there was something more, the access to which I had thrown away? And would I be haunted by his words—the words that cycled through my mind at night until I wrote them down simply to rid myself of them—indefinitely?

I returned to the tea shop, unsure what I meant to do or say. But the back table was empty, one of the girls from the counter already gathering the cups, the pot of water, the discarded tea balls onto a tray.

As I left again, his words pursued me in his absence, a specter at my back whispering visions of heaven, of the devil, in my ear.

5

My hands burned, seared by the throne that threatened to blind my vision and melt down my wings, but still I held on. I was strong strong and weightless, as though I had come from a place with five times the gravity of this one. And there was Lucifer, spanning the heavens above me, his light so bright now that the wings of the others were nearly translucent with it, their bodies white conflagrations so that I thought, *We, too, are transformed.* And I was broken by gratitude that I should feel kinship with that splendid creature. It was a new and marvelous identity that swelled my immortal chest.

I wasn't the only one. I clamored with equally awed seraphim and archangels, their hands grappling with mine. We had witnessed his glory. We had bent the knee. I could no sooner turn back than I could annul the oath of my allegiance. I had undone the contentment of my prior existence with words and acts irrevocable.

We sped heavenward, drawn up after Lucifer like a magnet, inspired by a single will—Lucifer's. The cosmos had shrunk to this: the expanse of his wings blotting out the sky, his brilliance diminishing the stars, the great power of his ascent piercing its way to heaven.

But then something happened. The higher we flew, the closer we approached the summit of the mount of God, the more a sense of inevitability crept over me. It crawled like plague over my body, settled like ache in my bones. I told myself that I was simply in unfamiliar territory; only Lucifer himself had ascended so high, to stand in the throne room of the Almighty.

But no, it was more than that. Something was wrong. I felt naked, even in glory.

Now, with the corporate thrum of our wings loud in my ears, I noticed strange things: seraphim regarded me jealously. One of them even pulled at my hands to wrest them from the throne. I knew what he was doing, and I was filled with rage. That seraph would seek higher favor with Lucifer by assuming my better hold on the throne! It didn't matter that he was my superior—this was the anarchy of ambition, and I felt no loyalty to rank order. I hated him, and though somehow certain I had never before raised a hand against anyone, I tore at his wing, ripping it.

He clawed at me, face contorted with rage, fingers biting like talons until I let go with a howl, unable to match him. But I was insane with anger and pursued him, clinging to his feet, pulling at him, wanting him to fall. I cursed him with new and foreign words. Unholy words. And now the others around us were clamoring, too, each determined to find favor above his fellow with this new god, jealous of those closest to him, resentment plain in their eyes. Revolt, glorious to us before, had sprung full-grown and hideous from our hearts. Our fervor, our ambition, careened into violence. And the higher we ascended,

DEMON: A MEMOIR   47

the worse it became, until there wasn't an angel without menace on his face, no seraph without pride in his better strength, no archangel without possession in his eyes.

We had found a new order, appointed our god, and brought chaos to the world.

The stars wouldn't abide it. Before we could ascend beyond the second heaven, the sky flashed. I felt anger again, but it wasn't mine. This anger was righteous, so different from that chaos permeating our knot of rebels. The Host was upon us. I recognized faces I had once loved. In the dream I knew them. And I was struck by their pure, sanctified power. They outnumbered us, and for the first time I felt the force of their strength—a strength I had once been a part of. I saw the hands of kin raised against me, and I feared for myself.

And then I feared even more because I had never before been afraid.

The throne fell from our hands and dropped through the tangle of our arms and wings and heads, plummeting away, a radiant speck in a blackening sea. I watched for a horrified moment, the bellow of Lucifer loud in my ears, as the golden throne grew smaller and smaller until it was gone, fallen back to Eden.

And in the dream I was so familiar with early Eden that I could picture the throne there, shattered in glorious shambles among the shining stones of forgotten harmony, the physical wreck of our plan. But no—when I looked, Eden, that land of brightness, had gone dark. I could see no mote of light there at all. Careening from those heights, fleeing for the lower heavens away from the hands of the Host arrayed before the third heaven, I realized that the only source of light at all was Lucifer.

Where were the bright stones of that garden, the great refracted brilliance of our prince, even from this distance?

I had never seen the earth from so far away, had never looked down on it like this. Even so, I knew something was horribly wrong. And then I saw black engulfing the shadowed land, covering it like ink, rising up over it and creeping across the earth until it had seemingly digested it whole, the garden drowned by a sea of pitch.

My world had gone as dark as a planet covered by a shroud, the black cloak of what we had done blotting out everything else.

Lucifer veered away from the onslaught of the angels, and I woke as the rebels, having nowhere else to go, took after him. I saw him, through the loosening fibers of sleep, leading them away: a bright light trailing stars, a comet and its sparkling tail.

IN THE SPACE OF a night, the ambition for heaven and darkness of Eden had become more real to me than my own home, than the tangled sheets of my bed. The face of that seraph was more horrific than any terror conceived of my own mind. I smelled the brine of sweat, felt its grime on my arms. Never had I experienced emotion in such terrible, pure form. Not even in the torture of facing an unfaithful spouse.

Perhaps this was his revenge for my walking out of the tea shop. If it was, I had no way to confront him, no knowledge—if I had ever had any—of when I would encounter him again.

The next morning, as I sat at my desk, erratic script emerging from my pen, I was seized by a thought. Opening my laptop, I turned it on and pulled up my schedule.

10:30 p.m.: *L.*

12:00 a.m.: *L.*

And again, in blocks between 1:00 a.m. until 4:00 a.m.:

      L.

            L.

                  L.

6

Bodies flowed around me in Park Street Station like water around a stone. Some regarded me with passing curiosity. Some of them looked me directly in the eye. I stared back, half fearful that I would find recognition in their eyes, half afraid that I would not.

I'm going crazy.

A woman in her fifties paused to assess me. "Are you lost, hon?" she asked with frank kindness. "Do you need some help?"

Is that you, Lucian, you devil? I sought the dark glint behind her eyes—that hint of shadow—but jerked away when she might have touched my sleeve. She shook her head and left me there, even as my attention landed on a man in a trench coat. Was he wearing an expensive watch? Or there—that young mother with the curly haired toddler. Or the tourist studying the *T* map . . . or that woman with the circles under her eyes. Her hands were cracked. Perhaps she worked as a maid in one of the inns off Newbury Street. She looked tired and worn. Was she ever visited by demons?

I eventually became aware of a young man studying me from several feet away. The faint hint of a moustache dirtied his lip. He was as pale as a computer junkie; he had that fueled-by-Fritos-and-Red-Bull look about him. A brown, stubby pony-tail spurted from the back of his head, half-obscured by the rumpled collar of his long, open jacket. It hung loosely on his shoulders, oversized on his thin frame. Skinny, dressed straight from a thrift shop, he should have looked like a charity case, but he managed to come off grunge-band cool, his unflappabil-ity as much a part of his ensemble as his faded *Animals Taste Good* T-shirt. I had been intimidated by that brand of tattered-jeans confidence in others when I was his age. As he dragged an appraising look up and down over me like a store checkout scanner, I found that the feeling carried over into adulthood. I suddenly felt grossly inadequate—not to mention preten-tious—in my Eddie Bauer jacket and loafers.

"Are we going to stand here all day?" he asked.

I searched for a witty comeback, but I hadn't had one when Jake Salter had picked on me in high school, and I didn't have one now. I followed him up the stairs, onto Tremont.

"And you needn't worry any more about Jake." His speech and the slight, strange accent were at weird odds with his human mundane. "He died a few years ago."

I had been on the verge of railing at him for hijacking my dreams but faltered at this news.

"I didn't know." The Jake Salters of the world still seemed untouchable to me, their flannel shirts and army boots armor against a society in which the greatest peril was a white-collar eventuality.

The demon shrugged. "Why would you?"

"How?" I envisioned a drug overdose, alcohol poisoning, a motorcycle crash. A knife fight.

He cocked his head toward the same invisible horde of insects I had noticed that first night at Esad's. I shuddered.

"A boating accident. On the Missouri River. He drowned and left a wife. Ah, and three children. Would you like to know more?"

"No," I said, numb, and then again, "No." *Family. Kids. Even Jake Salter had his act together. I couldn't even stay married five years.* And then I felt guilty. Act together or not, Jake was dead. Why did it always seem to happen like that?

"It always does seem to happen like that," he said, far too young in human years to utter such words, far too dispassionate regardless of his true age.

"Stop it! Stop reading my mind! And what was that with the dreams? How dare you!" A couple stopped to stare as I turned on him. I had become one of those people I always steered clear of.

"Do you think I could have done that differently? I couldn't have. I need you to *know*. It was the only way." He had said something similar that first night at the café. I heard the echo of it now, bits and pieces of that first conversation flitting along with it.

"How about just telling me next time?" I said over the iteration and counterpart of our first conversations, as someone shouts with headphones on. I clutched at my head, realized with belated awareness that I was close to hysteria. I hadn't slept well. I had lost enough weight in the last two weeks that my pants were loose—something I would normally be glad of but under the circumstances found slightly alarming— and was so behind at work that I had started to wonder if my job might be in jeopardy. It had been well over two months since I had brought any proposals to the editorial committee, and I was behind in getting the ones that had made it through ready for the publishing board with sales and marketing. The slush pile on my desk—the queries and manuscript samples sent in by agents and would-be writers—had grown to such a proportion that I had been forced to clear a space on my bookshelf to accommodate what wouldn't fit on my credenza. I had more than a hundred e-mails in my in-box and fourteen voice mails that I repeatedly resaved under the delusion that I would return them before week's end.

To top it all off, I just noticed this morning that I had begun to sprout bumpy hives on my chest, underarms, and back.

"I have so much to tell you, Clay. And we've so little time," he said, the echoes of prior conversations subsiding with this statement. There was nothing youthful in the shake of his head.

"You're obsessed with time, you know that?"

"You would be, too. Maybe you should be."

"What do you mean by that?"

"Come on. It's a lovely day."

THE COMMON WAS ALIVE with the desperate festivity that comes with the last warm day of the season. Couples pushed children in strollers. Brownstone Brahmins walked their dogs, and couples dozed, curled up in quilts. A coed football game was in progress on the lawn, and leaves were everywhere, the trees having thrown their autumnal parade seemingly overnight, leaving behind a slew of red, yellow, and orange confetti.

I hadn't been to the Common since last year's July 4 when we—Dan, Sheila, Aubrey, and I—had decided to camp out on a patch of grass to get a good view of the fireworks. Aubrey was distant that day, and her moodiness had irritated me. Two days later, I found the e-mail from Richard.

Now here I was again, this time with either a demon or a psychopathic, albeit talented, hypnotist—part of me still clung to the shrinking possibility that an explanation might still be found in this corporeal world—and last year's Fourth of July seemed as surreal a life as my new one had become.

We were walking toward the Soldiers and Sailors Monument, in the direction of the Public Garden, but even now I could see the blackness of Eden, the blaze of light that was Lucifer, the trailing stream of angels that followed him in a fleeing Milky Way of bright bodies. But before I would hear more, I wanted something.

"You said that first night that you came at great risk."
"Yes."

"What's the risk?"

Lucian sighed heavily, as though it would take great effort to explain. "Is it not enough that I have assumed it?"

I was silent.

"I'm sure you would agree that this is highly unconventional," he said at last.

To say the least.

"It would not be looked well upon, my talking with you."

"By whom?"

"By just about any of them. Us. Enough now. This does not serve my purpose."

"Your purpose? What about mine? I've spent an entire night falling from heaven, and you know what? I'm exhausted."

"What do you want, Clay?" He sounded weary, and this aggravated me even more.

"I want to know why! If this is dangerous for you—and I have no idea what kind of ramifications this will have for me—I want at least to know *why* you're doing it."

"I told you you were safe. Any 'ramifications,' as you call them, will be those of your own making. As for why I'm doing this, I've already told you that as well. I'm not going to waste our time answering the same question twice."

I had hoped, if he answered it again, that I might glean some small detail more because, although I had heard his reasons, I did not understand them. Why would a demon want his memoirs published? And why by me? He had laughed at my first notion, that he was here to strike a devil's bargain. But despite his irritation at my asking again, I could not help feeling that there was something more.

"I saw Lucifer leading you away, but I didn't see where he took you."

The demon tromped alongside me, his pasty skin and black boots a decided 180 after the stylish redhead, the dignified black man. "We assumed he would lead us to a place of our own. A place of his making—as though he had truly become, in that short time, a god. As though he cared for us and would recreate that garden and walk in it among us. But he led us nowhere." He looked up toward the tops of the trees, their branches like the sparse scalps of aging men.

"There was no other place to go. We hovered on the edge of the earth in fear—fear and silence. And I longed for Eden, settling even then beneath those murky waters, the beautiful facets of the gems within it reflecting nothing but darkness. I was sick for it, would have given anything—if I had had anything to give—to have it all back as it was."

I remembered the day Aubrey left our apartment.

"But here was the most terrible thing: El went down to Eden and laid himself out over the waters, there to brood in trembling sorrow. And it infused me, this sorrow. It saturated my being. Beside me, seraphim huddled with long faces. Some of them wept. I had never seen such tears before—dark, remorseful, bereft of joy. There was only sadness and dread, that terrible sense that had I been a god, I would have set it all back. I would have erased everything, returned it all to the way it had been."

"Why couldn't you?" I said. "For that matter, why couldn't God?"

The kid gave a jolt of laughter that sounded slightly hysterical, and then his lips curled back from his teeth, and spittle flew out with his words. "I'll tell you why: Because we were *damned*! Oh, not that I knew it then—how could I? There was no precedent for any of it. Wrong had never existed. Lucifer had to manufacture that first aberration himself. Until then, there had been one law dictated by the sole fact of our creation: Worship the creator. And now, as surely as Lucifer's throne had broken into a thousand splinters, we had violated that order."

"I thought Adam was the original sinner."

"You humans always like to think of yourselves as the first at everything."

I ignored his open sneer. "What if you had apologized?"

"*Apologized.*" He spit onto the edge of the path. "Let me tell you something: Apologies are a funny thing. Half the time they're insincere. And even when they aren't, there's nothing a person can do to undo whatever he did. Oops, I ran over your cat. So sorry. Meanwhile, the cat's dead, entrails oozing out of its mouth. Now I can buy you a new cat, but it hasn't changed anything except that I now have an opportunity to run over your new cat as well. If Aubrey had apologized, would it have made it all better?"

I didn't answer that.

"Besides, even though we knew we had committed some *thing*, we had no idea how irrevocable our actions were. Not yet. So there was only remorse—black, clinging like tar, eating like acid.

"Meanwhile, there was the shaking of El's spirit like the keening of a banshee, as though the whole world had died. And I suppose it had. It was unbearable, that sound—a pain without end or even the hope of death to escape it. I could not watch, was unable to stand the sight of that spirit hovering over the darkness, though I couldn't block out the sound of it.

"But this was the most terrible thing of all: El had turned away." He tried to tuck a rogue strand of hair behind his ear. When it wouldn't stay put but teased along the edge of his cheek, he yanked it out with a savage pull. I stared as the patch along the side of his temple sprouted angry red dots against the white of his scalp.

"I didn't know why." He seemed not to notice the deviance of his own actions as he flicked the hair off his fingers. "I didn't understand that we had opened an unbridgeable chasm between us. All I knew was that he couldn't stand to look at us. Oh, but to know that everything is wrong with the universe, and to know that you had a part in that irrevocable drama, is just about too much for any mind to take. I had lived always for the moment—that was, after all, all there had been—and now

I could see no end to it. Regret ate at me like a ravenous worm. Had I been human, I would have gone insane."

Are you sure you didn't? I remembered his strange laughter but said only, "Obviously it did end."

He shrugged. "Eventually. And I might have spent only an epoch like that. But it felt like an eternity."

We walked in silence. What did one say to something like that—*I'm sorry?*

I had almost forgotten who I was talking to.

The demon pointed down the hill. "Look! The Frog Pond. When winter sets in, we should go ice skating there."

DESPITE MY LIMITED KNOWLEDGE of Lucifer, I couldn't picture him—her, it, whatever the devil was—sitting idle after that. When I asked Lucian about it, he shook his youthful head.

"He kept to himself and wouldn't even look at Eden. He was like a child who abandons a toy after he's broken it. What was Eden to him now? Even if it had still been perfect, it might as well have been ruined; he had set his eyes on heaven. As for us, we no more existed to him than Eden did in those days . . . those nights. It was all one night to me, those hours like years, as Lucifer raised his head to heaven and narrowed his eyes at God."

The demon squinted at the sun. "We huddled on the fringes of Lucifer's light—all the rest of the world was darkness but for him—never venturing any closer for fear of his anger or any farther away for fear of the darkness. And all the while there was that terrible, shuddering spirit of El.

"Meanwhile, Lucifer grew bolder by the day. He blasted El with sharp, serrated words. I thought for sure the Host would come for us, that El would send us away or worse, scatter us like salt over a field."

"Did you think he would obliterate you?"

The kid shrugged. "I had no concept of death, though I will say I expected something terrible. And I even thought by then that I might welcome it. But El was absorbed by grief, which only seemed to incense Lucifer."

"Why wasn't he afraid? He had been the favorite; he had the most to lose."

"Exactly. El had never ignored the voice of his favorite before. And as his silence continued, Lucifer grew more venomous. I had never seen this kind of resentment. The violence of our uprising seemed like children's quarrels by comparison."

Children's quarrels? The horrible face of the seraph in my dream hovered before me.

"Lucifer ranted and stalked. And we trailed him like ermine on the train of a king. Then, just when I thought he had forgotten us, El broke his silence."

We were nearing Charles Street. What happened next was something I would replay over and over in my mind for weeks. A woman jogger was running toward us. She was all blonde hair and black running pants, a hot pink iPod strapped to her arm. I thought with some irony that this was the extent of my social life of late: appreciation of women going the other way.

Assuming, of course, that they were not demons in bookstores.

Just as she was about to pass us, Lucian tripped, his hand grabbing at my shoulder as he practically fell into the woman's path. It was such a queer incident; I had never seen him anything other than fully composed. The startled jogger, for her part, managed to skirt him just in time to avoid a collision that might have kneecapped her, and Lucian escaped the fall, thanks to his pulling at my shoulder which nearly took me down with him. As I stumbled, shoving the demon's hand away, I saw alarm and confusion on the woman's face. But, as we more or less righted ourselves, she seemed to decide that Lucian was neither an attacker nor injured, and she ran on.

Lucian stared after her with slatted eyes. He murmured something under his breath.

"What was that about?" I demanded. It was bad enough that he looked like a punk. Did he have to act like one, too?

"You wanted her."

It was close enough to the truth to shut me up.

I would come back again and again to this interchange, would remember that narrowed look on Lucian's face for weeks and months to come.

OUTSIDE THE GATE OF the Garden, a bearded man played an electric guitar. It was plugged into an amp, and now I realized the source of the music we had heard from the Commons softball field. As we crossed Charles Street, I asked, "What kind of special curse does one reserve for someone who has ruined everything?"

"We're talking about Lucifer, not Aubrey. And El didn't curse Lucifer." He pulled a cigarette out of his coat pocket.

It was bizarre, seeing him light up. It was the first time I had actually seen him ingest anything.

"He didn't strike us down, either."

"So what did he do?"

"He drew breath." He exhaled a stream of smoke that drifted before and then over us, diffusing like ectoplasm. "And with that inaugural sound we, with keen immortal perception, knew that something was about to happen. Something *different*."

"How could you tell?"

"How can I explain this?" He kicked a Dunkin' Donuts cup, an escapee from a nearby trash bin. "It was a pregnant sound. Expectant, like a hesitation on the verge of speech. It vibrated throughout the universe like the tight pulse of a tuning fork." He flicked his fingers, sending a ripple of invisible energy into the air and a spatter of ash toward the ground.

We veered down a small path toward roped-off flowerbeds and domed shrubs. I thought back to my nightmare, to the vision of the newly fallen drifting away, fading into the residue of sleep. I didn't know what happened next. I had to know. I was jonesing, pure and simple. I stopped. "Show me."

His brows rose, as though he were waiting for a punch line.

"Show me," I said again.

He pulled the cigarette from between his lips and flicked it away. "I will never understand humans," he said and then grabbed me by the upper arm.

My experience the night before had been birthed into the warm vessel of sleep. But this was an electrifying jolt, like the first chug of a roller coaster on a track. Just as I felt I had reached the apex of that first hill, the universe unfurled before me, as though I were standing in the narrow part of a funnel looking out toward the opening of *everything*. I was aware of the vastness of it, the infinite amplifications of space before me, the stars. And I knew, somehow, that each of them had a name known to El.

There was Eden. When I dreamed it—no, when I *saw* it— the darkness had been a moving thing, a living tar creeping across the rocks and flashing stones. It was as black now as a shroud, vacant as an eye in a corpse's head. I heard a sound like a sob and recognized my own voice. Eden, infused with sorrow, stood ruined, a monument of grief covered by a dark and terrible presence trembling on the water.

The spirit of El himself.

I pulled away, unable to endure another moment of it, and doubled over on the lawn, sucking breath.

"Did you hear it? The keening?" the demon asked from above me.

"I didn't hear anything."

"Human ears," he said, the way a debutante might dismiss a bottle blonde.

"What did I miss?"

"Didn't you see the shifting over the water?"

I shook my head.

"Did you see anything?"

"Dark Eden. And space."

He rolled his eyes. "What you missed, my dear"—the words were thoroughly odd coming from him in this getup— "was the sense of his hands. El's. Covering the vast wreck of the world the way a sculptor's fingers roam a block of marble, carving with the inner eye before touching the chisel. You missed that sense of him moving over the surface of the deep, as though there was no memory of Lucifer's cherished garden, ruined beneath the chaos of violence like an insect trapped in amber. You missed that this was no longer a ruined Eden but an Eden roiling with the potential for a new thing. And you missed when he spoke."

I regretted having pulled away so quickly from the vision, though I knew he would not have allowed me to see this far.

"Spoke?"

"He called for light."

"As in, 'Let there be light'?"

"As in."

"'Let there be light.' You're telling me it actually started that way," I said, my hands on my knees.

"Actually, we weren't sure what was happening. All I knew then was that upon hearing that voice—that beloved and awesome timbre—I wanted to weep. Only then did I realize how much I had longed for it, how strong and reassuring it was to the fibers of my heart. And, because of what we had done, how foreboding."

"I thought you said there had already been light. That Lucifer gave off light."

"This was new light—different from that of my master," he said, gazing past the footbridge toward the statue of Washington. High-rises jutted up like teeth into the sky beyond the statue. "And light, as you know, is many things. Energy, for one."

"Are you talking about the sun?" I straightened, my patience thin. He was specific when I didn't want him to be and maddeningly vague when I wanted specifics. And the kicker was that he probably knew it, too.

"Among other things. But you're missing the point, and it's this, since I have to spell it out: We had never heard words like that before—wonderful, terrible words. These were more than words of power—they were infused with creation and the giving of *life*. Think about it. What one of us had ever witnessed an act like this? We don't recall our own beginnings, after all, so this was the first creation we had ever witnessed. And you call an earthquake an act of God."

"So this light—"

"It was brilliant, the first of its kind, generated by El himself, exploding out into the heavens. Even Lucifer, who was by now more disdainful than ever, was in awe. Speechless. He could never have done this."

"Wasn't Lucifer still giving off light?" Perhaps I had found a hole in his story. The inconsistency would never explain the other things—the dreams, the hallucinations, if that's what they were. Hope surged, and maybe a companion bit of despair, that I might have caught him in an incongruity. "If he was fallen and damned, why was he still giving off light?"

We had come to the footbridge with its pale blue lampposts and railings. The demon leaned a thin shoulder against one of the pillars and crossed his arms. Behind him, the water of the lagoon reflected the brown of maples and elms and the sharp arch of long-limbed willows bowed low to the water's edge.

"You need to understand something. Outwardly, Lucifer hadn't changed. Despite the venom he hurled at El, he still illuminated the lower heavens. He was still brilliant. Consider Moses after he came down from Mount Sinai. He glowed from having stood in the presence of El, and that after only forty days in El's presence and he, a flawed human made of mud—a rather unreflective surface overall."

He smiled blandly. "So you must imagine our Beautiful One, perfect master-work that he was, shining with an *infinity* of reflected Shekinah glory. Even we, who do not breathe, are breathless at him still."

"So this was a different kind of light."

"Yes. And when Lucifer left, retreating to the periphery of the lower heavens to look down on the muck of Eden, he took with him the light from the world, which was his own. So when El made this new and spectacular light that chased away darkness so that even the murky waters reflected it like facets of onyx, Lucifer was taken aback. He took it as a personal blow, in fact."

"Because he felt replaced."

"Yes. But El wasn't finished. Now he did something he had never done: He partitioned time. It sounds so fantastic, so mythical, doesn't it?" He paused to study my wrinkled brow. "You do understand that time, in the measured sense, had now begun."

"I really don't," I said at last. "If you're trying to sell me on seven days of creation, you'll have to pull a few more tricks out of your demonic bag. That's folklore."

Of course, the fall of Lucifer had been folklore, too.

He scratched at his temple, and I realized he was just now discovering the hardening scab on his scalp. "I know all manner of theologians and even scientists hold debates about this. How long was a day? Isn't a thousand years like a day to God? Isn't a twenty-four-hour day too literal? Surely God created evolution. They ship speakers into churches and seminaries and universities to debate it."

He gestured in the general direction of Cambridge. "But what they fail to realize is that creation defies rationality, mathematics, and reason no matter how you try to quantify it. You might as well try to quantify El himself—something you'll never find me wasting my time on."

I thought of MIT, practically across the street from my office. Of divinity school scholars at Harvard. And I realized then that I could more easily publish the memoirs of a self-professed demon than I could share with another scientific or religious-minded human the truth of my interaction with him. The thought left me feeling alienated, like some frail and sickly member of my species separated from the human herd.

"Listen now," he said, fixing me with a bright gaze. And

I saw that same darkness behind it, as though a cloud had passed behind the sun. "He called it a day, and the significance is this: There had been no days until this point. For all I know, our revolt might have erupted an eon or an hour before that. Only misery had made it seem like an eternity. But here was this new and revolutionary thing: the day. An invention for all time—literally. Can you understand what it was to us, having languished in our inertia? Can you imagine our relief and fear at once?"

"I think so," I said, lamely. "Conceptually, perhaps." And then: "No."

On the other end of the footbridge, a laughing couple held hands. Joggers ran the path beyond the bronze lantern. The juxtaposition of this modern life-in-process and religious prehistory put me at tenuous odds with reality, and I began to fear that my mind, overwrought in recent weeks, might lose discernment of where between the two extremes reality lay. Maybe I had already lost it. Maybe I was even now doped up and strapped to a bed in a mental ward. I had wondered more than once if I had dreamed up this demon, if somewhere along the line I had developed paranoid schizophrenia.

As I thought all of this, I began to feel a heaviness in my chest, as though I were trying to breathe steam in a sauna that had become too thick, too hot, too fast. Dizzying numbness sank into my skull through my eyes. I clutched at the rail of the footbridge, my heart pounding even as I tried to appear normal in this public place. And I thought, *This is how it is to die, to realize that something is wrong and to try to appear as though it is not.*

"Are you doing this to me?" I managed.

"No." But he watched me intently, in the same way scientists must observe lab rats after infusing their cages with cigarette smoke or injecting them with red dye.

"I feel ill. Something's wrong." I hauled in a slow, heavy breath, considered my lack of sleep, took inventory of all I had eaten today: cereal, coffee . . . more coffee. Not enough. I was exhausted, and my blood sugar was low.

"How tenuous and tedious it must be, keeping that balance of rest, food, and sleep." He spoke dispassionately. "Come on. We'll find something to eat."

We passed the bronze statue of George Washington atop his horse and came out through the Garden's iron gate onto Arlington. Walking seemed to help, as though the motion had reagitated my coagulating blood. I was headed toward Newbury Street to a coffee shop that served gourmet sandwiches and bottles of imported sodas. I veered left, looking for the next crosswalk, thinking I could hear Lucian's boots half a step behind me.

I was halfway across the walk when I heard the stuttered screech of tires grabbing pavement and a thud off to my right. I started at the sound, braced, stupidly, toward oncoming traffic. Someone screamed.

But it was not me.

Half a block down the street a car was just settling to a stop. Two more abruptly halted behind the first, narrowly avoiding an accident. Pedestrians stood frozen on the sidewalk, hands covering their mouths. More, emerging from the Garden, stopped short.

A man got out of his car, a cell phone in shaking hands. Shouts for an ambulance. Traffic backed up. Someone began to divert it to the far lane where cars filed by, heads swiveling behind the wheel.

I ran on shaky legs toward the car with the crystalline web for a windshield but stopped with a white-hot chill when I saw the crumpled form on the asphalt. I had thought he was behind me.

A bystander announced she had called 9-1-1. A man ran toward the curb, bellowing at someone snapping a picture with a camera phone. A mounted policeman rode out of the Garden, the horse cantering too prettily and far too slowly.

More people joined the clot of onlookers on the Garden side. A young woman in a peacoat hurried to the small cluster on the pavement, obscuring my view, saying she was a nurse.

Get up! I thought, angry, terrified. What was he doing? Making a scene? Playing dead? Could demons die? One of his sneakers rested on the asphalt, some fifteen feet away.

He hadn't been wearing sneakers.

I pushed through to the knot of people kneeling in the street, unable to hear anything but the thudding in my chest.

It wasn't him. The leg splayed out in macabre yoga was distinctly female. Blood pooled in an inky blot beneath her head, black against the pavement. It mottled her hair, which had come loose from its ponytail to stick to one side of her face in sticky, crimson-blonde fingers. A shattered pink iPod was still strapped to her arm.

Somewhere bells were ringing, church bells, perhaps from Park Street Church across the Common, maybe from Arlington on the corner. I stumbled back and searched the growing crowd for Lucian. But he was gone.

I was sick with the kind of horror one feels upon realizing he forgot to lock the gun safe—the one from which a neighborhood kid steals a handgun and shoots someone. Or upon waking from a drunk to the realization he's had unprotected sex with a prostitute. It was the kind of fear in which one realizes he has courted danger under the guise of negligent normalcy.

And now a woman lay dead.

I backed toward the curb, the gruesome bouquet of tire rubber, blood, and urine in my nostrils, as the woman in the peacoat administered CPR. Eventually, she sat back on her heels, breathing heavily, arms dangling on her knees.

A fire truck and then an ambulance arrived, sirens wailing. The way the medics left the body where it lay—the way the police shut down the street, took aside the traumatized driver of the car, interviewed some of the bystanders—it all seemed so haphazard. Like a chaotic game of pickup sticks, as primitive as surgery conducted with sharp stones. I had had such faith in this city, in the civic marvel of emergency response and modern medicine, and a woman had just died on the asphalt.

I lingered even after the ambulance drove off, silent and empty. I fixated on the policemen, trying to gather the courage to say something. To tell them that I knew. That I knew who—what—had killed that woman.

I couldn't stop thinking of those too-old teenager's eyes, narrowed at her after his staged fall, those young man's lips murmuring seemingly to himself.

I never got anything to eat. Instead, I found a liquor store and bought a bottle of merlot—a bottle with a screw cap. I carried it home in its paper bag inside my coat and gulped from it in long, less-than-covert pulls on the *T* like a common wino. I hissed and then shouted at random buildings on the walk home, calling Lucian out, calling him a murderer. People walking by gave me wide berth, and I let out one of Lucian's hysterical laughs in response.

I WOKE WITH THE cold claws of panic inside my chest. I had been prone to anxiety attacks in the past and could feel the old eddy now, offering to suck me into the spin cycle. *Don't think about that. Get up. Move.*

Queasy and unsteady on my feet, I pulled open my apartment door and stumbled down the stairs to the bank of mailboxes inside the foyer. I averted my eyes from the glare of midmorning sun pouring through the glass double doors; I didn't want to know what or who I might see standing there, peering in with too-knowing eyes. I snatched one of my neighbors' paper.

Back in my apartment, the door locked firmly behind me, I folded the *Globe* open on my kitchen counter, paged past the national section to city and region. There it was, page B2, just a tiny mention: *"Woman Dies, Hit by Car."*

*A woman was struck by a car and killed yester-
day on Arlington Street at about 4:48 p.m. She was
pronounced dead at the scene. The identities of both
victim and driver were withheld last night pending
investigation.*

I searched through the rest of the section, but there was
nothing more.

I felt infected—by dark words, images, and influences, by
my own willingness to expose myself to his particular strain of
evil. While his first appearance had been a startling aberration,
his presence in my life had become more real, more normal
to me than the facts of my everyday existence. Just yesterday
I had stepped willingly from the corporeal world into an alien
spiritual realm.

What did it mean that a demon could infiltrate my life? And
what were the implications for me that I had willingly met with
him since? That death followed him even as he spoke of heaven,
of God?

Worst of all, I could not erase the memory of that sound. Of
a human thrown into a windshield. It should have been hard,
the crack of a body breaking. But it had been sordidly dull, as
muffled as a gun fired through a silencer.

Someone knocked at my door. I jumped, sweat breaking
out on my back. Was that him? Would he come here? I wished
I had my laptop open to my calendar. I never wanted to see that
cursed *L.* again, but at least I'd know if I should answer the door
or stay here, trembling and silent.

I sat very still. There had been no buzz from the front
door, but did that matter? Would he force his way in if I didn't
answer? Somewhere I had a list of this building's tenants and

their numbers. If I called, maybe a neighbor could investigate for me. But no, that was stupid; I wouldn't know what to tell them to look for. He could be a twelve-year-old selling Girl Scout cookies for all I knew.

"Hello?"

I didn't move.

"Clay? It's Mrs. Russo. Are you there?"

I exhaled and moved on slack legs to the door. I had unlocked it and started to pull it open, relieved at the thought of seeing her short gray hair and smooth olive skin, the crow's feet around her eyes, when I was leveled by a frightening idea: Could Lucian show up as someone familiar to me?

Again the eddy, the cold fingers clutching at my chest.

Panic is an illusion, a small voice inside me said. *Open the door and face her—it—whoever it turns out to be.*

I pulled the door the rest of the way open, ready for anything.

A plate of muffins. Blueberry, by the look of them. Across our shared second-floor landing, Mrs. Russo was just closing her door. Upon hearing me, she came back out.

"Well, there you are!" She smiled and retrieved the plate from the mat. I stared, making certain it was the same Mrs. Russo who had brought me lasagna the day I moved in, who had helped me arrange my furniture—which consisted of little more than a few items on sale from Crate & Barrel and a desk my grandfather made for my eleventh birthday—and who had declared the result "elegantly Spartan." Mrs. Russo, the widow whose husband had died of the kind of complication people sued hospitals over—though I don't think she did that. It would have seemed beneath the woman who often referred to those things that can and can't be changed, and to the will of God.

Mrs. Russo, whose mail and newspapers I collected when she went to visit her children and grandchildren. Mrs. Russo, who was always baking, warm and homey smells drifting out onto our landing from her apartment as they did now from the plate I accepted from her hands. My stomach cramped.

"Clay, dear, are you all right?"

"I've been sick." It wasn't far from the truth. Dehydration had taken its toll. I was sure that my face was pasty, my eyes shadowed and hollow. My breath was certainly bad enough.

Have you ever been harassed by a demon? I wanted to blurt.

"Have you? That must explain why I've been thinking about you so much these past couple of days." She reached up to lay the back of her hand against my cheek. Her crisp white shirt crinkled when she moved. A double strand of pearls hung in the neckline like a beady smile around her neck. She was made up for the day, her lipstick the color of new bricks. Her hand smelled like Jergen's lotion.

"Well, you don't have a fever."

I wanted to tell her everything, from the first meeting in the café to the dreams and the accident—the horrible accident—to unload it all like tears spilled in a mother's lap. But one long, stream-of-conscious sentence out of my mouth and that matronly look would change to alarm or worse. Mrs. Russo would disappear behind her door, and this moment of relative normality would be taken from me as surely as the peace had disappeared from my life that first night in the Bosnian Café.

What peace? I had not been at peace before this. But even my discontent and general aimlessness had been better than this.

"Are you sure you're all right?" She frowned, her hand going to her hip. Her camel pants were smartly pressed, and I realized she was about to head out for the day. I nodded, angry at finding myself on the verge of tears.

"I think I need to lie down. Thank you, Mrs. Russo, for the muffins," I said. She looked as if she might say more, but I gave her a weak smile, thanked her again, and closed the door, hoping I hadn't offended her in my graceless haste.

İ SPENT ALL DAY thinking about who to go to. Who I could tell without seeming like a lunatic. And I came up with only one answer.

No one.

İ LOCKED MYSELF İN my apartment for two days. I slept in fits on my sofa, refused to open my laptop for fear of what I would find on my calendar, and ate Mrs. Russo's muffins. Though I had never suffered from agoraphobia, I began to understand how easily I could become one of those people who refused to leave their home. I wondered if any of them had been stalked by demons.

On the second day I found myself rationalizing what happened in the Garden. Lucian really had tripped. When he murmured, he was merely talking to himself, calling himself clumsy and cursing his human body. Maybe he made an appreciative comment—she had been an attractive blonde, after all. That he disappeared when he did meant nothing; he routinely disappeared when I wasn't ready or whenever I wasn't paying close attention.

Anything to explain it. The truth was too appalling.

Sometime into the second day, after calling in sick again, I retrieved the stack of notes from my desk drawer. The summary account of my demonic encounters to date consisted of portions of two notebooks, of random pages stuck inside the cover of one, and the backs of a few pages from the recycle box. The last of these pages was scrawled in wild, volatile script. I had started to write about the Common and the Garden the night of the accident but never finished—mostly because I could not reconcile reality with Lucian's strange behavior and the events that followed.

The other reason was that I was drunk.

Lying on the sofa and reading through my notes up to that day, I began to feel a strange sense of control—over my words, if nothing else, as though I had captured and contained events that defied rationality. The page brought order, a shape to all experience, the comfort of events scripted into story.

I picked up my pen and began to write, chasing reason, meaning, sanity.

After three days in my tiny apartment—the false, mundane world shut out beyond my door—my denial made its pendulum swing to reckless acceptance. The mad ruminations, the nightmares, the panic gave way to exhaustion until, in my depleted state, it became very simple: I could never return to my in-transit, post-divorce life. My life might never be normal again, but I could not keep to these sequestered shadows forever. I was tired of playing the specter in my own life, of huddling behind the flimsy lock of my apartment door.

Lucian had the power to kill me—he had proven that much. And if that's what he wanted, there was nothing I could do about it.

But I didn't think that's what he wanted.

For whatever reason, he desperately wanted to tell me his story. He wanted it written and published. And though I had no intention of doing either, I had the power to give him both.

Like a fever, my fear broke.

The next morning, I lowered my chin into the collar of my coat. I did not look into anyone's eyes on the street, nor did I make my routine stop at the bagel joint near the *T* station.

Even so, I half expected some stranger to hail me by name, to signal me in the front lobby of my office. To turn toward me on the elevator as the doors closed.

Nothing like that happened.

When I passed Sheila's desk, she asked how I was feeling. She had circles under her eyes but managed a small smile that still managed to look attractive. She had always been like that—almost prettier when suffering. It used to tug at my heart, and it brought back the old envy I had felt toward Dan when he first started seeing her. Even when her mother died, she had been beautiful, a weeping Madonna at the funeral. Today, however, that trait struck me like a line repeated one too many times. I murmured something about the stomach flu and feeling better. I didn't want to talk to her.

"Oh, Clay," she called after me. "Your nine o'clock is waiting for you in your office. She came early."

I hesitated. I hadn't opened my calendar in two days and therefore had no idea who was in there.

No, I had one idea.

I veered off into the bathroom. The trembling was back in my hands. I heard again the hopping skid of tires against pavement, the thud of the collision. The back of my neck felt clammy despite the chill of the morning lingering in my fingers and on my cheeks.

So much for bravado. He had never let me escape him for long. The last time—the only time—I walked away from him, he had infiltrated my dreams. Breathing deeply, I walked myself through my conundrum to the conclusion that had freed me from my apartment prison: For whatever reason, I held the keys to something he wanted very much.

I reshouldered my bag, which was stuffed full of the same

untouched proposals I had taken home with me last Friday, and walked resolutely to my office. The door was ajar, and a vibrant female voice seemed to fill up all the space behind it. I knew that voice, and it was no demon. Well, not technically.

"Clay!" Katrina turned from the window, clapping her phone shut. Her coat was thrown over the chair in front of my desk, the upside-down Burberry tag staring out like the vacant smile of a doll. "You look good. Have you lost weight?"

I unloaded my bag as she told me about her train ride in, her new apartment in the city, her latest stash of exciting new proposals, her growing stable of up-and-coming writers. I docked my laptop but didn't turn it on.

"I'll take a look at whatever you have," I said. Despite the fact that she tired me out, she never gave me shoddy stuff, and I needed some fast acquisitions.

She hesitated, and I realized she was weighing the stacks of proposals, queries, and boxed manuscripts on my credenza and bookshelf. I was either more backed up than usual or had grown in popularity.

"They haven't hired a new editorial assistant, have they." She sat down on the Burberry-covered chair with crossed arms, peering out at me over the fine arch of her nose—which was probably as designer as the rest of her. Her nostrils tended to look like slits—until she got excited about something, in which case they flared. "How are you doing Clay, really?"

I sat down, sighed, and gestured at the paper skyline. "I've been sick. I'm behind. I could use about five solid projects right now to fill out our next season. I'll never get through all of this in time. So anything you want to send when you get back—"

"You know I will." She paused and then, on seeming whim, reached for the bag covered with Coach's trademark Cs. "You know I don't bring a lot with me"—she pulled several packets from her bag—"but here are a couple that might trip your trigger."

"I'll read them this afternoon." I meant it. I needed to patch at least one more project together this week or next to take to committee. Still, I took them with the sense of one accepting a meal from a questionable Samaritan.

She pulled another few pages from her magic bag. "And then I have this strange little orphan. Highly experimental. Frankly, I'm having some trouble finding a home for it."

She handed me a mere two pages, an odd length for a proposal—more like a query, I thought. I added it to the top of the pile. And then my gaze caught the title: *Demon: A Memoir.*

My eyes slid down to the next line: *A novel by L. Legion.*

"It's dark, edgy—it'll get in your head. Don't read it unless you want to seriously question what you think is real."

My heart accelerated, loud in my ears. "I'll look at it as soon as I can—just back from being sick," I murmured, already turning to the first page past the cover. My blood iced over at the first words printed there:

Don't stop reading. I need you to know.

"Well, let me know what you think." Katrina gathered up her coat.

"Who—who did you say this author was?" I blinked up at her.

She gave me a blank look. "Someone my assistant discovered in the slush pile. I think it has potential."

I don't know what I said after that. I saw her to the door, the manuscript clutched in a sweaty hand. When she stopped to talk with Sheila, the voices of both women assuming a personal tenor, I shut my door and carried the pages to my desk.

> *Don't stop reading. I need you to know. This story is about you, after all.*

I sat down hard in my chair.

> *I know what you think, and it's not true. Hear me out; I have nothing to gain by lying to you. You're very important to me.*

My fortitude, so carefully bolstered by my logic, cracked. *Go away*, I thought, my voice like a child's in my mind. But even as I thought it, I knew that wasn't really what I wanted.

> *I'll tell you that thing you want to know, answer the question haunting you. You just have to hear me out—hear it through—first. Let me tell my story. All of it.*
>
> *I am not a mindless monster. I do what I do for a reason. Question what you think you know about me. I've only told you the beginning. You don't completely understand anything yet.*
>
> *Time is failing us. Don't let your natural instincts keep you at bay. You cannot trust them. They're human, after all.*
>
> *I promise you'll get what you want in the end.*
>
> *For now I offer you a rare gift. Take it.*

That's all there was: a teaser paragraph, the title, and Katrina's contact info. I read it again with an editor's eyes. Yes, it might be mistaken for an intriguing, if nebulous, prologue.

I set the pages aside. Silently, robotically, I turned on my computer, logged onto the network. Opened my calendar. There was Katrina, at 9:00 a.m. That was all.

It appeared as I was staring at the screen:

> *9:30: Come outside. I'm waiting. L.*

Insanity. It was all I had known these last few weeks. I put on my coat.

The taxi waited on the tree-lined east side of my office building. I stared at it until the driver leaned over and opened the passenger door. "Get in. We have to talk."

"I don't have to do anything."

"Just get in!"

When I didn't move, he leaned farther across the front seat. He was ruddy skinned and thick set. His head was shaved and his brows might as well have been; they were so pale that they hardly appeared on his face except when the light caught them. A thick stainless steel watch escaped the ribbed cuff of his leather bomber jacket. "I tried to delay her. Startling her was supposed to slow her down."

I thought again of his strange stumble that day in the Garden.

"And prevent her getting killed?"

"That was the idea."

"Why would you do that?"

"Because I didn't want it interfering with our time together."

"You're not even going to pretend that you cared about saving her life."

He paused. "No."

I believed him. That the expediency of his purpose and his personal convenience took precedence over a life was both brutal and, I believed, the truth. The bald admission triggered something irrevocable within me, and I knew then I could no sooner walk away than I could return to my former life—be it the one with Aubrey or my aimless existence since.

There were things I needed to know. Would I kill for meaning? No. Would I accept that my informant, teacher—whatever he was to me—was a party to murder?

I got in the car.

"You were tracking her," I said.

"I only provided her location."

"Why?"

"It wasn't my mission."

"Then whose mission was it?"

A muscle in his jaw tightened. The hand on the steering wheel looked better suited to fixing a sink or punching someone than driving a car. I tried to reconcile them with the slender fingers of the redhead, with the fastidiousness of the man in the café picking at the lint on his trousers. I couldn't—until he glanced into the rearview mirror and I saw the murky shadow behind his eyes.

"Think about who you're talking to and remember that we have our own chains of command. Our ranks and hierarchies. Must I remind you that I answer to an order, that I am, as you say, 'low man on the totem pole'?"

"You say it like you're in a war."

"We are!" And then, more quietly, "We are."

We drove in silence along the Charles. In the middle of the river, a crew team skimmed along the water like an insect skating on the surface of a pond.

"It seems somehow too cliché for you, killing innocent people." I had found a follow-up mention in the next day's paper: *Sarah Marshall, a native of Michigan, was 35. She is survived by her husband and infant son.* The rest of the story had been about placement of the crosswalks on Arlington.

"No one is innocent, Clay."

"Am I going to end up smattered on someone's windshield?" I saw again the blood in the crackled glass—blood and blonde hair.

"I told you; you're very important to me right now. Besides, they're not concerned about you."

"They who?"

"The Legion."

I hesitated before asking, "Why not?"

"Because you pose no threat."

"And that blonde runner did?"

"I promise you'll understand soon."

I sat back against the leather seat and waited, but he made no effort to explain. "Where are we going?"

"I want to show you something," he said, speeding down Memorial Drive.

I gazed out at the aluminum sky, the lusterless yolk of sun. Lucian's account had left off with the creation of that very body, with the coming and going of a day.

The demon nodded as though I had spoken. "After that, El drew back the darkness covering Eden like a dusty cloth from forgotten furniture. It had been formless since the rebellion, a watery wasteland. Now he separated those waters, lifting a canopy of them into the sky. And then he parted the deep, raising Eden up from beneath the water.

"Lucifer began to take interest in that planet for the first time since the great stones toppled like Titans into the murky ocean. My heart quickened. I knew what Lucifer must think: that El had seen the merit of a second god. And maybe even now he restored the earth for us—no, made it into a new and better thing. We would be happy there again. Our star would ascend after all, even if we never entered the throne room of Elohim ourselves. I didn't care about any of that anymore. All that mattered was the relief flooding my taut immortal veins. El was going to take us back."

"But how could he? You said—"

"I know. And if I had thought about it at the time, I would have known it was impossible. He could no sooner welcome us back than he could change his own character—righteous, perfect. And we, as we had become—we were changed. No, that's a pallid euphemism for the truth, which was this: We were ruined. More ruined than the wasted earth mere days—an age—before. Still, we hovered nearby, hopeful, waiting to see what would become of it. And Lucifer stood stoic witness, waiting to see what El would create for him. The earth, after all, was his."

He was quiet for several minutes before he said softly, "It was tremendous. It surpassed imagination. We had seen Lucifer's garden. We knew what we expected, though there really was no reason for El to reproduce it. And he didn't; this was an entirely different work, this new Eden. Earth and water, deep and mountain. We watched, despite ourselves, fascinated with what El might do next, trying with our vast minds to anticipate the impossible. But even we couldn't predict the green things that sprang up from the earth. You have to understand the revelation of this great wash of green."

"It was a novelty to you," I said, almost to myself.

"Of course! This was no rock garden but a rich and lush new world, teeming with life! Who could have fathomed such delicate complexity? It awed us. And for another reason, too: All those strange green things had within them the power to create, to reproduce, each of them manufacturing miniature versions of themselves. *Imagine!*"

It had never occurred to me what a bizarre concept reproduction might seem to a race of finite number.

"I was enthralled by the veins on the back of leaves, by the seeds growing inside fruit and pod," he said, lifting his hands from the wheel as though to hold—as he must have held—each leaf between his fingers, each pod, broken apart to reveal the seeds within. "The sticky pollen on the stamens. It was bizarre. It was awesome. This was beyond your science fiction to us. I had never even dreamed such things. And by the look on Lucifer's face, neither had he.

"There were new and foreign bodies in the heavens now, too, their courses precharted for millennia to come. And the water, once dark and stagnant, moved by the pull of the new moon. I was instantly in love and left the others to walk by the muted light. I stood by the shore and watched the tides leave their skeletal treasures on the sand, lulled by the rhythm of a world that seemed to say, *Be at peace; know that I Am.* I longed for it, for all that was within it, and to be a part of it."

We had turned off Memorial onto Mount Auburn, and I was gazing at the scratched Plexiglas divider between us, seeing in its surface the mottled white of the moon, when a Lexus abruptly cut in front of us. Lucian hit the breaks and flashed a distinct bird over the steering wheel.

"Don't do that!" I said, alarmed. "For all you know he has a gun!"

"He doesn't have a gun," he said, and flashed it again. Some time after the car had sped on ahead, the demon continued. "These new celestial bodies took on great meaning to us. It was like watching the creation of an hourglass and all the sands within it. Sands within an hourglass are measured a closed set, a finite amount. And they were now set in motion. I would never look at the heavens the same; where I once saw the artful strew of El's stars, I now saw the cogs and pendulum of a great clock, ticking the finite measure of time."

"Who says time has to be finite?" I studied him in the rearview mirror. He had a faint scar against one temple, again suggesting a history that was not his. I wondered if it was the demon equivalent to designer jeans, faded and pre-ripped right off the hanger.

"Things with beginnings also have ends. The beginning of time is also the beginning of an end. And so that great hourglass to me was like your fabled Doomsday clock, ticking, ticking, every grain one in a too-limited series, the granule of an instant, passing and lost forever. I understood that things now and hereafter set in motion would be things of consequence, of inevitability. The passing of every moment since has disconcerted me. See the clock on the dash?" He tapped it. "You're deaf to it, to the death of each second. But I am not."

I had thought his fixation with time and timepieces a fetish until now. Now I thought I understood the preoccupation, the compulsive checking. Every timepiece I had ever seen him wear had been expensive. Was it that time was precious?

And to think that in the last year I had done nothing but pass time since my separation and divorce, tossing first days and then weeks and months at the iterant routine of work, of the T. Waiting out the pain, waiting for clarity and direction, waiting for the day that something shoved me from inertia.

And something had.

The demon was driving with one hand on the wheel, the other fingering his watch with more thoughtful delicacy than I would have thought those fingers capable of. "I didn't understand it yet, of course. I was preoccupied, if unsettled. Each new day brought new wonders to Eden. The next day El spoke again, and the water swarmed—and so did the air."

"Are you talking about fish—fish and birds?" I saw the distinct image of my own hands—small, as they had been when I was a boy—pasting animals onto a paper earth in Sunday school, something I had forgotten until this moment.

"Yes, and we had never seen anything like them. These were no spirit-beings but strange and alien creatures, swimming in the water and flying through the sky. So queer and diverse. Even Lucifer watched, stark eyed, beside himself with amazement. And I knew, with a vestige of that single accord that we had once shared, that he coveted this strange new world and all the things inside it. He had wanted to be a god, but in that moment I believe he remembered why he was not.

"But now, a stinging blow! El did something he had never done before: He blessed them. Never before had I heard such things spoken, even to Lucifer, and he had been the anointed one. Coveted words! And then, to these creatures, these base and strange new things, he gave license to create more of their own for as long and often as they dared. *Imagine!*"

In the rearview mirror I saw fever in his eyes.

"These were no gods—no spiritual beings even—these *creatures*. But they had been given the power to create."

I had never seen him this emotional.

"We had no such power! They had been blessed. We had no such blessing. Can you understand?"

"Maybe," I said, thinking how a firstborn must feel at the birth of a younger sibling—how I had felt at the birth of my sister when I was six years old.

"That day," he said, at a stoplight now, his hand a fist on his chest, "another new thing sprouted, this time inside me, its roots embedded in the soil of my changed heart. By nightfall, jealousy had wound its tendrils through my innards, choking me from the inside. From Lucifer's face I knew I was not the only one.

"And now, with the passing of another day, there came new creations more exotic than before, walking on legs, many of them without wings, roaming over the land. By any logic they should have been miserable—censored, condemned to swim, to roam on land without flying, to fly and not swim. I wanted them to be miserable. But they fascinated us with their strangeness and variety. And they ate things."

He chuckled, but the sound was hollow. "Never before had we seen such a phenomenon. Terrible, fascinating—the devouring of green, living things for the sake of a too-mortal body. Mesmerizing. Horrifying. We watched them do it for hours, transfixed—mouthfuls of green, leaf and branch, fruit and seed, even the tiny plankton of the sea—all devoured by bodies with appetites we did not understand. So strange, so novel. We couldn't get enough of it."

I thought back to the coffee in the café, the scone at the bookstore, and the demon watching me. Even in the tea shop, he hadn't drunk from his cup but watched me lift it to my lips so intently I had wondered if he had poisoned it.

"Yes!" He laughed. "So now you know why I will never tire of watching you consume things."

This struck me as deviant as a foot fetish. "Then why don't you ever eat?"

His expression slowly twisted. In the rearview mirror, I saw acid leak into his eyes. "Because it all tastes like the *dirt* you come from!"

I fell back against the seat, startled into silence as he drove on, eyes boring into the road before us.

We entered a residential area of large, rolling yards. Iron fences enclosed wooded drives, old elms screened houses buttoned tight by latched iron gates. I recognized this Belmont neighborhood; in college I had attended a party here at the family home of a friend-of-a-friend. I had been struck by the sheer size of the house, awed by the French table clocks, chinoiserie secretaries, and mahogany sideboards that whispered "heirloom" and "old money," each of them at anachronistic odds with the modern security system panels and television sets. Someone had set a sweating beer bottle on top of a Queen Anne table and I had discretely removed it, trying to save the old oak the indignity of a ring.

For years I returned whenever I found myself in the area, to admire the gabled roofs and columned porticoes, the dark shutters and diamond-paned windows, to tell myself that when I got caught up at work, I would pull out one of my own manuscripts and finish it. And when that day came—the one with the six-figure advance and movie deal—I would buy a place here where my kids could play on the lawn or ride their Big Wheels in front of the garage, where our two family cars—one of them an

SUV and the other an Audi sedan—were parked inside. When the kids were old enough, they could go off to the local private school, complete with its own ice-hockey rink.

I indeed finished the manuscript and sold it in a three-book deal as the Coming Home series. But I never bought the house. The first book sold fewer than 3,500 copies, and the series was cancelled after the release of the second. Had it stayed in print long enough, I was sure it would have done better, but the unsold copies returned too quickly, their shelf space surrendered to higher volume tenants.

Lucian pulled over in front of a stately brick Tudor covered with ivy. I was not surprised to recognize the curved front entry, the door like an upside-down *U*, the turret to the side of it running up the front of the house, complete with a spire, the steeply pitched roof. It was the same house I had visited nearly two decades ago, the same one that had informed my every image of success, of a life worthy of Aubrey's expectations. A mark I had fallen short of.

The demon squinted at it through the passenger window, his forearm resting on the steering wheel. I expected him to crow his knowledge of my having come here, to regale me with the story of how I made out with Deanna Blair in an upstairs bedroom, then drop the bomb that she was dead or paralyzed or kidnapped in Colombia. But he was silent. I found it unnerving.

"Why are we here?"

He turned in the seat and regarded me. "I've thought a long time about telling you this, gone back and forth on it. I'm not sure about it, even now, but look—we're here, and I promised to tell you everything."

He seemed to wait for some indication of my understanding.

"The world is not as you see it," he said finally. "Look at that house. So grand, so very upper-crust."

"That it is," I said warily.

"But here's the thing: That house, the cars, the old furniture and interior decorating, even the landscaping—this physical world—is nothing but window dressing. Beneath all of that lies another realm altogether.

"The distinction between our two worlds is important for you to understand. It's important for you to know that beneath the aesthetics of every temporal veneer lies a stratum of infallible truth: a spiritual realm, the world wiped clean of cosmetics."

Now, as I looked again at that house, the heavy brick began to fall away, translucent as a frame in a ghost movie. And then the two upper levels silently collapsed, caving in the middle so that the stately old furniture, tables, and consoles with their curving legs and claw feet slid and then toppled through the crumbling floors. I had experienced Lucian's tampering with my brain before in visions and dreams, but this—here, with my eyes bearing open witness to the very thing before me—was disconcerting. I jerked in my seat, but it, too, had become transparent. And then we were no longer seated in a cab but standing on a street that was no longer paved, in front of a yard that was nothing but earth and rock.

In my vision, my waking hallucination, he turned to me. "I'm aware of every detail you've admired about that place: the great deck out back, the vaulted ceilings, the crystal light fixtures, and old oak floors. The grandeur, the status, the sheer custom cost of it all. But I see nothing more than your fancy tissue paper: brightly colored but fragile, fading, and easily torn, not to endure very well even the short span of your lifetime."

I closed my eyes, and when I opened them, where the house, the raised flower beds, the turret spire, and the iron gate had been, there was nothing but a pile of brick and rubble, dry dirt and stone. On the ground perhaps ten feet from me lay the splintered foot of a Queen Anne table, the cabriole wizened as though a century had had its inevitable way with it in the space of that instant.

A car motored past us on the street, and we were in the cab once more as a postman pulled over in front of the bronze mailbox. The house was restored to its opulence, secure in its legacy, anchored in privilege to the manicured lawn.

The demon tilted his head back against the window. "I see beyond the comforts of the amenities you seek all your life—the money, the hobbies, the alluring distractions that promise temporal gratification. Though humans claim to plumb the depths in search of meaning, I find they tend to settle for whatever drifts across the surface."

He had given me something. I knew that, for whatever reason, he had granted me a concession in showing me this thing, without which he might have shared his story just as cohesively and in a more expedient fashion. And I wondered why. To unsettle me? I was indeed unsettled—seeing the embodiment of my dreams ravaged before me resonated with strong, discordant notes.

He raised a finger. "Granted, every now and then a human comes along with extraordinary discernment, a gift for seeing the world—if only for momentary glimpses—with near-angelic acumen. It's unnerving."

"Why?"

"It's like peering into a roomful of shadows and having one of them step forward to look you directly in the face. Humans shouldn't see so clearly."

"Do you think angels—demons, whatever—have a monopoly on truth?" I asked, not without defensiveness.

He sat up, put the car in gear, and pulled away from the curb. "No. We're simply better equipped to see it. Why? Because we aren't looking at the world through soft and pulpous eyes like you, but through the iris of truth. It is neither obscured from us nor spared us."

"I want to know what this has to do with me."

"I'm coming to that."

Just then the two-way radio on the dash crackled with static. Though no voice came through, Lucian tilted his head as I had seen him do before to the invisible swarm of insects near his ear.

We had been wending through the country club area, but now he turned around with a curse.

"Helen's been asking about you at the office. When you get back, tell her you had a doctor's appointment."

"That's lying."

"It's on your calendar."

"It's not on my cal—" I stopped, aggravated. "Why did we even come here if you were going to take me right back?" Though I had been antsy about the time away from the office, I now had mixed feelings about returning.

"I didn't know they'd be talking that much about your absence."

"I thought you knew things."

"I hear things. I observe. I'm not omniscient." He sighed and rubbed his forehead, as though the very act of talking to me gave him a headache.

"We have a little bit of time left," he said, checking his watch and then tapping the clock on the dash as if it had stopped.

"So now listen: The world was new. All the creatures were vegetarian. The rending of flesh was yet to come. Creation enthralled and amazed us."

"Vegetarian?" I remembered his T-shirt that day in the Common—and then, inevitably, the shattered pink iPod strapped to a sickeningly skewed arm.

"By design. You weren't made to eat meat. Of course, you weren't made to die, either."

"What do you mean?"

"I'll come to that. For now, you need to know something more about Elohim: He is the ultimate force of creativity. He is the author of diversity. The richness of creation has been lost on your kind for centuries. Millennia. But it wasn't lost on us. Even Lucifer stared in amazement. Light. Earth. Water. Life. It was base and gorgeous. It was extravagant. We had never seen the earth like this, a swarming symphony of life. I heard with angel ears every call of bird and whale, the murmur of water, the rustle of tree. I thrilled to the sound of crickets, the collective pulse of mortal vein and plant stem. It was a visual feast as well, and I consumed it in long, wondering stares: the jade of glaciers, the desert art of sand dune, the simmer of lava, the effusive glow of firefly."

His voice fell and drifted off. When he spoke next, his words were distant, in that way in which we go back to our past to gratify or torture ourselves.

"I was intoxicated by the activity of the day but returned almost every night to the shore, to walk beneath the gentle light of the moon, which forgave in shadow everything the sun so harshly laid bare. I could have spent millennia like that, days and nights walking the earth, sating my senses."

I was, for a moment, moved. And though he had not cast me into the illusion of his memory, I stood vicariously beside him on the shores of Saint Lucia, where I had gone on my honeymoon.

"We longed for this world. We coveted it, and we hoped. Even Lucifer, though he wouldn't say it, looked on with greed-softened eyes, infatuated. I deluded myself into thinking that yes, perhaps Elohim had taken him back. Perhaps Elohim had forgotten all, would set him up as a god over this rich and wild new world. The next blessings to come from El would be his, and ours." He shook his head with a brittle laugh, the sound slightly too high-pitched for such a big man.

We had skirted the MIT campus to arrive on Main, a block from my office building.

"And why weren't they? Why couldn't they be?"

He pulled over, put the car in park, and turned to look at me.

"Because then he created them."

"Them?"

"You."

A scending the stairs to my apartment that evening, I felt drained but calmer than I had been in days.

The incident outside the Garden still haunted me. I heard, in unexpected moments, the sound of that impact, saw again the splayed and broken limbs of that woman. *I have something he wants*, I reminded myself before that tendril of panic could tease my composure. And I knew that I needed something from him in return.

I planned to spend the bulk of my evening writing by hand every bit of our conversation. I could feel the urge of it already, demanding release like an overfull bladder. But I hesitated on the landing and, on a sudden whim, went over and knocked on Mrs. Russo's door. Now that I was composed, I wanted to thank her for the muffins, for her friendship and her concern. Her timing had been uncanny and, considering my state yesterday, I wouldn't have blamed her for thinking I might be on drugs.

Standing on her threshold, I wondered if her keen discernment would sense—and recoil from—any lingering trace of the company I had been in today. And so I was relieved when, after waiting another moment, there was no answer.

That night, as I sat at my desk, my pen moving across the page, one thing in particular set my mind on edge: his capricious moods, especially in relation to me. Or rather, to humans. I returned again and again to his near-violent response—for a moment he really had looked possessed—to my question about why he never ate. To the way he had called humans *them,* as though we were a vile species.

Or a hated enemy.

few years ago I considered becoming a member of the Museum of Fine Arts. It was where Aubrey and I liked to spend days holding hands, standing with our arms around each other in front of the exhibits, murmuring into each other's ears. I had planned to take her here for our anniversary last year. Instead, here I was on yet another stop of my Location Reclamation Project.

A piece of calligraphy in the long Islamic gallery caught my eye. The Arabic was written in the shape of a boat. The placard translated: "I seek God's protection from the cursed devil." I wondered at the symbolism of the boat—but wondered more what had prompted the writer's need for protection.

I wandered into the Asian gallery, past busts from Angkor with curling hair and wide, broad lips, past Indian cave paintings faded into soft palettes of color, past the statue of an Indonesian demon with bulging eyes and a broad-lipped smile full of fanged teeth. The placard read: "The demon Manisha."

Demons everywhere. Why had I never noticed this commonality between cultures before? Why had I assumed demons to be property of the Christian church? I suddenly felt, as a

modern and educated man, that I might be living proof of ret-
rograde enlightenment.

Beyond the marble statue of infant Moses and his mother lay
the Nubian gallery, the room typically rushed through en route
to the morbid Egyptian collection. Even the museum guide had
printed, beneath "Egyptian Funerary Arts," the parenthetical
"(Mummies)" for those who had come here solely to see dead
people. Aubrey had always found the idea gauche, so we never
invested much time there; the impressionists, existential and
vibrant, were much more romantic.

I was considering the pieced-together shards of a bowl that
had been buried with the wife of a king when a woman in her
fifties came to stand next to me. "Nothing lasts, does it? It all
turns to dust."

"I suppose you'd know."

In my peripheral vision I saw her turn and stare at me as
I realized my mistake too late.

"I *beg* your pardon!" The skin between her chin and neck
shook as she said it. I imagine it did, too, when she walked
deliberately out the direction I had just come in from.

Across the small exhibition hall, I heard soft laughter. The
crimson stain was still on my face when the source of the sound,
a caramel-skinned woman, strolled toward me, mirth and the
devil dancing in her eyes.

"Not one of your smoother moments," she said, still chuckling.
Her hair fell in a wave past her shoulders, and I inwardly groaned
at the sight of it, even as I found myself wanting to touch it. She
was tall, svelte, her peacoat not reaching the hem of the short
skirt that bared her knees. They were coltish, those legs, skin
showing through the open weave of her tights like sun through
a thousand tiny windows. She had turned her heart-shaped face

to the broken bits of bowl, but I was staring at the profile of her mouth, at the pouty curve of her upper lip. She was the kind of beauty other women seemed to hate on principle.

"This is quite old, in terms of your history. Though it seems like yesterday to me. I'm dating myself, aren't I?"

"I hate it when you do that." I turned away.

"Do what?"

"Make your smug demon jokes."

"What else can I do in this divine comedy that sums up your human existence? It is a joke! It's all a joke."

Together we wandered past gold necklaces, amulets designed to protect the wearer from evil—Lucian seemed unfazed by any of these—past scarabs and Eyes of Horus to a collection of ninth-century BC jewelry.

She studied a weathered gold ring. "This is much closer."

"Closer to what?"

"The time when God came to Eden."

"Came to Eden?"

She looped her arm through mine. "We had no idea what he was doing," she said in a low, seductive tone. "Everything so far had appeared by word, had come into existence by the sheer will of God. But now El came down to this new Eden. We felt him moving over the land, rushing upon meadow and valley, the animals excited in his wake, their chorus raised to the sky. In the garden I felt him, circling as one paces upon the ground in consideration. He came to the edge of the river and lingered there, roaming through the reeds." She looked at me, her eyes luminous and wild.

"Why? What was he doing?"

"The unthinkable!" she said in a whisper. She seemed unusually convivial today. "There now, by the river, the earth was gathering upon itself, forming up from the ground as though El himself had bent down and scooped up mounds of the foul stuff in his hands." She covered her mouth, a strange half laugh seeming to escape her of its own volition, inadvertent as a hiccup, the sound of it peculiar and cracked.

"We on the periphery lingered in the humid air. What was he doing? There was God, doing something in the muck. We looked at each other. Even Lucifer stared, dumbfounded. You should have seen the look on his face!"

She broke out in sudden, trilling laughter. There again was that slight hint of mania. And as before, the abruptness with which she regained her composure startled me nearly as much as how quickly she had lost it. It occurred to me that anyone overhearing her—the way her voice shot up in register and low-ered to a whisper and then broke out in laughter—might have thought she was unbalanced.

She steered me toward an exhibit of gold bracelets and rings, preserved all these years in a Nubian tomb. I was conflicted by her casual contact and thought about pulling away from her whispered words, stirring the tiny hairs in my ear.

"El was sculpting the earth into some thing, some likeness, creating this time not by word . . . but in person." When I said nothing, she gestured imperatively, vainly, as one groping for words. "In person, Clay. As though *by hand!*"

I looked at her, baffled.

"We were all staring, gape-mouthed as you, by then. And then he surrounded this thing. He was everywhere around it, as if he had gathered the dirty thing in his arms and cupped it by the head. And then I *heard* it."

She was clutching my arm, her fingers biting into my flesh

so that I was glad I had worn a sweater, sure that she would have left half-moon punctures with her nails in my forearm.

"The sound, it was the same expectant sound at the dawn of all the world. A breath exhaled into the mud! Given to the mud thing as surely as if he had set his mouth against those dirty lips and breathed.

"Oh, divine exhale! It was *himself.* Much more than life, it was everything—the awareness, all the emotion, the propensity to love, to nurture, to create. And he endowed it all upon this new creature made of mud." The plush mouth contorted. Behind her irises, the unnatural light I had noted before blazed like a black nova. "And the clay chest filled, and expanded, and warmed. The man coughed and fell down, alive."

I stared. "But you're saying—"

"Yes, *Clay*"—her mouth smoothed into a chilly smile— "Image of El, breath of God. In such an unworthy vessel. Something far more precious than diamonds, denied even to us but entrusted to a container of mud."

"I take it Lucifer was as thrilled as you seem."

Again the brittle laugh. "His jealousy exploded in a fiery blast, the fallout infecting us with his cancer."

She shrugged out of her coat, and I instinctively moved to help her. She wore a sleeveless turtleneck beneath, and the skin of her arms was smooth, luminous. I wanted to touch it.

"Eden, once the seat of his government, had been made anew, raised up and recreated lush and living—and prepared for another." She took the coat from me and draped it over her arm, a delicate silver watch on her wrist catching the light. "No more stones like mirrors—this was a handcrafted cradle for no creature of our kind."

"So he—El—made it for Adam. I assume that's the man you're talking about."

"Yes. This new garden, planted by Elohim, became his home. The former throne of Lucifer now belonged to a cherished new creature made of mud."

"You said yourself that Lucifer didn't want it anymore."

"Not as it *was*. Not ruined. But El had done something special and made it anew—and given it away. Worse yet, El himself deigned to go there. He went down from the heavens daily. He left the mount and moved among the creatures, speaking with the man, walking with him in the shade and telling him things beneath the trees. Oh, intimate whispers! How my soul suddenly longed to be a clay creature!"

All this time we had been alone, the museum unusually quiet for a Saturday afternoon.

"By now Lucifer was no longer content to sit by. The earth was his, had been since its inception. He meant to inspect these new creatures and all this strange life now roving about and sprouting from this planet of his jurisdiction." She stopped to peer at an assortment of jewelry: shell bracelets and necklaces, their tiny conches perfectly intact. "From the Red Sea," according to the numbered notation.

"There had never been any question, in Lucifer's mind at least, as to who would rule this place, this new life, the creatures. The earth—all of Eden—belonged to him. He might disdain this refurbished Eden and its new tenants, but it was his. But El wasn't finished."

She moved farther to my left to gaze intently into the exhibit case, and I saw the object of her interest: an ivory comb. For several moments, she stood unmoving, her expression thoughtful, her lips pursed. And then she tilted her head and said with what I thought was sadness, "I knew the woman this belonged to. She used to sing to the moon at night, and I used to stop to listen to her, this human who seemed to see in that pale light the very thing I did."

I could not help but wonder if some accident had befallen that woman—the 2200 BC equivalent of being run down by a car. Just then it hit me: I stood shoulder to shoulder with a being older than any item in this room. Or the next. Older, even, than the very soil it was built upon.

She touched the Plexiglas. "How odd that I should share sentiments with a human. It was, I think, the most kinship I have ever felt with one of your kind." Her fingers fell away. "Of course, I realized sometime later that it had not been the actual woman I was drawn to, but those qualities within her that were the earmark of El. In the poignant yearning of her psyche, in the loveliness of her voice, I had heard El."

She fell quiet after that, her lips moving slightly, emitting no sound. And I realized that she mouthed the words to a song.

"You said El wasn't finished," I prompted.

She sighed. "No, he wasn't. In a sudden, great blow to my prince, he gave the animals to the man and told him to rule over them. Do you understand what I'm saying, Clay?" She leaned against the case, her face turned up toward mine. *"Gave them to the clay man!* He brought them to the man and gave him the power to name them. And the man, oblivious to what he did in usurping Lucifer's rightful place, did it. But it got worse." She shifted her coat, lifting a finger for emphasis. "For every animal there was a counterpart." She added a second finger and turned her fingers this way and that. "But for the man—nothing. Naming the animals took a long time. Caring for the garden was no small task. The man needed help. And he was lonely. Communing with nature is only novel for so long."

"He had El," I offered, wondering that such pious-sounding words should come out of my mouth.

"True, and that ought to have been enough. But El is extravagant. And what was good enough for us positively paled beside what he was willing to do for the mud race." There was a strange, ironic tinge to her voice.

"And so, like your bakers, who pinch off dough from one loaf and set it aside to leaven another, El took out a part of this man—no flesh, but fine, sleek bone—and crafted a new thing." She moved on toward the next room but glanced over her shoulder as though to see if I followed. I noticed that the smooth skin bore a small tattoo: a falling star. "And she rose up, a counterpart to the man, the female to his male."

She smoothed her hair back with her hand, her fingertips brushing absently against the side of her neck, pausing to trace the line of it, to feel, perhaps, the faint pulse there. "They were as regal a pair as could ever hope to spring from the mud. Both unique from all creation, both uniquely created in person by God and after his own image. I actually forgot, as El gave them the green things to live on and told them to fill the earth, that they had been born of the dirt."

She stopped to check her watch. I was accustomed, by now, to this ritual—and to the fact that it might signal her imminent departure. She tapped it as I had seen the demon do in the taxi with the dashboard clock. When it seemed to work to her satisfaction, she looked up at me.

"And?" I hated the way she made me wait on her. But I did it. I did it because I wanted as much to take back to my desk, to my expanding stack of pages, as possible. I did it in the hope of having more from which to glean her purpose, her unspoken reason in sharing her story in the first place.

She shrugged. "He sat back, called it good, and rested."

I waited.

She waited.

I raised my brows. "And?"

Her mouth curved into a smile. "You think I'm pretty, don't you."

THE "MUMMY" ROOM WAS dimly lit, miniature track lights shedding halogen pools onto giant sarcophagi and burial masks that were never meant to emerge from darkness. It was cooler, too, the change in light and temperature making for an appropriately tomblike atmosphere. Along the far wall, a small pantheon of gods stood sentry over the dead: Isis, Anubis, Maat, Thoth. Sections of an actual burial chamber adorned the adjacent wall, etched with symbols to protect the dead.

Thinking of the Arabic calligraphy and the amulets to ward against evil in the Nubian room, I wondered what the deceased had used to protect themselves while they lived.

Lucian sauntered through the display of sarcophagi, caressing the Plexiglas cases in a way I found thoroughly unsettling.

"I know this seems like a myth to you. Ancient history at best. But can you imagine, Clay, that all of this"—she gestured around the chamber—"stemmed from them, the original two?"

I assumed what she meant by "this" were the vestiges of an elaborate culture. Otherwise, for all practical purposes, this room was a cult tribute to death.

"After that," she said, "we waited. Even as the man began his life with the woman, feeding her and lying down with her, we waited to see what they would do, sure there would be more. But El was finished. And there was nothing for us."

She leaned over the sarcophagus of a princess, turning her ear to it as though to listen for tapping on the inside. "I wonder, sometimes, what it must be like to die."

I turned away.

"Oh, don't." She was at my side again, her arm twining through mine.

"I want to know what this has to do with me."

"If you don't understand the beginning, the rest will mean nothing to you, and we'll have wasted our time. And neither of us can afford that." She picked a piece of lint off my sweater.

A few other patrons drifted through the mummy room as I remarked again to myself at the lack of traffic. I wouldn't have minded more; a shallow part of me felt gratified to be seen like this with such an obviously beautiful woman on my arm. And another part of me remembered that this was no woman, no human, at all.

Wheels, skidding on pavement . . . blonde hair and blood . . .

"You picked the perfect place for me to tell you all of this. Here, among your artifacts that have managed to outlast millennia of humans like you. Can you grasp what I've told you? That I watched the first rising of the sun, strolled the best beaches on earth before human feet soiled the sand?"

Her head tilted toward my shoulder. "I know," she said with a sigh. "I'm giving away my age."

HER VOICE DROPPED TO a conspiratorial whisper. "Lucifer claimed it was spite." She might have been any woman gossiping to a friend. Across the room, a man in his twenties tried not to openly stare at her. He mostly failed.

"It was spite, he said, that El communed with these new creatures as though they were more than walking mud, as though they could ever be worthy of anything. He knew then what we hardly dared believe: that El had created a new favorite. I have a present for you, Clay."

I was startled by the sudden sound of my own name. "You do?" I frowned. "What is it?"

"You'll see." Her lips curled up, catlike.

I didn't like that smile.

She tightened her arms around mine, hugging it to her. "Now Lucifer addressed the Legion: '*What is to stop us from becoming their kings? Their gods? What else could we possibly be to these new creatures? Let us walk in the garden as he does. Let us be as gods to them and exercise our influence over them and turn them away from this fellowship with Elohim, as we have turned away.*'"

We paused before a statue of the falcon-headed Horus. I hesitated and then marveled at her implication. Did I imagine it, or had she winked at it? I shuddered. She nuzzled my shoulder, her eyes on the statue. My head was spinning.

"Lucifer became obsessed with the humans. I didn't know what to make of his fixation. I had never seen him like this. Even in the throes of his failed ascent, he had never been so intent, driven by such singularity of purpose. He studied them. He lost interest in the new world. He forgot us and even ceased to taunt El. The whole world had shrunk to this one thing: the humans." She leaned away, her arm never leaving mine, to inspect a burial mask with vacant eyes and dark, curling hair, to trace its shape on the Plexiglas.

"He prowled the garden, inspecting for himself the handi-work of El like the jealous critic who judges the craftsmanship of the master, turning the work slowly between his hands, searching for the slightest weakness." Her finger squeaked down the front of the display case. "And who, after long days and years of searching, finds it at last."

For the last ten minutes or so there had been a new flow of visitors circulating through the room, coming in and out of the entrances on adjacent sides of the gallery. And so I paid no particular attention to the couple that entered the room just then until I felt, rather than saw, one of them falter. I glanced up just as Lucian twined both arms around mine once more.

Aubrey.

I HAD DREADED AND anticipated this day. Would it be at Old Beijing on a weekend? On the pedestrian mall outside Macy's, or coming out of Peet's? Would I look up in the T station to see her waiting across the track . . . or would it happen at all?

In the weeks since Lucian's intrusion into my life, I had found new fears to rival my dread of running into Aubrey. Since then there had even been a growing number of days when I thought about Aubrey only once or twice. I panicked upon realizing this at first, feeling that the last traces of her were slipping away from me completely, too quickly. Later I tenuously congratulated myself, thinking that in the midst of this new madness I had begun to move on.

Even so, I was invariably conscious of her specter almost every time I left home—following me down Tremont or into the Harvest store in Cambridge, seeking me in places we had never been together before—whispering in my mind, *Is today that day?* And though I had exhaustively premeditated it, I knew when that day happened, I would not be prepared.

But I was less—so much less—prepared for it today. Especially upon seeing her with a man, the arm of whom she had instinctively clasped upon seeing me.

Richard.

Now at last I would confront him. But what I saw confounded me more than the faceless man he had been to me all these months: Other than his height, he did not resemble at all the chiseled-featured lothario of my imagination. Granted, he was tanned as if he had just come in from Saint Martin, and he had a full head of sporty brown hair. But his features seemed somehow soft, his eyebrows ill-formed over the pale color of his eyes. I thought his chin receded a little bit as well. In fact, other than the obvious understated quality of his clothing, he was disappointingly average, which evoked in me first relief and then incredulity. And I wondered, as I had a thousand times before, what the draw had been, that thing that caused Aubrey to gravitate toward him when she compared the two of us side by side as she must have done.

As I did now.

I noticed the black cashmere scarf draped around his neck: Aubrey's trademark gift. She had given one to me and her boyfriend before me. I wondered if he knew that.

Aubrey was tanned, too. They must have just come from some no-doubt exotic location. And it irritated me to think that as I wondered almost daily if and when I would run into her, for part of that time she had not even been in the city.

The introductions went smoothly—thanks, surprisingly, to Richard. *The* Richard. Smooth as Richard. To his credit, he stuck out his hand, congenially and formally, as though it were a peace offering. I saw my hand clasp it, heard myself say something not nearly as clever as I had said in my rehearsals for this moment.

It was then that I caught the scent of her perfume, the bottle of which, shaped like a blue star, had sat every day on the bathroom counter. I was suddenly besieged by memories: her shoulders in the dress she wore to her office party our last Christmas together, the indentation of her pillow in the morning, the hair across her face as she slept, her clothes, pooled by the side of our bed.

"Clay," Richard said. I detected, in the single syllable of my name, a slight accent. British. Wouldn't you know it.

"You look good," Aubrey lied. She seemed flushed, as though too warm in her cable-knit sweater and corduroys, a mixture of slight confusion and what I would recognize later as benign detachment in her eyes. Her lips, glossy and pink, were parted, as if on the cusp of a remark. I remembered the shape of that mouth, found myself first gazing and then staring at it. She had a front tooth that had always been at a slight angle so that it nudged her upper lip. She had been self-conscious of it, but I had thought it endearing. It kept her otherwise aristocratic look somehow approachable, more human. But now I was certain there was no discrepancy between those white edges. She had gotten it fixed! The lips closed, parted again as her blue gaze flitted from me, to Richard, and back like a moth, settling at last on the woman coiled at my side.

"Yvonne." The demon smiled in that magnanimous way women do when they know they're the prettier of the two. Her head tilted just perceptibly then, and I recognized with alarm a faint buzzing in the air. Her smile broadened. "Clay was just telling me how you used to come here together."

I was mortified. I wrapped my arm around her. Aubrey gave a slight smile.

"I'm surprised to see you in the mummy room." I wanted to accuse her—of getting her tooth fixed, of coming to the mummy room though she didn't like it.

"I insisted, having never seen it before. Quite spectacular, really," Richard said, coming to her rescue.

I hated him.

"So nice to meet you, Yvonne." Aubrey's expression was benign, betraying no insecurity or envy, only a bare hint of surprise. "Are you from the city?"

"Yes. I'm an attorney," the demon said.

"Ah." Aubrey was obviously impressed, her gaze bouncing from "Yvonne" to me, and back. And with ex-husband perception I heard her thinking that she would never have thought an attorney to be my type. "What kind of law?"

"I litigate product liability lawsuits," Lucian said with a smile. I had no idea what that meant but felt an instant alignment like gratitude toward her that both surprised and unsettled me.

Richard checked his watch. "Well, I'm a bit peckish. Do you mind much, Bree, if we head up to the restaurant for some lunch?"

Richard to the rescue again. Aubrey excused them both with a smile and nod. "It's good to see you, Clay."

When their footsteps had receded out into the American galleries, I turned on Lucian. "You had no right," I hissed, feeling the heat of the initial meeting still in my face.

"I think that went quite well." She let go of me. I stared past the funerary mask of the dead princess, quite unable to believe that it had finally happened and happened so uneventfully that they were even now walking into Bravo, the upstairs restaurant, as I stood blinking in the middle of the mummy room.

But now that it was over, I was angry. Angry at Aubrey's detachment, at being caught off-guard, at Richard's heroics. I hated Richard for stepping in the way he had, first into our marriage and now today, for saving her from the need to answer for herself, as though to protect her from me.

"Is that why we were here?" I asked Lucian finally.

"You chose to come here, Clay." She was smoothing her hair back in a way that reminded me of a Siamese cat. She peered up at me, then, her expression indulgent, the smile I hated was back again.

I2

♦

I could not sleep the night after the museum—not until I transcribed every word and expelled every nuance of that otherworldly drama from my memory. This process, normally focused to the exclusion of even hunger and fatigue, was interrupted regularly that night as I stared out the window or at the wall, seeing neither, seeing only the image of Aubrey's hand on Richard's arm, the pink curve of her lips over those perfect teeth, the imperfect shape of Richard's face, Aubrey's gaze fluttering between Lucian and me. And I searched that memory for any glint of her reaction to the sight of Lucian and me together.

Richard had called her "Bree." Aubrey used to hate that.

I replayed the scene in my mind, outfitting it with every witty rejoinder, smug comment, and cryptic well-wish I had rehearsed for months. But finally, upon contemplating yet again the distance in Aubrey's gaze, the fixed front tooth, I decided that she had retreated too far beyond me to be touched by any of them.

The image of them together, of the formerly faceless Richard, had preyed upon me in waking and dreaming moments for more than a year. But now that it was over, I found something disappointingly unremarkable about the reality.

I had always assumed he and Aubrey had no chance of making it, having started the way they had. But thinking back to Richard's quick rescues, I wasn't so sure. She had seemed in utter possession of the situation despite his protection of her. And I found something pathetic in his safeguarding her, in his willingness to be fitted into the mold of her expectations like a mummy in a coffin made for someone else.

I WENT TO WORK and sat in meetings. But even as I did, my mind roamed the heavens, walked the shore by moonlight, passed among the reeds on the bank of Eden's river.

At home I made my way through manuscript chapters, jacket copy, and e-mail, my gaze wandering often to that pile of pages, scratched in frantic pen and harried pencil, growing on the corner of my desk, to the rumpled receipt I had saved from the Bosnian Café that first night. It seemed a year, an age ago.

"I'm going to tell you my story, and you're going to publish it."

Staring at the pile, I considered the narrative tension of his story, the larger-than-life qualities of his characters (and how could they be otherwise when they included both God and the devil?), the unlikely point of view—like the monster of John Gardner's *Grendel* telling the tale of Beowulf ripping off his arm. A stepsister's account of being born ugly. A tale turned on its head, a sympathetic character from an unsympathetic source.

No. There was nothing sympathetic or likable about this teller. I thought again of Sarah Marshall, her hair matted on the pavement.

If it was a hoax, it was the most elaborate one I had ever heard of. And if it was, I found that a part of me did not want my disbelief proven, for through it the wheels of my creative mechanism, which I'd feared indefinitely jammed, had begun a familiar, albeit creaky, new motion in me.

I thought of Katrina's proposal. *L. Legion.* How clever. I tried to locate it, but it was apparently buried beneath a ream of paper-clipped proposals and sample chapters.

Later, well past 1:00 a.m., I returned to my account. I had combed it a dozen times in the last week but left each time feeling that something was missing. Even as he took me speeding through the heavens and introduced me to Eden, he was coy, refusing to put me at the edge of his understanding as I demanded my authors do in their narratives, holding back some vital piece of information.

I checked my calendar.

The blank grid stared back.

13

The parade was on TV. Apparently it was Thanksgiving. But all I knew or cared about was that it had been five days. Five days, and nothing. I sifted through the stack of pages comprising my record as an archaeologist brushes dirt through a sieve, searching for details, meaning, reason. *I have lost it.* At best, I was obsessed. The fact that I had not replayed to death my encounter with Aubrey at the museum was proof of that. I had thought I would be compelled to drink, break down, or at least stew for a few days, reliving the years of our marital routine, the arguments, the silent specters between us. But I did none of these, having already transferred my best energies to the account growing on the corner of my desk.

My pulse throbbed in my temple. I was more conscious of it of late, imagining that I felt its thumping shiver through the mattress beneath me as I lay in bed at night. This experience had drained me, this thing that I had fallen victim or privy to.

I checked my schedule by the hour—sometimes more often—lingering at the keyboard like a lover waiting by a silent phone.

In these idling moments of distracted nonproductivity, I looked up articles on Horus, searched for pictures of the falcon-headed god to see if I saw anything of the demonic scowl in the ancient idol's eyes. In dark, postmidnight hours, I browsed the Internet, following the links through a pantheon of Egyptian gods until, dozing in my chair before dawn, I dreamed convoluted dreams of bird-headed deities with clay bodies, of sarcophagi with wide-eyed funeral masks, of a woman the color of bone singing by the pale light of Lucian's moon.

I woke up in the afternoon, raked my hands through my hair, scrubbed at the stubble on my cheeks, and realized the holiday had passed. It was the weekend.

That day, as I returned to the account of my meetings with Lucian, I was disturbed by the fragility of the paper it was written on, the fraying edges of the notebook pages, the bloated ink where I had set a glass of water on one of them. I recalled the shambles of the house in Belmont, the splintered table leg. *Tissue paper*, he had called it.

I immediately decided that I should type the entire thing, commit it to a more lasting medium.

When I finished, it was well past dark. I sat back, considered the last line of my account, which ended in the museum with Aubrey and me parting ways again. With Lucifer searching for the weakness in man.

On impulse, I pulled up an online Bible and then faltered. There were at least two dozen translations to pick from. We had read the King James in confirmation, the "thees" and "thous" as mysterious to me as God himself. I randomly chose a more modern version.

> *In the beginning God created the heavens and*
> *the earth. Now the earth was formless and empty,*
> *darkness was over the surface of the deep, and the*
> *Spirit of God was hovering over the waters.*

It was so bare-boned. The image of God hovering over the water that had made Lucian shudder was recounted here with all the emotion of a recipe. I read through the days of creation, and though I found no inconsistencies between this account and the demon's, I found no mention of the angelic host or Lucifer, of the fall that precipitated the earth's emptiness. I read through the creation of animals and man. I found it retold in the next chapter, this time with more detail, even down to the exact rivers flowing into the garden. The specificity surprised me, as though one might actually locate the place on a map. I read the first two chapters again, this time with a writer's appreciation for the omniscient point of view, the declarative sentences, the repetition.

Still it seemed much the same as it had been thirty years ago in Sunday school: dry and rote, down to the repetition of the days coming and going in numbered sequence. I was disappointed, tired, and very hungry. My mouse hovered over the X that would close the online Bible, but then something happened: I heard the echo of past conversations with Lucian coming back to me now in fragments like the lyrics of a half-forgotten song.

> *Now the earth was formless and empty, dark-*
> *ness was over the surface of the deep, and the Spirit*
> *of God was hovering over the waters.*
>
> . . . the way a sculptor's fingers roam a block
> of marble . . .

Then God said, "Let the land produce vegeta-tion: seed-bearing plants and trees on the land that bear fruit with seed in it, according to their various kinds."

All those strange green things had within them the power to create . . . manufacturing miniature versions of themselves.

So God created man in his own image.

. . . the awareness, all the emotion, the pro-pensity to love . . .

"Rule over the fish of the sea and the birds of the air and over every living creature that moves on the ground."

He gave the animals to the man and told him to rule over them.

"It is not good for the man to be alone."
And he was lonely.

The one thing the demon had not yet mentioned was the tree in the second chapter. I scrolled to Genesis 3.

Now the serpent was more crafty than any of the wild animals the Lord God had made.

He prowled the garden, inspecting for him-self the handiwork of El like the jealous critic . . . searching for the slightest weakness.

It now came vividly alive. I scrolled ahead, excited, look-ing for more. But I found only Cain and Abel, followed by an entire genealogy of men who became fathers in their old age and supposedly lived for centuries. Lucian had said nothing of this part, having come only, as far as I could tell, to the end of Genesis 2. Looking at the screen, I thought with some alarm of the thick, dusty, leather-bound book on the shelf at home when I was growing up. Is that what he meant every time he said time was short—that it could take an entire lifetime to recount the whole thing?

I rethought my obsession, not sure if I was up for all of that. I was exhausted, hungry, and preoccupied—and Lucian had barely covered the first two pages of that dusty book. Did he mean to recount his observation of or participation in every event in the Bible?

And what did any of this have to do, as he contended, with me?

Something scratched at the back of my mind.

> *And there was evening, and there was morning—the first day. And there was evening, and there was morning—the second day. And there was evening, and there was morning—the third day.*
>
> Time, not yet created, had begun its phantom tick for us alone. Where I once saw the artful strew of El's stars, I now saw the cogs and pendulum of a great clock, ticking the finite measure of time.

And then I knew.

The demon's obsession with time wasn't about getting through the entire Bible. It was about his own limited quantity of it. In our conversation upon leaving the church that day weeks ago, he said he had never been to hell.

Yet.

On a whim I searched the Internet for *Lucian*.

Back came Lucian of Samosata, the rhetorician, author of *Dialogues of the Gods* and *Dialogues of the Dead*. How fitting. Lucian of Antioch, the saint. Why would a demon take the name of a saint? Lucian Freud, the painter. Various blogs, designers, an actor, even a boxer.

Well, what's in a name anyway?

I typed: "Name meanings: Lucian."

I received: *Lucian: Latin. "Light."*

Light?

I searched for *Lucifer*. I felt strange, deviant doing it.

Lucifer: "bringer of light."

I toggled back to the file containing my notes and scrolled to Lucian's retelling of Lucifer's attempted ascent, of the darkness after its failure. And then before that, to the flashing stones of Eden that reflected the light of its governor. It had all been noticeably missing from the account in Genesis. I wondered if it was anywhere in the Bible.

Returning to the online Bible, I searched for *Lucifer*. The only linked passage that came back was a reference from Isaiah:

> *How you have fallen from heaven,*
> *O morning star, son of the dawn! You have been*
> *cast down to the earth, you who once laid low the*
> *nations!*

I searched next for *Eden*. An entire list of references scrolled before my eyes. I dropped down to the index results, to "Garden of Eden." There I found more Genesis and more Isaiah but nothing that snagged my attention—until this:

> *You were in Eden, the garden of God; every pre-*
> *cious stone adorned you:*

I scrolled down through the passage from Ezekiel.

> *You were anointed as a guardian cherub, for so*
> *I ordained you. You were on the holy mount of God;*
> *you walked among the fiery stones.*
>
> *You were blameless in your ways from the day*
> *you were created till wickedness was found in you.*
>
> *Through your widespread trade you were filled*
> *with violence, and you sinned.*
>
> *So I drove you in disgrace from the mount of*
> *God, and I expelled you, O guardian cherub, from*
> *among the fiery stones.*

I grabbed my notes and reread them, my heart accelerating. It was the same story except that, as before, the demon's account was more fantastic. More compelling.

I had sworn I would not publish his story even if he were J. D. Salinger.

Salinger never wrote a story like this.

And again I had to wonder: Why me? I was no high-profile editor. Brooks and Hanover was a small publishing house. With titans like Simon and Schuster, HarperCollins, and Random House roaming the earth—with Houghton Mifflin, even, right here in Boston—why choose me?

It drifted back to me from the pile of pages: *My story is very closely connected to yours.*

But how could that be?

I searched for *Satan*, half expecting to see a warning on my screen.

Satan: "Accuser."
For a long time, I read and reread that single word.

I SLEPT, FINALLY, AROUND three in the morning but woke again just after five thirty.

I couldn't go on like this. *Maybe that is his intent.* I pictured myself five years into the future, a skeleton of a man, my eyes sunken into my skull, dark circles like black halos on pallid, sun-forsaken skin, ranting on street corners, and no doubt jobless.

I got up for water, thinking I ought to return to bed, try to sleep some more. But instead I sat down at my computer, setting the glass atop a pile of proposals I had read the night before, the content of which I could no longer remember.

I touched the pad on my laptop. A page of links on Satan and Satan-related topics sprang to pixilated life. I had asked about Satan on the verge of hysteria that day in the bookstore. Now here I was with a bookmark on him.

Lucian claimed he didn't know where I was meant to spend eternity. Staring at the screen, I wondered: Was I sealing my own fate with every hour, every minute I passed with him? I felt the cold fingers again, scraping the inside of my chest. Could one be damned by association?

Stop it. You'll make yourself crazy.

I looked out my window onto the darkness of Norfolk Street. All around me I was surrounded by so-called normal people chasing lives filled with normal things—money, relationships, losing weight. People who went home to families or empty apartments and went to bed worrying about the same, normal things.

I wondered if I would ever return to that life. Assuming Lucian never appeared again, could I ever purge myself of this more vivid reality and go back, reset . . . reboot?

Just as I lifted my finger to the power button, a new meeting notice appeared in the corner of my screen.

That Tuesday, Helen, my editorial director, called me into her office.

Helen Ness was a strange mixture of steely, old-school-style politics and a frozen-in-time femininity that, having manifested itself in young adulthood, had never quite progressed into the next thirty years. As I entered her office, she pulled off her glasses. They hung on a beaded chain and dropped down against her sweatered bust. I took a seat in one of the two chairs in front of her heavy oak desk. From here I could see that the lines at the corners of her mouth had directed bits of color from her lipstick away from her lips like tiny irrigation canals.

"I'm worried about you, Clay. Even when you're here, you don't seem here. Your skin is pasty, you look thin and worn out. You look terrible." She smoothed a strand of hair from her forehead. Shoulder-length, curled under at the ends. I doubted it had changed style since her days at Smith College. "I don't know if it's your divorce or your health or what. Sheila said you've been to the doctor a few times."

Well, see there's this demon.

"But I need you to let me know what's going on."

He's following me, and I'm pretty sure he had that runner on Arlington killed.

"Let me help, Clay."

I'm compiling the story of our encounters, which, by the way, has a nice subplot about Satan.

"I understand. I've—" I raked a hand through my hair. It needed a cut. "I'm just run down."

"I've had one viable project of yours make it through the committee in the last three months," she said.

That's because the editorial committee can't make up their minds. Despite my sick days and missed meetings, I knew for a fact I had three proposals stuck in committee limbo.

"I need a big project to fill a hole—something we can get into production by spring, summer at the latest." She dropped her hands to her desk. "Do you have anything you can get me? Help me out here, Clay. I know Katrina's been sending things your way."

Don't even suggest it, Clay. But I could think of nothing else. "Actually, Helen, I've been working on something," I heard myself say. "A novel about a fallen angel—a memoir-style story told from the viewpoint of a demon." Inwardly, I cursed myself.

"Clay"— a slow, appreciative smile eased across her features—"I had no idea you had gone back to writing."

Since the failure of Coming Home, you mean.

"Sounds intriguing. Religious fiction is getting hotter, and you do know we get first right of refusal."

I'm an idiot. "I know."

"Give it to Phil or Anu, and we'll take it to committee." She replaced the glasses, sliding them down her nose.

"It's not quite finished—"

"Just get us something to look at." She smiled, a second reminder that the meeting was over.

I thanked her, eager to get out of her office, to figure out what I had just done. Eager to get on with the day and to my appointment that evening.

I passed Sheila in the hallway, and the sight of her startled me. She looked drawn, thinner than I had ever seen her, and I realized it had been weeks since we'd had a real conversation. I had never seen her look quite like this—she was practically gaunt, and her lavender twin-set matched the smudges beneath her eyes.

"Clay, how are you? I talked to Aubrey over the holiday. She said she saw you. And that you're seeing someone." She smiled slightly.

That struck me as hilarious—in a manic, high-pitched laughing kind of way. "It's, uh, a casual thing. And you? How are you?" I thought of Helen and her "you look terrible." Apparently it was going around; I had never seen Sheila look so unattractive. I had never seen her look unattractive, period.

She took a long, shaky sigh. "Oh, Dan and I are separated."

"I'm so sorry." I said it because it was the proper thing to say. It was the thing I had grown sick of hearing from others about this time last year. But I wasn't sorry, not really. Despite her haggard appearance, I had a hard time summoning any compassion for her. Thinking back to what Lucian had told me, to the "have to see you" e-mail, I found my sympathies rested solidly with Dan. What was it with Sheila and Aubrey, the adultery twins? I should call Dan. I ought to be having this conversation with him.

"Yeah." She glanced down at the papers in her hand. She appeared to have been en route to the copy machine. "It's difficult. I don't know what will happen."

"Well, if there's anything I can do . . ." But not only was I sure there was nothing I could do—I was fairly certain I wouldn't do anything for her if I could.

"I'm glad you're seeing someone, Clay. I'm not sure Aubrey realizes yet how much she lost."

I thanked her and excused myself.

Her words stayed with me the rest of the day, as powerful, almost, as Lucian's.

I REALIZED AFTER MEETING with Helen that I might have a problem. I had just proposed a story based on the memoir that Lucian had apparently submitted—or gotten through otherwise demonic means—to Katrina. Maybe the stack of papers on my desk bore little enough resemblance to the scant pages Katrina had given me that it wouldn't be an issue, but I couldn't find the proposal she had given me to know for sure. And I did not like the idea that I was walking what felt like a thin ethical line, especially considering on whose behalf I walked it.

Closing my office door, I phoned Katrina, but she wasn't in. Not wanting to draw more attention to the matter than necessary and not wanting to talk to her assistant, I sent her an e-mail asking for electronic copies of the proposals she had given me on her visit two weeks before.

That was all I could do. That, and worry.

THE AROMAS OF WARM bread mingled with garlic, salami, and olives. It had once been an endurance test for me to make it to Prince Street without getting sidelined by every temptation on Salem. When Aubrey and I used to come to the

North End for dinner, we would stop afterward at the twenty-four-hour bakery to buy turnovers and semolina bread for lunch the next day. In our last year of marriage, we still perused these streets for new restaurants, but the discussions we once had over pasta and veal dwindled to the clinking chatter of our cutlery, and we often forgot the bakery.

On the corner of Prince and Hanover, I paused before the iron gates of Saint Leonard's, which bore the emblem of nail-scarred hands folded in front of a cross. In the summer, especially on feast days, church ladies sold Saint Anthony's oil and religious icons at a table around the corner. Tonight the heavy wooden doors beyond the gate were locked tight, as though against sin itself—in addition to editors who cavorted with demons and spent entire nights contemplating Satan. Standing before the crumbling plaster of the church, I felt like more of a stranger to that churchgoing world of my youth than I did to Lucian's spirit-inhabited realm.

But most unsettling, I felt less and less a part of the secular world in which I lived.

It was nearly seven o'clock. I hurried down Hanover, the smell of the ocean briny in my nose. In summer the restaurants—barely more than little open-kitchen joints boasting no more than eight tables apiece—threw open their doors, spilling tables onto the sidewalk to catch the influx of tourists and saints' feasts celebrants. Tonight they were closed up against the coastal chill, menus peering out from windows, the flames of tiny candles dancing on the tabletops inside.

On the second-floor entrance of Vittorio's, I experienced a brief moment of déjà vu when the host informed me my party was already waiting, and again when he led me to a candlelit booth where a woman in her thirties waved at me.

She was a wholesome, if average-looking woman. A gold chain and single diamond pendant dangled over the folded neck of her navy blue turtleneck. Her blonde hair was pulled back in a ponytail.

I slid into the booth and took the menu from the host. When he had gone, I said, "If Aubrey is going to show up, tell me now."

Her eyes widened slightly. "Not as far as I know."

I shrugged out of my coat, still winded from the walk, my ears tingling from the cold. Then I noticed the glass of red wine on the table. Had she ordered it for me, to antagonize me? Did she know about my night with the bottle of cheap red wine that day after the walk through the Commons?

I ignored the wine, saying little as the waiter brought us bread and took orders for dinner. "Mussels Fra Diavolo," I said, gazing at the woman across from me. Lucian rolled her eyes.

"Your name means 'light,'" I said without preamble when the waiter had gone.

"Yes."

I tried to see past the faint laugh lines around her eyes, the diamond stud earrings, the indentations through her sweater where bra straps bit into her shoulders, the wedding ring on her finger.

Such elaborate lengths, I thought, slightly sickened. "An angel of light?"

"Sometimes I still take that form."

I tried to imagine what an angel of light would look like, but it was like trying to summon a modern-day leprechaun.

"You can't fathom it, so don't bother." She leaned back.

"How long will this go on?"

She tilted her head and seemed, for the first time, to have no ready answer. Finally, she said, "Until it's finished. Or we run out of time."

"Until what's finished?"

"Your story."

"You mean your story." I thought of my discussion with Helen, of the proposal from Katrina. I needed time to sort it all through, to figure out how much of a hole I had dug for myself and how I would get myself out. Meanwhile, the only thing that mattered was having more of her story to take home with my leftover pasta tonight.

"Tell me about Adam." I began the mental calculation of when I might get home and how late I might stay up scribbling, perhaps even in bed, and how many hours of sleep I might get. Helen's blunt conversation with me today had returned at least a portion of my focus to the routine necessities of my job, no matter how empty they were to me these days.

"All right," she said, tracing the edge of the table through the tablecloth. "About Adam . . ."

"Wait. How do you know the Bible so well?"

She laughed then and seemed surprised. "Because I lived it! I understand Scripture intrinsically and intellectually better than any of your so-called enlightened churchgoers. Lucifer himself is a master theologian. Better than any of your preachers or seminarians, I assure you."

Intrinsic understanding. A theological master. It was the claim of thousands of spiritual gurus, self-proclaimed prophets, Kool-Aid killers, and Branch Davidian leaders.

"Now, about Adam"—she propped her chin in her hand—"history and popular myth have done him a great disservice. Let me tell you that Adam was perhaps the best-looking man I have ever seen. Of course, at that time, there was nothing to compare him to, and for the better part of a few centuries, humans were all clay freaks to me. I guarantee you, if your backyard compost pile suddenly got up and started taking over your house, you would feel the same. But in retrospect I can honestly say he was handsome."

I wondered if I should point out that I didn't have a back-yard, which reminded me—

"How come you've never shown up at my apartment?"

Her impatience turned into a moue of distaste. "Please. I'm trying to tell you something. Can we come back to this later? Listen to me now: Adam was an admirable man. For as much as I resented him, I also found myself drawn to him. Sure, the plants were nice to look at, and the animals were entertaining, albeit predictable—all that eating and rutting—but Adam . . . he was dynamic. I never tired of watching him, and neither did Lucifer. Of course, Lucifer hated him because of who he was and who had made him. Adam not only bore the Creator's stamp; he bore his likeness. He was a brilliant thinker, a creature of reason. He observed the things around him. He was a scientist. He was also an agriculturalist, a botanist, a zoologist, and a horticulturist," she said, ticking all the "ists" off on her fingers. "He was a husband, a man with responsibility: He cared for the garden; he ruled the animals; he was a family man. And he walked with God. Literally."

As she spoke, I noticed that she moved differently than she had as the woman in the museum. It reminded me of the effect costumes had on actors.

"And what about Eve?"

She stroked the stem of the glass, silent for a moment. "In Eve," she said softly, "of all creatures, I saw something that might have inspired me. Something with which I could most identify. She was second-generation mud, of course, but she was intelligent, intuitive, and beautiful—striking in fact. She reminded me a little of myself."

One of the cooks in the small kitchen had started singing. I recognized the strains of Puccini's "Nessun Dorma":

> *Depart, O night!*
> *Set, you stars!*
> *At dawn, I shall win.*

She propped her chin on the back of her hand. "Life then was beautifully predictable and secure. Oh, the bliss of that age! I watched and dreamed and experienced peace vicariously." She glanced down at the tablecloth, scratching at it with her finger. "But Lucifer remained vigilant, a spider on the periphery of his beautiful web.

"The first glance. Remember it? I did. So did Lucifer. *Your eyes will be opened!* Lucifer told her. *You will be like God.* He was sure of himself, but I less so. The woman was brilliant, perceptive in ways that even Adam was not. I thought to myself: *She is made in the image of God—she will know what you do. She is made in the image of God! What more can there be for her? She will not choose it.* But in the end we were more alike than I had realized. How I wanted to rail at her! Was it not enough that she and her man were the new favorites of God? How greedy they were! How much more did they expect, could they need? And yet I, too, had once known bliss. Still, I began to hate her after that."

"And so it happened again," I said.

She nodded slightly. "In Eve's tempting, all the combined drama of what had gone before played out again, like your play-actors on a miniature stage with the script of a well-known story.

"That day, as I watched Adam and his wife realize for the first time they were naked, I was overcome by sadness—and déjà vu. I cut the strings by which I had vicariously experienced their contentment, unwilling to go through the emotions again. I remembered too well what it was to be exposed—when all the blithe routine of life slips away, and there is only regret and the overpowering knowledge of an irrevocable act." She sighed. "It was futile, their hiding. We all knew it. And El—"

"Cursed them."

"Quite the biblical scholar now, aren't we?" Her brows arched. She looked like the quintessential soccer mom. A scolding soccer mom. "Yes, he cursed them. But I didn't stay to watch. I could recall too well the shivering grief of that spirit over the deep, crying out in the dark. I couldn't bear to witness it all again, even as I admitted that a tiny part of me took delight in knowing we weren't the only ones to fail El. Perhaps I was even a little smug"— she lifted her glass by the stem as if to gauge the color of the wine—"but my satisfaction sweetened nothing."

"Why not?"

She gazed across the rim of the glass at me. "Because it is a sad tale I'm telling you. Do you weep? No. Of course not. You can't imagine the loss of perfection. This is the only world you know." She set the wine glass down on the tablecloth, turned it this way and that. "You literally had to be there—before—to understand the gall of that remorse as it stained . . . the cup . . . of my heart." Her finger traced the stem, too hard, and the glass toppled over, practically in slow motion.

I started, bumping my hand on the edge of the table as I tried to grab the glass in time. I wasn't fast enough, and the wine bled out over the tablecloth in a plum-colored blot, creeping in all directions.

"Of course, the remorse has faded some since then," she said, gazing dispassionately at the blooming stain.

I daubed at the spill, irritated. When the waiter arrived with my salad, he set it on a nearby table and went about cleaning ours, going so far as to remove everything on it and to spread a pressed, pristine white linen across the scratched and worn surface beneath.

Lucian the soccer mom watched all of this with strange impassivity, saying nothing when the waiter assured her it was no problem. I said we were terribly sorry and urged him not to go to all the trouble. As the waiter set everything back, I noted an ironic, if slightly bitter, look on the demon's face.

After replacing the settings and condiments, he served my salad and carried the dirty linens away.

I picked at my food in silence after that, and she watched me, her chin resting on the back of her hand.

"I supposed El would turn his back on the clay humans," she said at last. "That he would destroy the garden as he had destroyed Eden once before, leaving them as naked and as miserably at odds with him as we were. And I wondered why El had done it, had put himself through it again—the disappointment of a creation all too free to choose ill. As I sit here with you, I've yet to find an answer for that."

Lucian seemed to be looking through me, as if trying to answer the question for the millionth time.

"Either way, Eden was finished." I speared a pepper.

"Yes. Though it didn't come about as I expected. This time it was different." She rubbed her forearm, as though to smooth away goose bumps. "This time there were consequences."

"The curses."

She nodded. "With words that rang prophetic, El cursed the form Lucifer had taken. I didn't understand it all at the time and would not for some time to come. We had never heard prophecy before. El cursed the ground from which Adam would grow their food and foretold the pain with which the woman would bear children and drove them both out of the garden and into the rest of the world. Those of us watching the human mimicry of our own first Eden pulled away in a corporate shudder. Adam and his woman would die."

The waiter appeared then with my pasta. He turned to Lucian. "Would you like another glass of wine, ma'am?"

The demon gave a slight smile. "No, thank you. I'll only spill it again."

"There's something I don't understand." I wound pasta around my fork. "They didn't die right away. At least Adam didn't." It hadn't said anything about Eve, but if the biblical account were to be taken literally—and I didn't see how it could—Adam had lived some nine hundred years.

"Of course not." She pressed tiny indentations in the table-cloth with the prongs of her fork. "But they changed physically and spiritually. They were marred now, at odds with the world and destined to struggle against it and against themselves. Strife is, after all, the constant companion of imperfection. Even so, it took time for Adam's body—clay, but genetically perfect by any standard of yours—to submit to the sentence of mortality."

"Why didn't God just kill him?"

"Trust me, at the time nine hundred years seemed frighten-ingly short—it still does. I really don't know how you cope with your eighty-something life spans, and that's a best-case scenario, isn't it?" She gave me a pert little smile, her lips pressed into the shape of a heart. "Suffice it to say, we were horrified by the entire concept of dying, even if we weren't the ones with the death sentence. None of us had experienced mortality, not even as spectators."

To have never seen death? As her story progressed, it sounded less like the biblical account of stodgy old men and more like a SyFy Channel movie.

"Here's something for you"— she pointed the fork at me— "you asked about the light-bringer, Lucifer. If Adam and his wife were the first and best specimens of your race, slowly but surely giving in to the inevitable, Lucifer, too, had begun to change. On the outside he was still radiant—is to this day—never cursed with mortal death as your kind is, only losing the glamour of the Shekinah glory by miniscule fractions through the ages. But inside he had changed. Even by the time of Adam there was little left of that perfect governor, of that shining prince. He was a new creature. But then, so were we all. And the world changed, too."

"Why would the world change?"

"Just as one renegade gene creates a new thing, the world had begun to mutate." Her casual shrug said it was nothing important. "It was the natural order, a trajectory set in motion by a single aberration that signaled perversity to come."

I thought back to every beautiful place I had ever been—to the red rocks of Utah, the shores of Saint Lucia, the peaks of the Guilin Mountains along the Li River. I thought of Aubrey's travel books, of Ansel Adams's black-and-whites.

"Yes, I call your beautiful world mutant and perverse. So would you if you had seen the original. If you had, you would know how far we've all veered, how like a cancer things have grown. In fact, I almost felt sympathy for El when I saw how saddened he was again. But I, too, had begun to change."

She had turned her fork over and was on the verge of pressing another row of indentations into the tablecloth when she started, as though something had caught her eye across the room. For a moment she was still, her eyes narrowed, seeming to peer through booths and walls and kitchen. She reminded me of an animal, ears back, hackles raised, haunches tense. I followed the line of her gaze trying to see who—or what—had captured her attention. But then her posture relaxed, and she was back at the tablecloth with the fork.

"So as I said, the world was mutating," she said, prick, prick, pricking at the cloth, looking up at me once to make sure, I assume, I was listening. "From the earth sprung hateful and ugly things that flourished amid all that was lush and good. There would be no more accord among the animals now; they would follow a different order, no longer subsisting exclusively on plants but also on one another. Adam's flesh was no longer the same, though it would take centuries for disease to manifest itself, for bodies so genetically pure that a man could marry his sister to corrupt down through the generations to the point where a man dare not marry even his cousin. In fact, it took, as you have read, 930 years for Adam to die, and his children lived similarly long lives."

I couldn't believe it. She had actually made a kind of sense out of something I was sure would prove a faltering point.

"Of course it makes sense." She lifted her chin. "As surely as the old doctrine of sin handed down from the father to the sons has remained thematic throughout your time. Look around you. See the truth of it manifest today: the imperfection of your eyes, the weakness of your immune systems, the proclivity of some of you for disease and cancer, asthma and allergies, genetic disorders of all kinds."

I did look around, my gaze settling on the large table of twelve in the center of the small restaurant. They must have been a family, I thought, feeling a slight pang of envy. And now I took tally: At least five of the people sitting at the table wore glasses. One of them, a young man in his twenties, was in a wheelchair. The oldest person at the table was a white-haired lady, her nape bent by a bump. She ate slowly, chewing her food with dogged purpose. I guessed she might be 85.

Eighty-five . . . versus 930. What had Adam looked like at 85?

"He was virile," she said. "Quite the stallion."

Now there was a thought that was going to fester.

"It isn't just you, though. You haven't had the nutrient wholeness of those first foods in ages. Look at what you pass off as food today. Frankly, I'm surprised you live twenty years on that stuff." She gestured toward my pasta. "Add to it the fact that you're missing the full health of the earth as it originally was, and you realize how far things have come. Do you think your ancients went around slathered with sunscreen? Do you think they had to infuse their soil with chemicals?"

I looked at the remainder of my pasta. Just earlier I had congratulated myself on actually eating a hot meal.

"And so the earth itself began to die a little, though like Adam it would survive a long while yet."

She was looking sidelong at that table of twelve. What was it that had her attention? With an uneasy sense I wondered if I would see someone die tonight. Would that old woman with her white hair choke and fall over, expire as horrified family members performed the Heimlich, CPR? *Please*, I thought, not sure who I thought it to—maybe all this talk of God, of creation and sin was affecting me—*please no*. I needed to hear this, uninterrupted. I needed more. I needed to have this time.

Someone could die tonight, and I'm worried about getting my demonic fix.

"Meanwhile, all over the faltering planet, the clay humans raised up others just like them in a world plagued with aberrations and depravity, fostering a new culture of death," she said, her eyes on the table.

"Don't you think that's a bit dramatic?" But her words called to mind the mummy room at the museum, her comment that all of it had come from those first, original two. And I had thought she had been referring to sophisticated Egyptian culture.

Her mouth curved, her attention solidly fixed on me again. "It does sound grim, doesn't it? Well, it's not. At least from my point of view. We had learned, by then, to take delight in what we saw, in what we perceived as the prolonged failure of El. Because, you see, if he failed with his new creations, these new heirs, it only served to make us look a little better. CLAY, LOOK AT ME WHILE I'M TALKING TO YOU!"

My attention snapped from the family back to her.

"I'm not here for my own edification! I know this story, remember?" The soccer mom's voice had raised in angry, demonic glory.

"I-I'm sorry—"

She jabbed her finger into the tablecloth. "Every time you *fail*, it proves something. Every time the humans *failed*, it made us feel better. We reveled in every instance of human ridiculousness," she said with biting annunciation, her tone lower but intense, her lips pulled back from her teeth.

"I understand." I wanted her to know I was listening.

"No, you don't. El didn't ignore the clay humans. He did not cut them off. Not at all. He took an interest in their daily affairs, though he no longer walked with them in the afternoon. And *that* is significant." Her blue eyes had come to dark, frightening life.

"He made concessions. He persevered through their constant and abiding imperfections and wrongdoings with more patience than I thought existed in all the created universe. He taught them how to make appropriately bloody, laborious, and horrible sacrifices in symbolic atonement."

For a moment, I thought she was going to leave it there. But I knew there was more. Knew I wanted to know it. "And?"

"And then he *forgave* them."

She was staring so intently at me that I found myself averting my gaze as one does from oncoming headlights. When she said nothing more, I glanced up to find her still staring at me, as though the implication of her words were sinking in for her, all over again.

She was seething.

"Think about that." She reached for her coat, then, with a quick glance toward the other end of the restaurant again, slid out of the booth. "We will have to do this faster." She put the coat on. "Time is getting away from us."

She slung her purse over her shoulder and walked out. In the middle of the restaurant, the table of twelve broke into a round of "Happy Birthday," as the old woman blew out the candle on a piece of ricotta pie.

15

ime is getting away from us?

I committed the encounter to paper, spending the urgent recollection of every word in the act of writing it. When I had finished, I spread the pages out on the kitchen table. They were scribbled in hyperactive script on paper from the recycling bin, across the backs of newsletters, pieces of mail—anything that had been near to hand.

I opened my laptop and started to type.

Around 1:00 a.m., as I transcribed the end of our dinner together—my dinner—I found I had missed a major point. I had thought there was something significant about the family at the table, that something about them first drew her interest and then piqued her. But that wasn't it, the thing that precipitated the moment—that startling, stunning moment—that she snapped at me. It was the coming revelation in her own story. The thing she knew she must say.

"And then he forgave them."

I had thought nothing about that statement at the time. Forgiveness was, after all, the vernacular of religion.

Even for demons?

I scrolled back through the electronic account to an earlier appointment, the words leaping at me as I came to them:

> *"Had I been a god, I would have set it all back.*
> *I would have erased everything, returned it all to the*
> *way it had been."*
> *"Why couldn't you? For that matter, why*
> *wouldn't God?"*
> *"I'll tell you why: because we were* damned!*"*

I scrolled forward.

> *"He forgave them."*

I sat back in my chair, staring at the screen.

LATE THAT NIGHT I received a response from Katrina, but the proposal she attached was not one I recognized. Confused, I paged through the brief teaser of *Dreaming: A Memoir,* by L. LeGeros.

It was the personal account of a paranoid schizophrenic.

16

The demon chose two more plates and pushed them across the table toward me with a short, stocky arm.

"Please stop," I told him as the woman with the dim sum cart stamped her red symbol on our tab and pushed on. I meant it not only because I was full but because the rapt interest with which he had watched me eat for the last half hour disturbed me. He had inundated me with sweet buns, pork buns, shrimp dumplings, and vegetable packets with tiny green peas perched on the twisted peak of their wrappers. They squatted now in orphaned ones and twos inside their bamboo steamers; I could not possibly accommodate them all.

"Very well." He folded those arms before him. He had hung his jacket over the back of his chair but, seeing the way his dress shirt strained at the shoulders, I thought he ought to have left it on.

"About your proposal to Katrina . . ." I wasn't sure how to go about what I meant to say next. I had feigned an e-mail problem, had asked her again to resend it, stating even more carefully that I needed the short one, the additional one she had given me as an afterthought the day she came to my office. But when she resent it, I found myself scrolling again through the scant pages of *Dreaming: A Memoir* by L. LeGeros.

"What proposal?" He seemed to wink, though his eyelid never moved.

So that was it. Another of his mind tricks. No one had seen the proposal for *Demon: A Memoir* but me. Katrina had no awareness of the story evolving into a living thing on my desk and hard drive, waiting for me to wake in the morning and come home at night, to feed it the nutriment of my preoccupation. An excitement tapped in my chest, a metronome in time with my heart.

"I see," I said carefully. *More,* I thought, *though it will risk his anger.* "Then in that case, I need to know what happened after El forgave them. The humans, I mean."

He sat up, fussing with the little teapot, over pouring a small trickle of chrysanthemum tea into his untouched cup. It seemed he could not dive headlong and cold into this topic, so I waited, considering his bushy eyebrows, the unremarkable face with the suggestion of jowls on either side of his thin-lipped mouth. I had thought him vain after our first few encounters, though of late he seemed to care less and less about the beauty of his guises.

"El's acts of forgiveness became tedious in the way that something routine is tedious. Like a sound that grates on your patience so that where you had only disliked it before, you come to hate even the merest suggestion of it. Like a smell that has the ability to incite nausea. I didn't know who I was more astounded with—El because he constantly forgave them, or the humans because they made constant and abiding mistakes again and again. With disgust and amazement we pushed ourselves to see how far we could go with them. We dared. And El sat back

again in pain amid the chaos of all this teeming life, once so
wonderful, multiplying over the great ball of earth and water.
But he would not relinquish them. During that time I realized
something had happened within me."

"What do you mean?" I said, surrendering my chopsticks
with an overfull sigh.

"Like nerves after they've been severed, I could no longer
sense El as I had before, even after falling away. But in that
same way that I knew myself—better, even—I knew El to be
unchanging. For as little as I could perceive of him by then, I
understood well his sentiments about all that was happening."

"And Lucifer?"

"Oh, he had determined to rule over this great, floating
ball of land—had, in fact, never given up his claim to it. Now,
having snatched Adam's birthright from him the moment he
abdicated it, he threw wide the doors to this world as though
to a mansion and invited the humans in, creating banquets of
diversions designed just for them: new and bizarre religions,
strange philosophies, indulgences for all appetites. He had by
then set himself up as all the things he had ever wanted to be:
a power, a ruler . . . a god. Gods. He answered to a variety of
names, and the humans offered him sacrifices and performed
great acts of murder and bloodletting for his sake. It was gory.
And grand."

"So he had what he wanted at last."

"After a manner, I suppose. You must understand that he
didn't care about the offerings, the blood, or the lives. It was that
people did it that delighted him. That with every little betrayal,
the people moved farther away from El. Eventually, they forgot
him. Those were wild, accelerated days—like a dancer, twirling
faster and faster until she falls; like your dreams of falling off

buildings, the wind shrieking in your ears. And I watched it all with a sense of inevitability."

Sometimes when he was like this, when it seemed he was transported back, I wondered if his own memories were as vivid to him as they had been to me the time in the tea shop or that day in the Commons.

As vivid as my memories of Sarah Marshall's death.

I had almost managed to go a whole day without thinking about it.

"But even the forbearance of El in his grief had limits. And the day came when he could abide it no longer. Of course, I expected him to slam down the heavy fist, but the day came and still he held off. Like a mother giving a child to the count of three, El gave the clay people 120 years to change their ways."

He sat back and crossed short arms, his shirtsleeves encasing them like sausages. "I was put off! Had he ever been willing to play the suffering parent toward any one of us? Toward Lucifer, first and best-created of El, prince and anointed cherub? But El had not offered him so much as a glimmer of the patience he showed humans. Never so much for any of us."

As he said this, the distant and disowned look seemed to creep first into one eye and then into the other, like a lizard slithering through his skull.

"Had I been human, I would have considered myself lucky." He thumped his chest. He was pudgy enough that it didn't make much of a sound. "But they were oblivious to the indulgence they had been given. They went about their ways as pleased them best. And the years went by."

"All 120 of them."

"All 120 of them," he agreed. "In the end Lucifer crowed his triumph. He had brought about the destruction of El's world and the spoiling of his clay creatures like so much fruit left on the ground. Now El would be forced to acknowledge him; there would be no more of the clay people to talk with, commune with—and who would want to by now, anyway? Unworthy, fickle, unfaithful. . . . The humans were a failure. It was time to destroy them."

I shuddered at the slight jeer with which he said this.

"Only you Westerners fancy what happened next as the stuff of myth. Most ancient cultures have taught it as history: water covering the land, swallowing up creation as it had Lucifer's rock garden an age before."

Indeed, I was having trouble reconciling the picture-book accounts of animals two-by-two with this story of failed humans, gleeful devils, and a forbearing God. "So Eden was destroyed again."

Lucian's brows drew together. "But it didn't exactly happen as I thought it would—as it had before. The deep didn't swallow up the land, and El didn't hover over the deep. Nor did he put out the sun or destroy my beloved moon. I didn't have the experience to know then what I know now: that El is unlikely to do anything twice or predictably. That he spared an entire family was unpredictable indeed." He lifted his cuff to glance at the elegantly thin timepiece on his wrist.

"Noah's family," I said, feeling as though I vied with time itself for his attention.

He dropped his arm back to the table. "I was indignant! Why bother? What was the point? For those forty short days that Noah's little boat bobbed about on the flooded earth like a piece of cork on a lake, I agonized over it. And when the rain was over and the water subsided and the people crawled out of the boat and made yet another sacrifice, I realized something:

Here was El's weakness, if ever he had one. He *loved* these creatures, these people made of mud. They had failed and he had grieved. He had punished them and they had died, but he couldn't bear to obliterate them all."

Ice crystallized in his eyes, like the frozen surface of a pond under too much weight—or the shattered windshield of a car on Arlington.

Just then the cart lady appeared again, pushing a large wooden vat. She waved a flat golden spoon as though it were a fan. "Hot almond pudding?" she asked, smiling at Lucian.

"Things obviously didn't end there," he said, nudging the plate of gelatinous custard closer to me. It was surrounded by a moat of syrup, and I accepted it without any intention to eat it. He was amicable again, as congenial as a round-faced elf. I found the increasing capriciousness of his moods more and more unsettling, as though indeed I walked on a thin layer of ice over a coursing black current.

"On the contrary, the Flood marked a new beginning. And when it was over and the family had survived, El did something he had never done before: He made a promise—not to us but to the clay people. He promised never to destroy the earth with water again. And he gave them a sign, like a token given to a favorite friend.

"Now let me say that not one of us has ever received such a token. What's more, it was the first promise of many. In subsequent generations he blessed them again, named a branch of them Israel, and made them his special nation."

Now he lifted his empty hands. "Promises . . . tokens . . . blessings. Who was God to be accountable to men? Who was

DEMON: A MEMOIR 159

man, to procure a promise from God? And then he gave them laws, specific rules for living, since they seemed to need things spelled out for them. He taught them intricate rites of atonement and for communing with an all-perfect God so that despite their wrongs, their tainted lineage, he could stand to be near them.

"But it wasn't just that he tolerated them. They had done the irreparable in separating themselves from him forever, and it was as if he couldn't bear to be apart from them."

Though he maintained the same even tone as he said this, it was too controlled, so that rather than seeming genuine, the effect was one of moderated effort.

"Do you hate humans?" The instant I said it, something dark slithered into his gaze with the silent stealth of a reptile entering the murk of a swamp.

"Compared to Lucifer's, my hate is nothing. His odium, his grudge against El grew—grows—by the day." He checked his watch.

No, not yet.

"Come on," he said, pushing back from the table.

"Where?" I was instantly on my feet.

He retrieved his coat and slapped a bill—a fifty—on the table.

BY THE TIME WE left the potpourri of food, stale cigarettes, and urine that was Chinatown behind us, I was breathing hard, my heart beating spastic percussion against my sternum. I towered a good six inches over him, but his short legs were deceptively fast, and I trailed after him like a hapless kid tagging after the schoolyard leader, down Washington Street past St. Francis House.

On either side of the street, homeless men loitered in ones and twos, smoking, scanning the pedestrians with dull, roving eyes, as if watching a play through a window. Though I had never been homeless, I knew that look, had been that person—the editor cleaning up the prose of would-be writers like a janitor sweeping up the refuse of others, contorting myself to fit my wife's boxed worldview, going about my life as silently as the Charles, flowing out to sea.

Lucian kept a brisk pace, looking around us with interest, seeming to enjoy the jaunt. This irritated me. Despite my obvious need for it, I was not here for the exercise.

"And so?" I said with some difficulty against the cold. "What came after the promises and laws?"

The heels of his dress shoes tapped against the sidewalk with the rapid staccato of a stopwatch. "The rest is just history, frighteningly dull: wanderings, wars, migrations, judges, priests, kings, and concubines. Actually, the concubines are a little bit interesting. You can read all of that for yourself if you're simply dying to know. But far be it from me to encourage you to read it. It's only the history of your race from the beginning. Nothing overly significant, I assure you."

I hated it when he was sarcastic. I never knew when it would bloom into a fit of real anger. Each of his outbursts startled and disturbed me a little more—and I felt I could afford them less and less.

At Tremont, he veered toward a lightbulb-lined marquee and the large, arched entrance of the Majestic Theatre. It glowed from within, a fact hardly discernable beneath the wealth of lightbulbs until we reached the front doors. Lucian pulled one of them open.

Inside the foyer, dark green ran in lightning bolt veins

through burnt orange marble. Ram-horned, Dionysian heads smiled down from the tops of pillars on either side of the main auditorium entrance, and gold cherubs capered above and between them, playing the pan flute. The house was alive, chimes just signaling the end of intermission as though they might have indeed come from those golden pipes. The effect was grand and gauche, but for a moment I thought I saw them crumbling to scagliola plaster and gold paint all around me, as the house in Belmont had caved into a pile of refuse. A woman bumped into me, and the illusion dissipated at the sound of her startled apology. I found Lucian on a low landing, impatiently waving as he started up the stair toward the mezzanine.

I followed him up and then up again to the balcony, breathing hard, my heart thumping in my ears with each step. Ahead of me, Lucian slipped inside the left balcony entrance with the last of the intermission stragglers.

The lights lowered as I stepped inside. Blinking in the dark, I caught the stocky form of the demon making his way toward a set of empty seats as the conductor entered to applause.

"What are we doing?" I hissed, sitting next to him.

He said nothing, only folded his hands on his lap as the curtain opened on a simple Japanese set.

I sat stymied through the third act of *Madama Butterfly*, through the return of Pinkerton and Butterfly's surprised meeting with his new wife. The soprano might have been outstanding, Suzuki's mezzo-soprano brilliant—I don't know. I both heard and did not hear them. The sets—perhaps ingenious—served only to occupy my eye, which roamed the lines of the shoji screens like the corridors of a labyrinth as I paced back through all that the demon had said at the China Pearl, wondering again, as I inevitably did, what this had to do with me.

By the time Butterfly committed suicide and the red Japanese moon bled down the front of her house in a modern projector trick, I was ready to jump up, to leave here for someplace where the demon might talk just a bit—any bit—more.

But when the curtain came down on the last ovation and a river of well-dressed bodies took up coats and scarves and shuffled to the exits, Lucian stayed in his seat, gazing thoughtfully at the stage.

"What a silly story," he said, finally. "Puccini never got things right."

"Why, because his heroines always die?"

"Yes, and what is left?"

"Honor?"

His words were an exasperated exhale. "But that's so *boring*. Butterfly should at least murder the second wife."

I was the one noting the time now, calculating how late I might be up tonight. I needed to get through the stack on my desk before I allowed myself the indulgence, the release, of transcribing our meeting today. And then there was Helen, expecting to see something soon on this "demon memoir," still the only viable project I had to give her—not because I didn't have anything of merit from another author, but because it was the only one that mattered to me.

"I would think you might enjoy the tragedy."

He crossed one leg over the other, brushed at his pants. "Tragedy is this: creating something excellent and having it go wrong . . . and then choosing a new and certainly less-deserving favorite. I had begun, by the time of the receding flood and the birth of El's favored nation, the Israelites, to see this pattern. And I have seen it repeated now for millennia."

The curtain had lifted, and stagehands were pulling apart the set. Beneath us on the mezzanine, ushers patrolled the rows, picking up discarded playbills.

"But here now, is the crux of it"— he stared at me—"there are those of us damned for one single, failing moment while you have the favor of an utterly partial God, willing to offer second chances again and again and again."

THAT NIGHT I FELT my focus like fervor. It was well after 2:00 a.m. by the time I went to bed, spent, never having touched the stack of reading in my bag.

As I lay in bed calculating the maximum number of hours I could sleep and still get in an hour of reading before leaving for the office, it occurred to me that *that* was the real demon, the thing I dreaded, to which I gave my reluctant and disinterested eye. It did not move me; I did it because I must.

Sometime in the last three years, I had resigned myself to the fact that I was a better editor than writer. That I was not destined to see my name in print again except on the acknowledgments page. Now I began to admit to a dancing modicum of hope that I had been wrong. In the last week I had felt more creatively alive—if physically drained—than I had in years, even if the story I sculpted was not my own. Lucian's story had taken root in the last fertile corner of my imagination, where surviving pieces of hope, ambition, even professional pride had gathered in silent refuge. I felt manipulated, and I still did not understand his motive in telling me any of this. But for the first time in more than a year, I felt a seed of volition in an existence that otherwise had none.

17

On the subway, I fought to stay awake. I drifted, my limbs slackening into a rolling lull where neither deadlines nor demons existed, where I was neither editor nor divorcé, where there was nothing but an oblivion that I had not known since infancy.

I shifted the bottle of Shiraz to the seat next to me. It was wrapped in a gold bag with a piece of evergreen twisted around the top, courtesy of the woman at the liquor store.

I had initially decided against attending Helen's party. But after nearly ten hours of staring at twelve-point print, I could no longer pretend to care if my newest author's manuscript consisted of three long, Dickensian sentences spanning 250 pages. I was weary of coming-of-age stories, of personal pain disguised as literature, of Ayn Rand-esque discourse that would take me as long to get through as it took to write *Atlas Shrugged*. By five o'clock it was all tasteless.

Sitting on the subway now, however, I regretted my decision to go. The three hours it would take to attend Helen's annual holiday function were three hours I might have spent in the accounts of my meetings with Lucian, which had just recently begun to cohere into a single narrative.

But it was too late. Phil, whom Sheila affectionately called "Philly," would be waiting at the Newton stop to take me to Helen's upscale house in her upscale suburb where $520,000 might buy eleven hundred square feet in a hundred-year-old home if you were lucky. Of course, being lucky would mean you were too poor to belong there.

Aubrey had been enamored with the idea of moving to Newton—once her job in marketing took off and I had written my best seller, she said. Which meant, of course, that it was really just a pipe dream to support and inspire me; we both knew her income would always be the greater of our two. I never spoke about my vision of Belmont—Newton had been her dream, and so it necessarily eclipsed mine. After a while it didn't matter; even her encouragements had begun to feel like a perpetual list of grievances, and I had retreated into silence.

Until that night.

I blamed her, yanked the covers back from the bed where she was sleeping. I yelled at her and called her a whore. But as furious as I was with her, I was angry with myself, incredulous that years of proving reliable, of doing the right thing—of being a *good* man—had amounted only to this: that I would never be able to do and be those things she required.

I rubbed my forehead, the back of my neck. At Copley Station I pulled the wine back onto my lap to make room for a woman with several bags. She had a long, gray ponytail that reminded me of my college anthropology professor, a sprightly woman in her fifties who routinely came to class in her dressage boots, smelling of horse sweat and leather.

My seatmate gave me a slight smile, and I half expected her to address me by name, to begin talking about clay men and Lucifer's personal vendetta against them. But she got up at the next stop, and I watched her go, thinking of the dressage boots that had carried from the classroom into my fantasy life, regardless of our thirty-year age difference.

A rough-hewn Asian woman in an army jacket smirked at me from across the car.

"She does bring to mind Professor Deptula."

My heart twitched inside my chest as she came to sit in the seat where the woman with the gray hair had been. Her face was round, the kind of face a Korean friend of mine used to call a "pumpkin." Her hair spiked in soft black tufts from her head, providing the angles and interesting dimension that her face did not. No fewer than four earrings dotted her earlobe. She was all cargo pants, leather, and camouflage, attractive in a rough-hewn way that refused to chase the classic Asian beauty she could never have achieved at any rate.

Her presence startled me—not for the fact that it came unannounced but because she had been sitting across from me for two stops before she made herself known. Had Lucian observed me, lurking in plain sight on other occasions? But at least one demon must always have been there for their swarming network to have such ready knowledge of my actions throughout my life. And while I knew this fact in theory, I found the reality of it unsettling.

"I didn't see anything on my calendar."

"I thought I'd drop by."

Yes, unsettling.

"And what if I had stayed at home?" Every day upon opening my door or stepping from my apartment building, I wondered if someone I did not recognize would be standing there with a too-familiar smile.

Lucian fell back in the seat, expelled a sigh, then raked a hand through her hair, making it stand up straighter than before. The thick strap of a leather watch was bound around her wrist. "Well, that might have presented a problem."

I didn't like the sound of that. "Why?"

"I don't care for your place."

This admission stunned me. "Why?"

"It has a fair amount of, shall we say, spiritual static. Let's keep it at that."

I felt a wash of relief, followed quickly by a flash of anger. How long had I felt as vulnerable as if I lived in a fishbowl?

"What do you mean, 'spiritual static'?"

"Clay, I didn't come to discuss your apartment's feng shui. I need to address an issue." There was warning in her voice, seeming to imply that if I pressed her, she might get up at the next stop, leaving me with no answers but silence.

That thought frightened me most of all. "What issue?"

"This debacle of Job."

Job? I was only vaguely familiar with the story, and more for literary reasons than biblical ones.

"Listen. Lucifer's days of proving his own worthiness and superiority were gone. He was beyond that, delighting only in El's disappointment, which had become a motivation all its own. To that end, he became fixated on pointing out human shortcomings, even predicting them in advance like a billiard player calling a shot. Lucifer loved this particular game. And the more El favored the human, the more tempting the human—and the game—was to him. He derived great enjoyment from the infidelities of El's favorites and in pointing out their failures. For these acts Lucifer first received the name Satan—'Accuser.'"

As she said this, the fingers of her one hand enclosed the wrist of the other, seeming to check that the leather band of her watch was securely fastened. One of the earrings dangled against the corner of her jaw: a silver knife.

"Now understand that like your scientists with their mice in their mazes, we knew well the predicted outcome, the percentages, the overwhelming empirical evidence. We have, after all, been there since the beginning and understand something of human proclivities."

I thought of the night he waited for me at the Bosnian Café. At Vittorio's. At the distraction I felt at the sight of her in the bookstore, the smooth skin of her décolleté and the ankh stroking it.

"During that time Lucifer—brazen, beautiful as ever, brilliant with the light that was still *him*—became obsessed with the man Job."

"Why?"

"Because El said there was no one on earth like him. And this made Job irresistible to Lucifer, who meant to show El that even the best among the clay people hadn't the faithfulness to show loyalty in the face of adversity. It's one thing to love a god who protects you, showers you with wealth and all the worldly things that seem to matter so much in the short space of a lifetime. It's another thing to love him when those things disappear.

"Now I'm going to tell you something. In all our work we go where we wish; Lucifer does what he will. But a barricade had been erected around Job, an unbreakable bulwark of protection. The Host were thick upon him, and we couldn't touch him—

until the day that El dispersed the hedge around him, and we were free to do what we would."

There was an ominous sound to the lilt of her voice, and though I knew she spoke of the past, I was reluctant to hear what she said next.

"We spent the wealth, attacked his livestock, killed the servants. And then we targeted his children. I came in as a storm and Belial as a great wind, and the house they were in collapsed and killed them all. We reduced one of the richest, most noteworthy men in the world to nothing in the space of a single day."

"In a day?" I echoed with morbid wonder.

"A day. And the next day Lucifer took his health. Simple, decisive measures with one outcome in mind: for Job to curse El. But he wouldn't do it. Suffice it to say, Lucifer's still sore about it." She leaned forward, resting her elbows on her knees, fiddling still with the band of her watch. "Mind you, a single failure every now and then still keeps our success rate well over the 99.9 percent mark. Not quite perfect"— her smile was crooked—"but in my humble opinion perfection is overrated. And Job was a freak."

"There was no one else exceptional enough for Lucifer to test himself against?"

"There would be, but he hadn't come along yet. In the meantime, we grew bored, toyed halfheartedly, and shook our heads at El's long-suffering. At times I wondered what would happen to us, but that uncomfortable sense, that inevitability in my immortal bones, had by then dulled to the phantom ache of a severed limb.

"When I felt it, I distracted myself by thinking instead about the mud people and what would happen to them. There was talk of judgment after death, and though the details seemed obtuse, this made sense. Surely El must eventually deal with them; this could not go on forever. He would reach an end to his patience. He would, I was certain, see the constancy of human failure—the only consistent thing about them—and destroy them all yet, for they grew worse, not better."

She was pulling at the watch now in a way I found strange and distracting. And then I noticed with alarm that she was not toying or fiddling with the watch at all but digging her nails into the skin of her forearm above it so that it rose up in red welts and had even begun, in one place, to bleed.

Something about the sight of that struck me as particularly destructive—more so than if a human had done it—so that I instantly wanted, needed, to get away from her. I felt unable to breathe in the confined space of the car and got quickly to my feet as the train pulled into the station.

"Go to your party, Clay," she called after me. "Go to your party, *Clay!*"

There was something about the way she shouted my name that propelled me out the door, the skin on my back pricking as though it expected a knife thrust. I felt her eyes on me even after I hurried up the path to the street and the train receded toward Riverside.

Standing on the curb, I was glad for the chill, the sound of voices, the idling cars waiting on commuters. Despite the fact that I would not have had this latest portion to add to my account had I stayed in my apartment, I thought I never should have left.

As I searched for Phil's gray Honda, I was disturbed, unable to push from my mind the image of her clawing at her skin as though it were a growth, a leech to be pulled away. And now, with that image in my mind, I must make conversation over mini-quiches, crab claws, imported cheeses, and macaroons— ask the appropriate questions of my colleagues' spouses about their jobs and families. They, knowing of my divorce, would ask me about my work, which I did not want to talk about. I would deflect their questions with inquiries about their children and be regaled with Carolyn's latest lacrosse accomplishments or Dayle's college application or little Ravi's latest rash. And because Helen had a particular talent for being everywhere in a group at once, she would no doubt make up for my deficit of family news by inquiring about the status of my manuscript in front of my peers. And I would have to come up with some way to explain the thing unfurling on my computer, including what it was called and when it would be done. Questions for which I had no answers.

A disturbing thought struck me then with such force that I halted on the curb just as Phil, double-parked down the street, opened the door to his Honda to wave at me.

I was not only writing an account of my every meeting with Lucian and each thing he told me; I had offered it as an excuse for my absences and lack of productivity. As an editor at Brooks and Hanover, I had a contractual obligation to show any of my work to our committee first.

The account could never have been published as memoir. No credible writer would claim it as nonfiction.

And then I knew: Lucian hadn't expected me to. I was an editor of fiction with a yearning to write—and more important, publish—again.

You're going to write it down and publish it.

The fiend had played me perfectly.

18

In the days following Helen's Christmas party, I told myself I was finished—with the story and possibly writing in general. Even if I saw the demon, I would write no more. But then, I knew, would come the lilt of his voice, wending its way through my memory. I wouldn't be able to bear it if I couldn't expel the words onto the page like a medieval surgeon bleeding himself into a bowl to cure himself of ill humors.

So I would write only to rid myself of it, but I would shred the pages. And I would delete the account beckoning to me from my hard drive like a Lorelei.

But even as I thought this, I knew I wouldn't.

At least I wouldn't publish it. I would tell Helen it wasn't working, that the well had gone dry, that I had a phenomenal case of writer's block. She would have no choice but to accept it.

But I didn't talk to Helen because the truth was this: I wanted it. I wanted the story, and I wanted to publish it. I had access to something no one else did, a story too fantastical to stay in the drawer. And like Cassandra of myth, I could never purport to be telling the truth without being seen as a liar, a lunatic, or worse. But I could sheath it in fiction, where lies were warmly welcomed.

Meanwhile, as though to punish my vacillation, five full days passed in silence.

I stared at the papers on my desk. I returned to the chronicle on my computer.

SHEILA CLOSED MY DOOR and came to stand at the corner of my desk, her arms crossed not so much in front of her as around herself, her hands clasping her upper arms as though she were cold.

"Yes?" I didn't bother to disguise my impatience with her hallway request to talk to me. I was practically unable to look at her of late and found the way her wasting state garnered sympathetic inquiries from others nauseating.

"Clay, I need a favor."

"Yes?" I repeated.

"I know you haven't seen Dan much since your divorce. . . ." She unfolded her arms and pulled at her hands as if they ached. Her lips looked chapped, as though they would crack and bleed if she merely grimaced. "But right now, I don't know what's going through his head."

I looked at her.

"I thought if you could talk to him, it might help." Her eyes were shining but did not seem to have the energy to well over.

"Excuse me?"

"I wondered if you'd be willing to call him."

Anger surged up my torso. It wasn't enough that she was cheating on him; now she had to pull me into it? What—to win sympathy? To say, as Aubrey had, that she had tried every-thing?

"I'm not going to do that," I said, flatly. "You need to straighten this out with Dan yourself."

Just then, an incoming chat request from "Light1" jerked my attention to the corner of my screen.

My heart stuttered in a mixture of relief and anger. I could hardly look away from it. I was vaguely aware of Sheila nodding, of her hesitation. The way she loitered, as though waiting for more, or to say something more, annoyed me. I lifted my gaze meaningfully to her.

She looked on the verge of breaking down, as if she would have already, had she the strength. For a moment I almost recon-sidered my response. I would not talk to Dan on her behalf, but maybe I could be gentler. I could encourage her to talk to him herself. To consider what she really wanted and how she was going about it. But she murmured something unintelligible and let herself out, her hair shielding her face.

I turned my attention to the blinking request on my monitor and clicked Accept.

Light1: As much as humans strive to be individuals, they have one universal weakness: the susceptibility to temptation.

BandHClay: You played me.

Light1: Like the two little eyes on a coconut, the perfect place to crack it open. Eat enough coconuts and you know.

BandHClay: You knew just how to do it, didn't you—how best to tempt me. Is that what you're saying?

Light1: With what would I tempt you?

I stared at the screen. Did he not think I would realize what he was doing? After several minutes, he sent:

Light1: Have you been writing?

"When haven't I been?" I wanted to type in large, angry caps. I wanted to yell through that chat window that I was like a man possessed, that I was running on an average of four hours of sleep, Chinese takeout, coffee, and whatever happened to be in the office break room, that he had manipulated me, that I was never going to give the story to Helen, and that the sooner hell was invented, the better.

BandHClay: As though I could help it, as you very well know. You know you could have written it all down and really submitted it to Katrina—or even here—yourself.

Light1: And languish in submission and publishing hell? Please and no thank you. Besides, I told you: My story is ultimately about you.

BandHClay: I still don't understand!

Light1: You will.

I must have broken a sweat at the first appearance of the chat box. It beaded now against my nape, my hairline.

Light1: Distribute the proposal for next week's meeting.

BandHClay: What makes you think I have a proposal? I need a synopsis for that, and to write a synopsis, I need to know how it ends.

Light1: Just give her what you have. Helen will love it and ask for the full manuscript.

BandHClay: Don't you get it? There isn't a full manuscript!

Light1: There will be.

19

The old woman's scalp was just visible through the feathery curls of her hair. Beneath the fake fur collar of her wool coat, her back curved up into a bump at her nape, reminding me of the woman at Vittorio's as she blew out the candle on her cake. Over the tops of her gray boots, stockings a shade too tan bridged the distance to the hem of her skirt, the skin beneath as veined as pink marble.

I was shopping for my niece, studying an elaborate nativity scene. Aubrey had started Susanna's collection two years before we married, and that had been our gift to her every year since.

The woman's head swiveled on her bent neck as she looked from one Christmas tree to another, each of them crammed with ornaments like a chicken breast stuffed with bread crumbs. Above us, glass baubles hung from the ceiling in a fantasy rain of giant, multicolored drops.

"How I love the trappings of the season." She plucked an ornament from a nearby tree: a rendition of a snowman worthy of Dr. Seuss.

My happiest childhood memories were of Christmas, when a covert visit from Santa was the pinnacle of the season; before

I learned that some children got more gifts than others, that visits from Santa cost money. Before I got my first job and the holiday got reduced to paycheck bonuses, unpleasant gatherings, and a pile of trash left out on the curb on January 2.

"And how I adore your nativity scenes. Porcelain and pristine, so pretty." Separating the syllables of "pretty" as my grandmother used to do, the demon passed along the edge of the table, looking down at the nativity scene the price tag of which was quietly displayed on a corner of the stable: $2,499. She plunked the snowman down in the manger on top of baby Jesus.

Watching her, I could have sworn something moved behind the milky iris of her eyes.

"Of course—" she picked through elaborately painted wise men, turning Joseph over as though to see what he had on beneath his robes—"it never really happened that way. The wise men didn't show up at a quarter 'til ten, the animals didn't gather round, and Mary didn't wear blue. She wasn't wearing much of anything, come to think of it."

"Lucian!" I hissed. The thought of a naked Mary offended even my vestigial religious sense.

"What? She was in labor." She dropped Joseph on his back in the middle of the sheep.

I left the nativity table, disgusted, wanting one sacred thing—even if it was an amalgamation of pagan feasts I would likely not take part in this year—to hold onto. I had come here under the guise of shopping but mostly to experience the holiday vicariously, to seek out the commercial trappings of a season that had once meant happiness.

"Your Christmas ditties, the ones about the actual incident and not about dancing snowmen, flying deer, or fat men in red, always make me chuckle."

To any passerby she might have been any little old lady talk-ing about her grandchildren, her white hair fluffing around her head like the spun fiberglass snow of the village display at the store's main entrance.

"Had it not been for the identity of the baby, it would have been an otherwise unremarkable night, and your polite 'Greensleeves' would have been an appropriate soundtrack, after all. But it wasn't an ordinary baby. It wasn't an unremarkable night."

I felt, rather than heard, a suffocating silence close in around me like the endless void of space. Then I saw the blinding flash of a star careen toward its zenith.

It wasn't silent at all! I was falling and seemed to fall forever. A deafening pulse filled my ears, reverberated through my body as if through the taut skin of a drum. I staggered, blinded by the throbbing in my head that jarred my vision as though with the beat of one giant heart. But then that thrum slowed and lengthened, stretching like a coil pulled straight until I thought I couldn't stand it, feeling that if it stopped I might die, as one dies with the last beat of a heart. And then it was not a sound at all but a wave of energy, surging as an ocean crashing upon a stony shore.

As it receded, that rocking quickened, rolling over itself, picking up speed until it was a taut vibrato, until it had become the vibrant hum that was energy itself—there! A burst of light! A bright highway of light shot out before me like a ribbon road to eternity. And somewhere that was both above and below and behind me came the heralding din of horns that were not horns, having to them a stringed quality that could not be strings. It crescendoed until I thought my eardrums would burst—or that my heart would. And in that sound I heard the cadence of unrest, the meter of a ticking timepiece, fulminating seconds, the phrasing of an impending end.

It fell away sharply at the single cry of a baby.

I was grasping the edge of the table, my skull feeling too small to hold the sound that had just burst within it. I thought I might vomit.

Nearby, someone had opened a music box. It plinked away a toy version of "Greensleeves" one tin note at a time, but I could still hear the throbbing in my ears.

"You—you did this," I said to the demon as she put a surprisingly strong arm around me.

"No," she said. "You started to black out. Come on. We'll get you a cookie."

IN THE FOOD COURT I sipped soda and picked at a giant cookie. The nausea and light-headedness had left me, leaving me as weak as if I had vomited off and on for an hour.

"There had been rumors. Prophets ranting about saviors." The demon's perennial cup of tea sat steaming in front of her, neglected. "Well, we have prophets, too, and they spout plenty of things, but that doesn't necessarily mean they're all going to happen. Plenty of people have purported to be messiahs. So we didn't worry about it much. Regardless, some of the clay people watched for him, eyes to the world. They hailed him, sight unseen, as a king. They hoped, and the hope was disconcerting to us. Hope changes the hearts of a people, lengthens their vision beyond their petty, everyday lives."

"Lengthens their vision." I considered that.

The old woman sat forward. "The day Adam ate mortal judgment to his body, he also ate scales to his eyes and myopia to his soul and to that of his children as well. Like one who views stars through the lens of astigmatism or through Depression glass, you can't see clearly. It's why you wonder why bad things happen to so-called good people, why there is violence, disease, the senseless things on the news, what have you. You're short-sighted, focused only on your immediate surroundings, your immediate timeframe. Is it any wonder that the world doesn't make sense to you?"

"Speaking of which," I said. "How are your cataracts?"

"Quite the annoyance," she said with a smirk, as though to say, "Touché."

She propped her elbow on the table then and leaned her chin on a wrinkled but soft-looking hand covered with random liver spots like stars.

"I had a frightening thought the other day. Even though I never ate from that tree, I wonder if I've fallen as surely as your first man. I wonder if I, too, am not quite seeing the world as it is, if my vision plays me false at times without my knowing it. I wonder even now if I'm looking through some watery glass of an eye, like a mirror hung too long on the wall." She squinted one eye shut and peered past me with the other. "If it, too, has warped in the age since my innocence." The lone eye turned on me.

"Then we're even."

"Oh no." She opened her other eye and sat back, reaching up to pat her feathery hair. "We may carry a great grudge and misplaced alliance, but being around since the beginning has a way of giving one insight. But it's so difficult for you to venture beyond the boundaries of your mortal world and comprehend the scope of truth—truth and eternity. After all, your life transpires in a blink. You're driven by the things you see, that you can touch and smell. By what you feel. Things as temporal as you are.

"But with all this talk of a messiah, a few Jews began to see beyond their everyday lives. And the longer they waited, the more we wondered. After all, if you watch someone look expectantly at the door long enough, you eventually start to wonder if someone is going to walk through it. So, in spite of ourselves, we started to watch, too. And then the news came: A messiah was imminent."

"How did you feel about that?"

She folded her hands on the table and smiled. "Oh, I wanted to see it! After all, it had to be a Herculean job, being a savior; it didn't seem possible for one man. And we began to speculate among ourselves which of his favorites El would raise up. Perhaps he'd be a man of breeding and education. A leader of men. A great general—a soldier, in the very least. A conqueror. But Lucifer . . ." She shook her head so faintly and so repeatedly that it seemed to wag on her neck like a doll's. "He wasn't interested in trying to outguess El. He wanted a preemptive strike. So he raised up a Jewish king, a man ruthless enough to tolerate no threat to his own power. And he, too, watched for this Messiah. This King of the Jews."

"This guy in Bethlehem."

"Worse. A carpenter's kid born of a teenage pregnancy." She covered her eyes with her hand and shook her head. "It was so ridiculous we wondered if the report was wrong. But no, the scout had seen the girl with *Gabriel*." She half spat the name, and I wondered, for the first time, what kind of history must exist between siblings, comrades, who have experienced eternity and parted to opposite sides in the conflict that ended it.

"El was making a clay child in the womb of some ordinary girl with a boring name. Not a queen, this mother of the new king. Not even a princess or woman of stature. An unremarkable virgin—and not even the best-looking girl I'd ever seen—pledged to marry some carpenter or another in some insignificant town. Suffice it to say, it didn't look promising." I felt now a strange tension in her, in the stooped back and the milky gaze, a tautness at odds with the withering body. "I thought Lucifer would laugh himself silly, would find this insanely funny. It became the brunt of our jokes. Really, El had gone too far with this one. He was making a buffoon of himself."

"He didn't laugh, did he?" Never once had the demon portrayed Lucifer as anything other than brilliant.

"No." She rubbed and then picked at an age spot on her hand. "He stood off, alone, silent. I had never seen him like this before. As he stared with fixed eyes, his hauteur slipped from his shoulders like a robe. And as the reason finally became clear, we realized El's plan was far more extravagant and unimaginable than anything we could have fathomed."

I felt the faintest aftershock of that rush of energy, the echo of that deafening roar.

"And as I huddled on the periphery of that night, I saw a shot of light, heard the heralding Host. The pulse of the world fell silent, one sound only filling the void where that deafening announcement had been: the first wail of a newborn human."

The babe. I had heard it.

She lowered her head to clutch at a soft tuft of white hair. "Had I blood, it would have frozen in my veins, for I *recognized* the voice in that human cry. And the knowledge of it rushed upon me all at once: Elohim, Creator Almighty, had sent that part of himself, the very part that had provided the light of that

first and re-created Eden, the part that had spoken the words for
the forming of the cosmos before my inception and for my own
creation, had planted himself in the womb of an insignificant
girl. He had arrived now in person."

Inside my sweater, the hair on my arms stood out from my
skin.

"Do you understand? Flesh! He had taken on flesh. Not
flesh in feel and appearance as I have done, or Lucifer might do,
as members of the Host have done since the early days, but true
flesh! The sentence of humanity. Why? Why!" Her arms jerked
like a puppet's, and I saw pieces of her white hair sticking to her
fingers, matted to them like blood on a windshield. "I racked my
brain. I writhed with it. Why would El go to such lengths for
these creatures—go so far as to demean himself by becoming
one of them? I burned with it.

"And I could only hazard a guess about how Lucifer felt—the
best-created, most favored of El—abandoned by his great bene-
factor, his God-King having turned his back on him for the sake
of a race of clay people. How it must feel to watch these insane
lengths El was willing to go to prove his love for their terminal
souls!" Drops of white spittle came out of her mouth as she spoke,
clinging in sticky strings to the corner of her lip, her chin.

"It came to me then with the howling force of a freight
train: He had never loved us so much. And then: *He had never
loved even Lucifer so much!* Had he ever made even the slightest
concession for any of us, let alone the shining cherub? But there
seemed to be no end to what he would do for the humans. But
here, now, was the thing:"—she raised her finger, albino strands
falling from it—"If El mended the rift between the humans and
himself in this sordid love affair, what would become of Lucifer?
Of us?" She held out her hands. "Of me?"

Had I heard those words from an old woman's lips in another time or place, it might have evoked pathos in me. But I had to remember: Never had Lucian seemed anything less than capable, crafty, and always more than he—she—purported to be. There was a latent cunning beneath the surface of everything she said, a taut power. And when she raised her eyes to me now, I saw something move like a shadow behind their clouded curtain, as one in the street sees a figure in a third-story window, looking down in silence, watching. And again I felt that surge of anxiety that I was missing something entirely.

"Then, with another squalling rush of clarity, I understood: There would be no new creation. He would not discard these mud people to begin anew with a greater or meeker brand of creature. He would offer his all to these mortals because they were the ones he loved."

"All this time you had been waiting for El to destroy us?" I said faintly.

Now that mouth, which had gone slack, spread wide, revealing crags of stained teeth. "Oh, *yes*." And the sibilance of that word was more menacing than if she had shouted, for I realized she had waited to revel in that very thing. Now she leaned back in her chair, tilting her head at an angle I found unnatural, especially for an old woman, as though she wouldn't mind at all breaking her own neck.

"And yet we were not without means. The world was Lucifer's kingdom, and El had just entered it in the flesh of a human. And as I held out hope, it lengthened my own, demonic vision."

I had hardly ever heard her refer to herself in this way except at the beginning, so it struck me with ominous force to hear it now.

"Our Jewish king, so carefully chosen and strategically placed, was ruthless. It was enough that this would-be king threatened his reign, and so he sought to kill the child."

"I take it he didn't find him."

That's when something strange happened. The demon became distracted, staring with squinted eyes off in the direction of a store somewhere beyond the food court. Following her gaze, I saw nothing out of the ordinary, only shoppers coming in and out of the store, two men standing outside it like disenfranchised husbands waiting on their wives.

"What is it?"

"He had every boy in the area under two years old butchered." Lucian's eyes darted this way and that, a dry tongue snaking out to lick at her lips.

I thought again of the nativity scene, so serene and idyllic.

"Not that it helped. Obviously, the baby survived."

 # 20

♦

I felt it like a bodily urge—like the irresistible need to cough, to vomit, to use the toilet. The story welled to a sickening head within me. I grabbed a stack of paper from my recycling bin and began to write, the physical act releasing it in fits. Even when I reached the end, I sat back, breathing slowly, deeply, waiting for it to subside, and then bolted upright to add in my thoughts, the description of her hands tearing at her hair, the grotesque moment when I'd asked her about human obliteration, her smile the rictus of a corpse.

Shortly after one in the morning, I went to bed with a headache severe enough to turn my stomach.

At 3:00 a.m. I lay in bed, unable to sleep, thinking about something the demon had said. *If El mended the rift between humans and himself, what would become of us?*

Of me?

I thought of the Genesis account. Of the messianic prophecy and the birth of the baby. Something dawned on me that I had not seen before, something that, even alone in my apartment, made my lips part in wonder: The growing pile of pages on my desk was not the story of a fall. Neither was it a demonic coming-of-age.

It was a love story. Of God for humans.

I supposed, too, it was the story of Lucian's own love affair and subsequent divorce.

If humans could be reconciled, what about demons? Lucian had said nothing about any hope for himself. At least not yet. Perhaps that was where he meant to go next.

But what if not? What if Lucian were truly disowned? Then he must resent people as much as he claimed. And that must, necessarily, include me.

MY SLEEP THAT NIGHT, all three hours of it, was riddled with restless visions. I dreamed of Pastor Feagan, seeing the deep lines around his eyes, the gold crowns on two of his front teeth, more clearly in dreams than I could in memory. But when he opened his mouth in children's church, he wasn't the pastor at all. He was Lucian, spewing his hatred for all things human across the carpeted floor of the sanctuary.

And then I was at my cousin's house. My father was still alive, and we had driven to Nebraska as a family to see his brother's family where they lived midway between Lincoln and the western panhandle. My uncle had moved there for some kind of work, and I used to love visiting my cousins there, where they burned their garbage in a big bin out back, and we played Kill-the-Carrier in their giant front yard. I was six again.

My cousin had, among his toys, a Sesame Street book about Grover, who was afraid of a monster at the end of the book. At each page Grover begged me not to go on, not to turn another page, and of course I couldn't resist. I was so enamored with the book that I wanted to take it with me on the car ride home. My aunt gamely told me I could have it, and though my parents protested, and my cousin, two years younger than me, started to cry, I wanted that book so much that I made the situation worse by continuing to ask for it. I knew my mother would scold me later, but I didn't care; I wanted to read it again and again with wild anticipation, Grover begging me at each turn not to go farther.

There's a monster!

I didn't care about the last page when Grover, alone at the end of the book, realized that he was the monster. It was the pages leading up to it that fueled my little heart, that kept me turning, fixated, despite repeated warnings.

And then I dreamed I was at my desk, thumbing through proposals stacked in towers nearly as tall as I, through manuscripts five thousand pages long. Peeking out from between two boxed manuscripts, I saw the thin book with its cartoon Muppet character. I picked it up and began to read.

There's a monster.

21

Voices drifted from the Bristol Lounge, punctuated every few seconds by the trilling laugh of a woman. I ambled toward that sound, feeling like an outsider.

I had loved to come to the Four Seasons in my first years as an editor. I was writing the Coming Home books then and used to imagine the day when I would spend every Friday afternoon in the Bristol Lounge's overstuffed chairs, perhaps in front of the fireplace if it were cold outside, expensive brandy rolling inside the snifter in my hand. There I would take drinks with fellow writers or my own editor—perhaps even an interviewer from the *Paris Review*.

It was four years now since I had last been here to take Aubrey's mother to enjoy salmon sandwiches, miniature tarts, and scones with clotted cream, all part of a high tea that we could barely afford.

I half expected the hostess to give me a polite but distant look, to say that they were full, so sorry, that I might try the Irish pub down the street. But she smiled and led me to an out-of-the-way nook just off the bar lined by a long, red leather seat. Between the bronze upholstery tacks along the back of the seat and the book-lined shelves above it, the polished cherry wood of the table and the attendant cozy chairs pulled up on the other side, the little nook gave off the flavor of an elegant personal library.

In another life, one filled with editor and writer friends, I could have claimed this corner as my own, reserved it each week to hold court and take that brandy, to grant that rare interview.

Tonight there would be no editors, no interviews, no brandy.

But there would be, at least, dessert. I ordered coffee and then got up to drift between tables of tortes and pastries and cheesecake and ice creams at that famous dessert buffet, returning ultimately with a glorious bowl of hot pumpkin bread pudding that was even now melting a scoop of maple ice cream into a white moat in the dish.

From where I sat, I had a direct view of the grouping of cushy chairs in front of the piano, where five women exchanged Christmas gifts over likewise melting desserts. The gift bags and boxes were wrapped with tulle and sprigs of fresh evergreen and yielded items like silver bowls, a polished wooden jewelry box, a Hermes-style scarf. On the hand of every woman was a rock so large I could see it from my corner, shining like a beacon.

Beyond the group, a long expanse of windows looked out onto the street and into the Public Garden beyond. I used to love the order of those flower beds with their iron ropes, the manicured lawns and spiral-cut shrubs. But now they seemed as meticulous and indifferent as a cemetery, as unnatural as the perfectly embalmed visage of a corpse.

"I'm afraid I'm the late one this time." A young man hurried into my morbid reverie and pulled out one of the cozy chairs. He

was dapper in navy blue pants and a button-down shirt, his tie
loosened so that it hung askew in a way that reminded me faintly
of a noose. He might have been an intern fresh out of college; he
had the mischievous, spring-faced look of an Ivy League a capella
singer, a Harvard Din and Tonic or a Brown Derby. His hair, a
light chestnut, curled around his face and over his ears in a way
that might have looked like a dirty halo if the wind caught it just
right. *Like a doll-faced cherub.* When he sat down, he crossed his
ankle over his knee and fell back into the leather as though, at the
ripe age of—what, twenty-one?—he had had a long day.

"Why are you so tired?" I said, a bit put out. I had come
straight from eleven hours at the office on only five hours of
sleep the night before.

"I'm a busy man," he said, smiling at me. He had a dimple
in his left cheek, and his skin was flushed pink. He looked like
a young man in the throes of infatuation. I had never seen him
like this.

"I don't need to tell you the committee liked what I gave
them, do I?"

"Of course they liked it." He smiled again and looked
around. "I haven't been here since they expanded." A waitress
came for his order. He smiled at her and, with a look at my cup,
asked for coffee.

"Helen assumes the content is mine, and that it's fiction,"
I said, shaving the corner off the bread pudding, taking just
enough ice cream with it.

"But of course."

"It feels dishonest."

He shrugged. "If you want to put 'as told to' before your
name, be my guest, though it won't do wonders for your
credibility."

"I plan to use a pen name." It would be my concession to a conscience that knew it could not claim full credit for Lucian's story—only my own.

"A nom de plume? How mysterious."

I did not say that it was also practical, a means of separating this work from my former, failed attempts at publishing.

The demon seemed to be elsewhere, just disengaged enough from our conversation to be unflappable, which bothered me. "Whatever you're comfortable with."

"I'm comfortable with knowing how it ends." It came out more calmly than I expected.

"Soon," he said. "You'll know. I promise." He returned his focus to me with an absent smile.

"What you don't seem to understand is that I can't even finish a synopsis without"— I stopped as the waitress reappeared. Lucian smiled up at her, and I considered my soggy bread pudding, not wanting to follow their small talk. I wasn't in the mood to witness any kind of interaction that I had not had since— since Lucian's trick in the bookstore.

"Don't be so sour, Clay," he said after she left.

"I'm not sour."

"You will be when you see . . . this," he said, lifting a scrap of paper from the table with a triumphant flick of his hand. I stared, exasperated, at a number with the name *Nikki* scribbled next to it.

"I'm trying to discuss this memoir that is so important to you, and you're collecting phone numbers?"

He tucked it inside his jacket. I couldn't help wondering what would become of that number—and the woman it belonged to.

"All right, you want to get to the end of the book."

The skin on my arms prickled.

There's a monster.

I suddenly wondered if I might have done better to stay home. I needed sleep. Television. A movie. I needed to focus on something normal—nothing, in other words—like any other anesthetized human for once. But I knew I wouldn't trade being here for sleep or time in front of a television I had not turned on for more than a month.

Lucian settled into his chair as though getting down to business and lifted his coffee cup. I gave him a quizzical look.

"First, a toast."

"To what?" I was almost afraid to know.

"To you, Clay. They're going to love your story," he said. "You'll have a contract within three months—not to mention a nice little advance."

Something lurched inside me, scrabbling at his words like pennies on the ground. I wanted to believe him. How I wanted to believe him! "You said you're not omniscient." But I lifted my coffee cup. He clinked it, sloshing coffee over the edges of both our rims.

"I'm not. But as you know, I play the percentages. And I would bet money on it."

I took a tentative sip, trying not to think about it, but it was too late; my heart had started a desperate little dance.

I had to admit I could use the money. Moving my books and sparse belongings to Cambridge and trying to replace the furniture I had given to Aubrey had not done wonders for my checkbook. I supposed I had Lucian to thank for providing me other matters to focus on than the minimalist décor of my apartment that Mrs. Russo had so generously called "Spartan."

"Speaking of which, you should look into some of those last-minute vacation specials."

"I can't afford it."

"Put it on your credit card. You deserve it. You can finish the story on the beach."

I dropped my head, slid my hands over my hair. The beach. I couldn't remember the last time I had seen a beach or taken a vacation.

"Meanwhile, if we have a book to write, we'd better get to it. Now then . . ." He scrubbed the back of his head.

"The Messiah was born," I said slowly, not wanting to remember the look of that withered face again, contorted in that terrible smile.

"Of course," he said, leaning forward in the chair, elbows on his knees, hands clasped loosely together, "by the time of that horrible, eerie night, Lucifer had made tempting the faithful and bringing them before El like so many unruly children his life's work. Not that it brought Lucifer much joy."

"It's what he wanted, wasn't it?"

"He seemed less and less satisfied by it, his tolerance and appetite had grown so great. So what else was there for Lucifer—for us—to do except dwell on our less-favored status, to watch our own dwindling hope sinking deeper and deeper beneath the surface of a black bog, out of reach? Actually, the more we dared to hope for El's renewed favor, the more we felt compelled to show these humans for the disappointments they were. And the more we carried out the commission of Lucifer— now Satan—the more out of favor we fell."

"Talk about diminishing returns."

"Exactly. And eventually, I suppose, the less we cared. By

then the means had become an end in itself—a way of life, a purpose.

"This had already been the case with Satan for some time, but then he had always been a creature of mission, a dark visionary. And now his vision ignited a new and unholy fire in us as well. I found myself less melancholy and more wholly focused on a new trade: no more to glorify Creator Elohim—never that again—but to degrade and despoil all his favored people in ways unknown before. Now there was true pleasure. Don't recoil like that."

"I didn't," I lied.

"It's not as though you've never wandered a step—and then ten more, each one easier than the last—down a path you had never thought yourself capable of taking. Did you ever once think you'd spend every night of almost four months drunk? That you'd wake up after a three-day binge to realize you were practically broke and still alone?"

I looked away. It was not a memory I wanted to recall, the weeks of drinking, the mad sobbing on my kitchen floor. A retaliatory one-night stand. Or two.

"But I'm not here to judge you. I'm only making a point."

I retreated into my cup, realizing I had forgotten the bread pudding. It was cold now, a sodden, lopsided heap.

"Lucifer is a creature of method. Since his first failed attempt to raise his throne and then that business of Job, he had grown allergic to failure. Even in the garden of the first man and woman, he devoted long years to observing the humans, studying behaviors, weighing their tendencies, watching them like exotic creatures in their habitat. He is the master of risk reduction. Never impulsive, his plans ferment a long time in the darkness of his heart. The Great Inventor meditates at length on his craft, always the innovator. It is the reason he so rarely fails.

"Now at last was a venture worthy of him. It set him on edge so that he craved it to the exclusion of everything else. He was insanely preoccupied, shut up like a scientist in his laboratory, a beast pacing behind the arena gate."

I thought I might know something about that kind of preoccupation. "And what was that challenge?"

"The spirit of the Almighty. God himself in the clay body of a man. *Elohim come to earth.*"

I felt my forehead wrinkle. "So you really mean it when you say he was God. Literally God and man." I was aware of my dubious tone. I had always placed Jesus in the echelon reserved for Gandhi, Buddha, Martin Luther King Jr. But they were all mortal men.

The look on the demon's face perplexed me. His lips were parted, turned up in just the hint of a smile. I felt he was somehow waiting on me, poised to see what I might say next.

Nikki, our waitress, stepped in, breaking the taut wire between us. I looked away as she refreshed my cup, cleaned up the coffee spilled from our toast. I was glad for the reprieve, unsure what had just happened between us.

When she left, he sat forward again, steepled his fingers. "Clay, what I tell you, I need you to hear. If you can't believe it, then consider it a part of the story, and I'll be content with that. I would be very content with that, in fact." His smile was a quirk on just one side of his mouth.

Of course. It only matters that it is part of the story.

"Right now you need to know that this God-man was too big a prize for Lucifer. Too tempting, shall we say." He laughed, and the dimple on his cheek squinted. I waited out the laughter as I had on other occasions. When it suddenly and disconcertingly stopped, he considered his hands, turning them over this way and that, as though he had not taken the time to examine them until now. "To thwart the son is to thwart the will of Elohim. This was too precious a goal for Lucifer to stand idly by. Too vital to Lucifer's state of mind. It was to be the summation of his life's work."

"You're saying he meant to tempt God."

"Yes."

"Isn't that impossible?"

"Not entirely." He looked and sounded, to all appearances, like the young scholar. He might have been a seminary student, ruddy cheeked and idealistic. "The clay body was the crux of it. No man, no soul in a clay body has ever been immune to temptation. In fact, every clay person since the first one had succumbed to temptation at some time or another, had experienced moral failure by El's standards at some point in his or her life. But here, suddenly, was the unfathomable combination: the perfection of El in a fallible mud body. Perfection and weakness fused together."

"Do you ever see anything redeeming in humans?"

He seemed on the verge of saying something then rerouted his response at the last instant. "It's the nature of the vessel, Clay: cracked. Something that, once ruined, should have been thrown from the potter's wheel to the refuse pile long ago. And what better way to prove it than to humiliate El with his own failure as one of them? He had *chosen* to become one of you. He chose the terms. If he wanted to fight with one hand tied behind his back, well then . . ." He shrugged.

"When you put it that way, it doesn't seem quite fair."

"He was as much flesh as he was El. But he was still El. And though Lucifer was practically foaming at the mouth, he chose his moment carefully. He waited until the God-man was fast-ing in the desert. Until he was hungry. There Lucifer exploited his hunger like a general attacking the weakest defense of the enemy. He questioned his identity. *If you are the Son of God,* he said. He is an expert rhetorician, experienced and so suggestive. *Why not turn these stones into bread?*

"But the man was steadfast. There was a purpose to the fast-ing, and he wouldn't be tempted to eat. He wouldn't yield to the dictates of his human flesh."

I thought of all the times I had been nearly incapacitated by low blood sugar. By plain hunger. By pain, by sleeplessness.

"So Lucifer appealed to his pride, taking him up to the top of the temple in Jerusalem. *If you are the Son of God,* he said, *throw yourself down.* It was ingenious."

"Why is that ingenious? Wasn't he essentially telling him to take a flying leap? To die?"

Lucian smirked. "I never thought of it that way. But no. The temple was the one place people expected to see the Messiah. And the Host would never have let him die from a physical fall; it was guaranteed in Scripture, and Lucifer knew it. You could argue that he was doing the God-man a favor—at least this way people would know who he was. And I heard Lucifer's thought: *Let them see him then. Let him throw himself down and prove who he is.*"

"But he didn't."

"No. His ego held no sway over him. Rather surprising for a man who went about saying he was God. By now Lucifer was showing signs of strain. So like a gambler on the last hand of the night, he held back nothing. He drew the God-man to a mountain and cast a mighty vision, a menagerie of nations, against the sky—Babylon and Persia, the government of Rome and commerce of the Mediterranean. Spices and olives and wine, fleets of ships, the jealous pride of kings and queens and emperors."

As he was talking, the tabletop shimmered, emitting more light than the reflected lamps of our corner nook. Between the abandoned bowl of bread pudding and his coffee cup, I saw the sun, setting in a dark gold disk. As it melted into the horizon, it became the wheat fields of Egypt. Then the stalks of wheat were not wheat at all but a field of people. A nation of people. Lucian's voice wafted toward me in what could have been the voice of a singer: *the mighty millions of the land of Han, flowing with silk, roads pulsing with trade.* The roads swept beneath me, beneath the surface of the polish, of my bird's-eye view, miles at a time until they became a sprawl of cities and I recognized pyramids—Egypt. No, not Egypt. These were the stepped ziggurats of an undiscovered west. *Teotihuacan, city of gods,* came the voice. I saw the gold masks, the priests in their robes, arms raised to the sun.

A coffee cup sailed over the image. Lucian had pushed it across the table toward me.

"Treasures of the East and fertile lands yet undiscovered, rich in commodities of a future age. Lands of people pagan and unconquered, of client kings and vassals and dominions to come. Like diamonds against black velvet, he showcased the world and all that might belong to the God-man so splendidly that those of us who had walked the streets and corridors and dwelt in the inner chambers of those places blinked and staggered at the sight of their collective glory. It was the mosaic of all of Eden's wealth. And Lucifer offered it all to the God-man if he would do one thing: fall down and worship. Just one, simple, singular act." He looked up at me. "It would have been so easy. I knew from experience."

"What good would that have done Lucifer?"

He shook his head. "It was the thing he had always craved and often won—except from the one from whom it would mean something. And now El stood a hand's reach away in the body of a man, with a man's cravings and a human's proclivities. We hardly dared breathe. For a moment it was as though I stood again in that ancient rock garden, the sand of the desert as hot under my feet as the rocks of that place had been. And I watched from below with spirit eyes as Lucifer, arrayed with Legion and surrounded by Host, aspired to the godhood he craved, his beautiful eyes as covetous as they had been that first day an eternity ago when he cast his ambition like grappling hooks up into heaven."

His gaze wandered. He seemed to be looking at something in the direction of the bar. But when I tried to discern what it was, I saw only a cluster of random business travelers, a few stray reception-goers bored with whatever was going on upstairs, a man and woman talking together. He seemed more and more distracted of late, and it was starting to concern me.

I looked from him back to the bar and considered the reception-goers more closely. They were two women, possibly sisters; both looked half Asian, one with curly, highlighted hair. She sat at the bar while the other leaned against it, turned in our direction. The seated one gazed sidelong in what I thought was my direction until I realized that no, she was looking at Lucian. *Figures.*

"This time there was no violence. Clay, listen to me! Our time is short."

My attention snapped back. "I'm listening." *As though I could do anything else!* I was fairly certain that whatever he said would return to me later, regardless of how closely I listened.

"This time there was no violence." He ran his hands nervously through his hair. "This time he would take heaven by word, by simple trade, offering the world in exchange for that proclamation of divinity."

"Was he offering that much, really? I mean, considering that El made it?"

"It was the sum of Lucifer's wealth, his kingdom, his all. He was jealously possessive of everything within it. Would he sacrifice it so readily for the sake of one dangerous temptation posed to God himself as he stood hungry in the desert, strained by human flesh? Yes. Yes, I knew he would. And it would be Lucifer's best and greatest moment. You have to know that wealth meant nothing in comparison to that—to this victory." He glanced over his shoulder.

Something is wrong.

"What were all the kingdoms in the world against the triumph of proving El's so-called son a fraud, a mortal as hopelessly weak in his clay trappings as the rest of them?" he said, his voice trailing over his shoulder.

"What is it?" I said finally, exasperated.

He blinked at me. "I'm fine. Listen now, this is important. There was something more than that, though. I realized it as I stood there, with Lucifer as close to the human act of sweating as a cherub can be. I didn't know it at the time, but Lucifer had seen in this man some great vision, some latent danger." He shifted in his chair, glanced at his watch. "And though he never said it, I saw in that moment that he was desperate."

I had never seen Lucian quite like this, and I was becoming nervous by proxy. I was worried he would leave too soon. And I needed this—every word he spoke. For the completion of my manuscript. For myself.

But his state unnerved me for other reasons: What could possibly make a demon uneasy? I glanced at the bar. The two women were gone.

Lucian pushed the coffee mug away, checked his pocket for something—the phone number of the waitress. As though sensing just that thing, Nikki appeared, all curves and cheekbones and lips. She set the check down on a tiny tray, and Lucian pulled a large bill from his pocket, telling her with a hasty smile to keep the change.

When she left, he said, "The man, weak, thirsty, hungry, buffeted by wind on that summit, refused Lucifer. He sent him away with the authority of El himself. And the kingdoms in the visions painted in the sky shattered like a great glass window, sprinkling shards onto the far horizons as the man collapsed to the desert floor."

He stood, rifling his fingers through his curly hair, seeming to look for the nearest exit.

It wasn't nearly enough! I leaped up. "And then? Then what?" I hated myself.

"Lucifer wasn't finished." He stepped around the chair.

He strode out, not even noticing Nikki when she tried to wave at him.

 **22**

The produce section of the co-op was filled with alien life forms: bell peppers, carrots, tomatoes. I could not remember the last time I had cooked anything from scratch. The concept seemed like a forgotten ritual, mysterious and Zen.

My eating habits of late had been abysmal. Often I forgot about food altogether. Coffee got me through the morning and early afternoon. At home after work, I ate leftovers from takeout the night before. Late into the evening, I emerged ravenous from a stack of reading or, more likely, from shaping my expanding account of the demon memoirs. And then I called and ordered enough food for a late-night binge before falling into a coma on my sofa.

I logged a workweek's worth of hours on the Internet and in the online Bible, researching demon fiction, demon encounters, and novels about angels for the marketing section of my proposal. I even researched accounts of angelic and demonic visitations. But I found nothing like my own experience. I wondered if all such accounts might be lurking in bookstores, already sheathed in fiction.

Sometimes I thought of Aubrey, though not by the hour or even the day as before. The most random things triggered my memory: A pillow beneath my sheets might remind me of her recumbent body, the sway of a woman's wide-legged slacks recalled her favorite gabardine pants. Looking at the bell peppers, I remembered how she used to stuff them with rice and meat; it had been one of my favorite dishes. I picked up a large pepper, turned it over in my hand, and then put it back.

If the committee accepted my manuscript as Lucian seemed certain they would, would she find out that I had published? But of course: Sheila would tell her. Would Aubrey read it? And would she see herself in it, even though I had changed her name along with my own? Would she put the book down in disgust that I had not spared her but had included candid glimpses of our life, delusions and dysfunction, of my myriad emotions toward her, or would she simply consider it part of the story and not recognize herself at all?

Aubrey, you are so stupid! The flare of my anger took me by surprise. *To do what you've done to a writer, knowing he has the power to crow it to the world!*

But even as I thought that, I had to wonder: If the book were received even moderately well—well enough for me to make some appearances, to take an interview (perhaps in the Bristol Lounge), to travel to a few cities on a short tour—would she think of me in a new light? Would she wonder how I was and want to talk? And would Richard, fully assimilated into the culture of Aubreyland, become a little less interesting to her in the light of my new, self-propelled life? And if any of these came to pass, what would I do?

The thought of her returning to a discarded husband, so like Lucifer returning to his ruined Eden, infuriated me. I vowed right then that I would never throw open the door to her, that even if she left Richard, I would not be easily won back, that if we were ever to reconcile, it would be with grave changes on her part and fewer compromises on mine.

I found myself staring into the glass of a freezer full of organic beef and free-range chickens. My solitary form peered back. There was something forbearing in the tilt of that head, as if patiently waiting for what I must inevitably realize: that this thing I longed for was impossible. Aubrey would never change, and I could never be transparent with her again. I could never tell her about all that had happened in these weeks and months, my encounters with Lucian. And not just Aubrey; I could not tell anyone. I, who prided myself on my principles and on my honesty—and who prized honesty more than ever after Aubrey's betrayal—could never be completely honest with anyone again.

A figure in a fleece pullover appeared behind me in the freezer window. He was broad across the shoulders, a little rough looking, some two days' worth of stubble encroaching on his brown goatee. His hair curled out from beneath his skullcap, the curls girlishly at odds with his stark masculinity. "You don't have time to cook."

"A man can dream." But he was right. I wasn't going to thaw and cook organic beef, buffalo, or formerly happy free-ranging chickens.

"Come on. You can get salmon in the café and something else to go. You don't have time for this."

"You want me to have more time?" I spun to face him. "Then you read the sophomoric thrillers, the *Lovely Bones* copycats, the *Sex and the City* rip-offs and Joyce Carol Oates wannabes in the pile on my desk. That would give me more time." I waved the empty green grocery basket, both relieved and angry to see him. There had been nothing on my calendar to prepare me for his appearance. Could I not be allowed even this semblance of a mundane life, a moment to mourn the closing of my chapter with Aubrey?

Apparently not.

Our little table in the co-op café reminded me of the brown, two-person one I had willingly shared with a gorgeous red-headed demon at the bookstore. I stabbed into the pink flesh of wild salmon, speared limp stalks of broccolini.

Lucian leaned into the curved back of his chair, stretched his legs out to the side of our table, and silently watched me.

You'd better start talking, I wanted to say, *because I told Helen I'd get as much of the manuscript as I had to her before I left for vacation.*

But I ate in sullen silence, having given up altogether on trying to complete a synopsis. The story wasn't finished, I told Helen, and I had no idea yet how it would end. "I just don't know where my characters are going to take me right now." It was one of those writer's claims I had always treated with derision, always contending that writers were in control of their characters, even if only subconsciously. I still believed this, though I had come to wonder if there were indeed other writers in my position, influenced by forces they could neither publicly own nor predict.

At any rate, Helen thought whatever I had might be enough for them to make a decision. They would look at it after the offices reopened in January, while I was sunburning on the beaches of Cabo during the day and holed up with my laptop at night.

Meanwhile, the attention I'd focused on when and where Lucian might show up and on writing the account was giving way to my growing fixation on how the account would end and whether our strange relationship would end with it. Would he disappear from my life once his precious story was published?

The thought brought me no peace.

Lucian locked his fingers behind his head and looked up at the ceiling. "Lucifer failed." He sighed. "I was confused. Nothing about this made sense to me, and my lack of answers only unsettled me more."

I knew that feeling. "What were you unsettled about?"

"Everything." He shook his head, the boyish curls brushing against the thick cords of his neck. "This God-man, this aspect of the Almighty in the body of a mortal, this Messiah, went about his business in exceedingly unsavory conditions. I mean, he hung out with whores and extortionists. I was flummoxed. Having gone to the trouble of becoming human, why not choose better company? Why not announce it with fanfare? A little panache? Hades. Why not awe the masses? This was the creator of the universe, after all." He threw his arms up.

"What did it matter to you?" I scooped couscous onto my fork.

"It galled me, the way people treated him—not because I wanted to see him welcomed or worshipped, certainly, but for the sheer fact of who I knew him to be."

Like so much of Lucian's account, it was something I had not thought about. The story of Christ was such a cultural fixture, such a central theme throughout history that I had never dwelled on these details.

"He had more coming. I simply didn't see it yet." He lowered his chin, studied the zipper dangling from the neck of his polar fleece. "He performed a few miracles at least. It was something. Still, I came away disappointed, waiting for more. This was Elohim, the Alpha and Omega!"

"More, such as?"

"A mass-healing. Something." He lifted his head and rubbed his goatee, his mouth slack. "Even your televangelists purport to do that much. But this was *El*. He could have reshaped the earth, restored Eden, shown even a portion of that terrible power that had spoken the green and wild earth into existence. He could have restored the humans to their original state. Hadn't he come to save them, after all? They were uninspiring creatures to begin with, but at least he could have done that much."

"Why do you think he didn't?"

Lucian's face went blank, "He seemed more interested in restoring individuals. I didn't understand it. Why mend one vessel when the rest are cracking all around you? Why mend one when the rest don't even like you?" He laughed. "But it got stranger: The priests of El himself called him a blasphemer and claimed he derived his powers from us."

I wondered where I had missed all of this, growing up. How pale, how superficial and ritualistic, had been my early experience with the church and their packaged God.

"As though our powers could compare. It was too ridiculous. El was humiliating himself and getting spat on for his efforts. And I came to think that now, at last, he would experience firsthand the misery of this mud race, and that in this way he deserved it. Still, as I look back on the hatred, the scoffing, the pointed fingers, I don't know how he stood it."

"Why did they do it?"

"Because he went against the religious establishment!" He laughed, the chords dancing in his thick neck, the sound of it arcing up now beyond his earlier chuckles to an octave it should not have reached, rankling. The man in the apron behind the café counter glanced our way. I was prepared for the instant composition of the demon's features but not for the haunted look that crept into them.

"Lucifer, for his part, wasn't happy about having this walking testament of his failure roaming the earth, embarrassing him. And something began to happen with him. His luminescent eyes turned shifty. He raged as he had not since the new Eden. We avoided him, entertaining ourselves with all the usual things— the running of his earthly government, temptation of the faithful—in hopes of raising his spirits. But he paced and stalked, and followed this Jesus wherever he went. He was obsessed, filled with loathing yet unable to stay away from him."

I piled crumpled napkin and plastic silverware on my plate. "How long did that go on?"

"Several years. Then, in the space of one night, everything changed.

"It was Passover, and though Jews knew it as the saving of the firstborn by the lamb's blood upon the doorframe, it will always be, to my mind, the thwarting of a perfectly good mass killing."

I stared at him.

"That night the God-man did a strange thing. He broke bread with his followers, saying it was his body, and he gave it to them. He gave them wine, saying it was his blood. But then he said something that chilled my immortal heart—now mark me well—he said it was spilled for them in a new covenant for *the forgiveness of sins*. Do you hear this? Do you understand it?" He leapt to his feet, pacing several steps away and back, not waiting for my answer. "Pardon my human reaction: my skin crawled."

He sat down again and leaned over the table, closer to my face than I liked. "We had waited an epoch for El to do away with these people, to, in the very least, give them their due condemnation. If we, glorious creatures, had fallen so far from favor, then we would never stand by and willingly allow these clay people—these *humans*—to replace us in his affections. Never."

The hairs along my neck stood on end.

"But those words spoken over the Passover table sounded with the hollow echo of a vault, sealing for eternity. As the first words of your creation had been full and pregnant, these rang now with the harsh sentence of exclusion, finality, and damnation."

"Maybe the forgiveness was for you, too."

He laughed, and this time the sound was low like thunder tumbling beyond the horizon.

"You are so blind, Clay."

For a long moment we stared at one another, and I felt the gulf between us as I had never felt it before, as one breed considers the other, and his own mortality with it, knowing that he will be surpassed and survived by the other, that the other has unwittingly succeeded him.

"With sickened sense I saw it all," he said softly, his expression expansive, eyes slightly widened. "They were going to kill him. It didn't matter that he was innocent. It didn't matter that his trial wasn't even legal. It was a fiasco, politics and government being the twin playgrounds of Satan. It didn't even matter that he was God. It was an appalling thought, the created killing the Creator. It went against every natural law."

The tinge to his voice was not sympathy or horror but a strange brand of wonder.

"But Satan was out of control. The danger ran off his back like so much rainwater on slick and well-oiled feathers. El would not bend to the temptation of his flesh. Well then, let him suffer in it! More, the God-man would suffer by the hands of the people he insisted on submitting to, these miserable clay creatures that he loved so dearly—and he would suffer greatly. Our prince rose up with a glamour to blot out the sun and roared, *Let him see how they love him in return!*"

"Are you saying you didn't want that, too?"

"Oh, I did. But this was error, this was folly. I saw too clearly the God-man's refusal of temptation, the immaculate life, saw in him the image of the Passover lamb. I raised my arms, my voice, took to wing, frantic for it to stop. I understood what was happening, and it had to stop—abruptly, violently, by any means, any force. But there was no one to hear me in the roar of voices both human and angelic. Lucifer and all my blind sibling minions were mad, frenzied as berserkers before a battle, intent on hauling this Jesus to the cross like a child before a runaway train." He rubbed his forehead. "I saw it," he said faintly. "I saw it coming. But I was only one being. I could do nothing."

"You didn't want to kill him," I said, incredulous.

"Oh"—and now his lips glistened—"a part of me wanted him laid open, flayed apart, rent in ways that humans were not meant to suffer and survive. And I reveled in the sight of his suffering. I wanted it, I lusted for it. But even then I knew it for seduction. And as I saw the blood running from his back and his arms and down his legs and into the ground . . . "

It was unsettling, seeing him like this. He was normally so cocksure, so arrogant. "What? What was it?"

He pressed the heel of his hand into his forehead. "I wished I had no foresight. For the first time in my life, ignorance would have been a mercy to me. Then I might have enjoyed our triumph, the sweetness of that moment." He rubbed his brows, pinched the bridge of his nose. "But El bore it all. As he had borne the ruin of Eden and the faithlessness of the humans before, with the same suffering with which he had wept down the skies onto the mud race he loved, he bore it. It was awful to me, the submission of Elohim to the murderous hands of his creatures."

"I don't understand."

"The spilling of blood—it was the spilling of blood." His voice cracked.

"Why do you keep saying that? What was it about the blood?"

"Idiot!" He was on his feet, walking away so that I stared after him—as did others in the café, heads snapping up from their companions and laptops. I started to rise, but he came striding back, shoved his weight into the chair and leaned over the table until it creaked and threatened to tip. His hair was disheveled, his skullcap missing. He wiped a hand over his beard and blurted, "Passover! The Passover lamb!" He was beyond himself, and I searched for something to say to calm him down. The man at the café counter was tense, and I knew we were on the verge of being told to leave.

"Death had come to every firstborn in Egypt—animal, king, slave—except in the homes of those Israelites who had painted the blood of perfect lambs on their doors. Death *passed over* those doors. Now here it was, running down the legs and arms of that God-man, the blood like that of those perfect lambs, their veins drained into basins, that vital, crimson reparation, the blood of atonement, once smeared on the doorframes of the Passover . . . now etched on the heart of man."

I had heard the phrase "Lamb of God" in hymns. I had heard the Jesus freaks saying he died for their sins. I had never understood what they meant.

Until now.

"I howled a banshee cry, but it was too late. They did the

unspeakable. They hauled him off to a public execution. In my ears and all around me was the motley fervor of Legion. And Satan had eyes for nothing but the son—that part of Elohim that had formed the cosmos and reshaped the terra and, most importantly, refused him—broken, as wretched as a human can be before a mortal body cries out, too broken to hold its own spirit."

I remembered the broken body of the jogger, cracked beyond life.

"'It is done,' he said. And I thought, *Yes. It is.* And the hourglass that had come into existence for me on that first day when time was created, that had signaled the measure of time until an unknown and inevitable end, was jolted, a wealth of sand— precious grains of limited time—tumbling through that channel, gone forever. I felt I could gather the crumbs of my future in one palm."

I saw now the rugged, multidial watch on his wrist, time in all its measurements, time measured and captured, no farther than arm's length. Time, owned and on occasion even stopped in the mechanism of that fine chronograph.

"Yes. Now you understand. And there it is." The watch was frozen, the second hand in mid-stutter, unmoving.

"As he died, I felt it—his departure, though I had become accustomed to the sense of him here, moving about the earth as flesh, and I had become numbed to it, too. The effect was that while I did not feel with acute awareness his presence here, I felt acutely the moment he departed. Felt it more deeply than the mortals who fell back as the sky went black. And when it did, I, without corporeal body, shivered, felt in my bones El's withdrawal from that place, like the sun fleeing a wasteland of ice.

"Around me, my comrades fell silent one by one, cries dying on their lips, giving way to a shifting, uneasy silence. I wanted to strike them all! What did they *think* would happen? Had no one listened, no one heard? But they had been caught up in their bloodlust, fueled by the rage and fervor of Lucifer even as Lucifer had surely come to the same realization as I had, too late. And now that it was done, as the broken body that barely resembled a body except in the most macabre of ways hung limply upon that tree, all we could do was stand and look on at the wreck of our design.

"That moment was, in all, the eeriest moment of my life since the day Lucifer's throne careened from violent, heaven-hungry hands, since the night darkness consumed Eden and water swallowed the earth."

I was silent. I had questions. But there was a hollowness in his eyes that made the dark light inside them look like twin black holes. I looked away from him, taking in the little tables, the people hunched over their laptops, their sandwiches and lattes—needing the comfort of their preoccupation, to hear the sound of the coffee machine, to regain the present. I did it in the way that one comes out of a theater, blinking in the light after a matinee horror movie, glad for the sun, the sound of the cars on the street. But Lucian pulled me back, and again I thought his eyes looked like holes.

"This was more than the shattering of ambition, of any last shred of our hope, however twisted and dark. This was what it meant to be damned. This was what it felt like to know that one already was—had been for eons—damned. Gall rose inside me, acrid and virulent. Terror beat at my heart. I writhed, grasping for some kind of resolution. I couldn't stand it. I hinged on madness. I craved malice, rage, the sound of Lucifer, our prince—the majestic Satan—howling his indignation, lashing out. Anything but this."

"And did he?" My voice sounded too loud, too crude, too human.

"Just as he had led us nowhere when Eden went black, he led us nowhere now. He did nothing. Our general, our prince stared on in silence. And what could I do but wonder at this new sense of the inevitable, this dread embalming my spirit? All was not well with me. All was not well."

His head snapped up toward the entrance of the store, and he straightened as though startled.

"What? What is it?" I twisted, trying to see what it was, but a thick grocery aisle blocked my view. Lucian craned his thick neck, as though to stare straight through it.

"We don't have much time."

"You've said that since our first appointment."

"No." He snapped his gaze to me and pushed his chair back with a skid against the tiles. "It's getting shorter."

It chilled me, the way he left, taking a long side aisle toward the door. I got up, made a show of throwing my plate and juice bottle away, tried to see who might have alarmed him so much. But there was no one in the store entrance or even down the middle aisle and only one patron in each of the three checkout lanes.

I loitered near the front of the store as cashiers scanned containers of rice chips and vegetable broth, of soy yogurt and tofu ice cream, each item registering with an electronic blip. Frustrated by Lucian's erratic behavior and uncharacteristic display of emotion, I left.

Fewer than five steps beyond the door, I ran into Mrs. Russo. She was wrapped up in her camel coat and carried her canvas shopping bag. Running into her shouldn't have seemed odd.

She was, after all, the one who had told me about the co-op when I first moved in.

"Well, Clay! Hello dear!" She clasped me by the arm with a gloved hand, and I tried to smile. "Did you come for some nice lunch?"

"I did. Wild salmon and broccolini." As I said it, my mind began to exercise a strange new thought.

"Oh, delicious. I might have to have some, too. It's a pity you've already eaten, or you could join me." She smiled, and I felt caught between wanting to pull away and longing to sit down with her over a plate of her famous lemon bars. There was something comforting about her presence, as though no harm could possibly come to me as long as one was with her.

"We'll have lunch together another time, Mrs. Russo. Have you just come from church by chance?" By way of explanation, I added, "You look so nice."

"No, dear. I'm meeting my small group tonight though. Is everything all right? You've been on my heart so much."

There was a time when I'd found her religiousness the only irritating thing about her, when I'd been as leery of her invitations to church or Bible group as I was of Amway. But now I bit my lip, feeling as if a wall that had both protected and alienated me might crack. "Everything's all right."

"If you need anything, you let me know. Don't you ever feel silly asking." There was a steeliness I had never seen in her before. And in that moment I thought she would have defended me to the death had she needed to. Not knowing what to say, I found myself fighting a wave of emotion, the product, I was sure, of exhaustion. I was so tired, in fact, that for a moment I thought I saw in her eyes an acumen as discerning as the intelligence in Lucian's was strange.

Ŧʜᴀŧ ᴨɪɢʜŧ, ᴀꜰŧᴇʀ ŧʀᴀᴨsᴄʀɪʙɪᴨɢ the strange interaction in the co-op, I tried to read one of my newly acquired manuscripts but was unable to concentrate.

Why was our time getting shorter? Did he mean that we were nearing the end of his story, or had something happened? Regardless of the reason, I should have been happier than I was—soon I might be free of him. I would have what I needed to finish the manuscript. And once it was published, I could get on with my life.

But I was unsettled by Lucian's distraction, disturbed that I could not pinpoint a reason for it. I had never seen him so emotional or emotionally at a loss. And to see him flee the co-op . . .

What could possibly compel a demon to flee?

The kindly face of Mrs. Russo floated before my mind.

Sᴏᴍᴇŧɪᴍᴇ ᴀꜰŧᴇʀ ᴍɪᴅᴨɪɢʜŧ ᴍʏ inbox chimed. It could have been incoming spam or a note from one of my authors—some of whom I secretly believed never slept. It might have been from Katrina, whom I had known to work through the night and half suspected of being a day-walking vampire. It could even have been a note from my sister, with whom I had had only sporadic contact since her insinuation that I had driven my wife away.

It was none of these.

From: Light1
Sent: 12:18 a.m.
To: BandHClay@brooksandhanover.com
Subject: More

I have to tell you one other significant thing that happened.

In the Jewish temple, El's spirit resided in the Holy of Holies. Do an Internet search if you don't know what I mean. All you really need to know is that it was the most sacred place on earth. Only the high priest could enter it and then only once a year and bearing the blood of atonement—one of El's many concessions to the clay people. The curtain concealing the Holy of Holies from the rest of the temple was heavy, requiring more than a hundred men to move it. There was no mistaken entry, and the symbolism was blatant: There had been no open communion with El since those days in the garden.

This is what you need to know: As the God-man, hanging on the cross like a common criminal, died, the curtain ripped. Access to God, so long denied to any but the appointed, was now laid open to anyone, the blood of atonement having been paid in full according to the old law. The heavy partition that had separated the spirit of El from the fallen soul of man was broken forever.

I hate you.

I stared at that last line for a long time.

On board flight 865 to Cabo San Lucas, I closed my eyes. I had worked straight through Christmas, marking the season with a roast-beef sandwich—homemade, no less—and a call to my niece, Susanna, during which she thanked me for the Chronicles of Narnia set that I had ordered and sent straight from Amazon. Afterward, I talked to my sister for a few rare minutes.

Despite my productivity in those quiet days alone on the second floor of my building—Mrs. Russo had gone to her daughter's house in Haverhill—I wasn't going on this so-called vacation without my laptop and the handwritten transcriptions of every meeting since that first night. I would have felt less compelled to carry so much with me—I brought along two manuscripts as well—had the majority of my work over the holiday been for my actual job. But I had been preoccupied with the memoir on my laptop hard drive, currently seventy-eight thousand words and growing.

I looked out the window from seat 21A onto a heavenly floor of clouds worthy of a fabric softener commercial, disappointed that I could not see the earth. On my trip to China in college, I had lifted my window shade midflight. And there, as the rest of the dimly lit plane slept, watched a movie, or worked by seat lights, I gazed down onto what I calculated to be Siberia. Chalky rivers snaked through stunted mountains like veins in marble, pasty snow-spackled crevices in the landscape like filling in the pores of travertine. I must have stared for half an hour at that fawn gray and virgin desolation, my breath fogging the glass as I wondered if, like Isak Dinesen, I was seeing "a glimpse of the world through God's eye." Did I look down on any spot of land previously untouched by any eye but God's?

It was the closest I had ever come to a religious experience, and though I had requested window seats and looked down on the earth from cruising altitude on nearly every flight since, I never saw anything like it again.

The man next to me—a short Asian with black, feathery brows and a hairline that had receded to the crown—leaned across the armrest between us to peer out as well.

"'And I thought, yes, I see, this is the way it was intended,'" he said, quoting Dinesen.

We were bound by the story, needing one another in our own ways, but in that moment I realized I hated him, too. Again I wondered what would happen when we both got what we wanted from this arrangement and what would become of us, of this contemptuous codependency.

The demon removed his shoes and tucked them beneath the seat in front of him. He was wearing GoldToe socks.

"What made you leave the co-op? What's been distracting you?" I asked without preamble.

He tilted his seat back and stretched his short legs. "I told you there were those who would not look well upon our time together."

I remembered. I also recalled that he had sidestepped the question, saying it did not serve his purpose.

"Who? The Host?"

He sucked at his teeth. His smooth skin belied his age, the few age spots on his face the only clue that he was, I guessed, close to sixty years old. "Yes," he said finally.

"Did you see them?"

"Let it be, Clay. You don't know what you're delving into."

"What does this have to do with Mrs. Russo?"

His expression sharpened into a glower. "Stay away from her."

"Why?"

"If you don't want to jeopardize the time we have left, do as I say."

I thought of the two men in the mall, the ladies at the bar in the Bristol Lounge. "What was it at Vittorio's?" I said. "I didn't see anyone."

"You wouldn't have."

"But—"

"We don't have time for me to explain this to you. I've answered your questions. With the committee meeting in your absence, I would think you'd be more focused on getting to the end of your book."

There's a monster.

I tilted my head back against the headrest, but it seemed to curve the wrong way and only succeeded in making me more uncomfortable. "They killed him," I said, but I was scouring our last meeting for oddities, recalculating the time of his nervous departure and Mrs. Russo's appearance in her camel coat. Mrs. Russo, who went faithfully to church and sometimes hosted a Bible group in her apartment.

Spiritual static, he called it.

"They wondered at his rising from the dead, but that didn't amaze me. I knew better than any mortal who this God-man was. Of course his power extended over death as well."

This brought my attention back to him. "You're saying he really rose from the dead."

"Yes, really. By then I knew for gospel fact, if you'll pardon the expression, that it would happen. Everything was coming to horrible fruition. I also knew El would call back that part of him to himself, and this God-man would ascend to heaven. Later, it struck me as ironic that he had achieved with ease the thing Lucifer attempted so long before—ascension to heaven and a seat at the right hand of the Almighty. Lucifer took it as a blow, but the reality was harsher than that: Lucifer's star had been eclipsed by a new Son.

"The followers of Jesus scattered to spread the news about what had happened. And people began to believe with an insight that incensed and amazed me. It was one thing for us to know that this Jewish carpenter had been more than a religious fanatic, but it was an altogether different thing for the clay humans to believe it."

"What did it matter to you?"

He sighed, and the Shadow Creek logo on his polo stretched and slumped back into a wrinkle. "Ordinary men, hitherto blind, began to see this redemptive blood for what it was and this man, this Messiah, for what he was. And they saw it because El gave them yet another thing: guiding discernment, the gift of his own Spirit, given first to the God-man before the spilling of his messianic blood and freely offered afterward. To anyone. It was awful. Gone were the days of Israel's elite, the heyday of the Jew.

Anyone could have this 'Holy Spirit' freely for the asking." He dropped his head back, reached up to adjust the airflow.

"I'll never forget the first human I watched receive it, this gift. Before my very eyes, he changed from a shattered thing of darkness, like a mirror reflecting nothing but shadows no matter which way its fractured surface turned, into something whole, reflecting El's radiance, so that I had to—could not help but—turn away. When I recovered, I saw that it was true; my eyes had not played me false. On the outside he was still flawed. But the soul inside had come alive, as though all defects had been erased. There was only that loveliness, that light, shining in him."

"But he was still human."

"Yes, but here was the difference: El drew close to those people who called to him as he had with Adam in the garden. Not only did he walk with them, he began to change them. And in them I saw more than the uncanny resemblance to that first man and woman. I saw something beyond what they were originally meant to be: 'Children,' he called them."

"Children of God," I said, with some wonder.

"I hated them! Never had I dared to aspire so high. Never had I imagined any such thing. Hades, I'm so tired of saying that I'd never fathomed this or that. But I hadn't. It surpassed any angel's dream, any human's deserving. How I craved it, jealous of your inheritance. Like Cain to your Abel, wanting you to die."

His last words jarred me, and I remembered the final line of his e-mail.

"For the first time, I saw the ill effects of the ages upon Lucifer, his waning brilliance, the wearing of the years taking its toll upon him like the first wrinkles of your human age. The moment I saw that, I wanted to hate him, too. Disdain and rage came naturally to me by then, and this time they came with such force I thought I would kill him had I only the power to do it."

"You used to adore him." Echoes of our first conversations washed over me like waves on a tranquil shore. *"Oh, my Beautiful One!"*

Lucian's laugh was hard. Gone was the slight mania, the high-pitched sound. "What reward had I gained in following him? What prize but the forfeiture of my soul? But even my hatred could not save me from misery. Every moment I looked upon these followers, these renewed people, these believers— and their numbers were growing—the more wretched I became. But as much as I wanted to kill Lucifer that day, I also wanted to rip from every one of those believers the brilliant vestige of their new souls, knowing El had no such designs for us. For me."

I searched for something to say as a beverage cart stopped in the aisle. Over the top of Lucian's head, a flight attendant smiled and asked if she could get us something to drink.

HE WAS SILENT AFTER that, not looking at me. I gazed out the window, sipping tomato juice and wishing it were a Bloody Mary, his words still reverberating between us.

"El had no such designs for us. For me."

Shortly before we landed, he unbuckled his seat belt and got up, ostensibly to go to the lavatory, but he never came back. As the plane taxied to the terminal, I noted his shoes, still under the seat in front of us.

I lay on the beach beneath an umbrella, the skin of my chest and back too pink to withstand the sun. That had happened the first day despite 45 SPF lotion. Between the sunburn and the swelling in my legs from the flights, I bore a stunning resemblance to a hotdog. But none of this mattered; I was glad to be out of Boston, to feel the air on my arms and chest, to sit with my laptop at the breakfast buffet and read—even with pen in hand—by the side of the pool. I could get used to wearing swim trunks every day, eschewing underwear, ambling over to the grill for a burger whenever the mood struck, and watching the bikini-clad scenery.

I passed on the Coronas and Dos Equis, which was no hardship, never having been a beer drinker, but a shot of tequila had never sounded so good.

I didn't need it. I had run up my credit card getting here, but it was worth every all-inclusive penny. The only thing missing was Lucian. It was almost as though he had truly disappeared on the plane that day, leaving only his shoes behind. I tried not to think about it; doing so sent my heart into strange stutters even when I was at rest. Obviously, I needed this reprieve. *And I deserve it,* I thought, as I gazed out over the pale turquoise water. Out toward the Cabo San Lucas arch where the Sea of Cortez met the mighty Pacific, wave runners scored the surface with raised white welts, and the sun dappled the water with platinum as they receded.

I want to show you something. Do you know what they look like, these believers?

I saw the daubing brushstrokes of the sun on the ocean—except that it was no longer an ocean. The water was running too swiftly, and I could see the bottom. It was a brook, a creek, and the stones of the bed shone beneath it. They were iridescent, glittering through water that ran clear in the middle but muddy in the eddies. A clump of dirt broke off from the side of the stream, and the water clouded, but several of the shining pebbles glinted through the mud and debris.

A child ran pell-mell toward the water, chased by his mother. The sound jolted me, and I realized I had drifted into reverie.

Sometime later I looked out at the water and thought of Lucian walking along the beach by the light of the moon. As I considered the water, the bright blue of the ocean, a cloud passed before the sun, dimming it. I could not see from beneath my umbrella that it was a thunderhead.

THAT EVENING, RAIN PELTED the balcony of room 408. A rare storm, they called it. So unusual this time of year, the hotel workers said. But nothing seemed usual or unusual to me anymore, the words having become meaningless to me.

I was, however, troubled by Lucian's near silence. I expected him to show up by the minute—every day, tonight even—to ramble at length into my internal tape recorder. I expected, alone at night, to purge myself of every word here, at this desk, before weaving them into the fabric of my manuscript like a bright thread. But despite his constant assertions that our time was short—was growing shorter, even—he never showed.

During the daylight, with burgers by the pool and smooth bodies lounging on chairs to distract me with thoughts comfortingly base, I could manage not to think about it too much. But by my fourth day I saw through the beautiful drinks on poolside trays to the cheap, plastic glasses and recognized the second-rate nature of the evening entertainment on the stage beside the outdoor bar as I ate my dinner from a scratched Fiestaware plate. I became aware of the fraying hems of the flamenco dancers' costumes, the gauche makeup of the girls. And I began to notice the plaster peeling from the edge of the stage itself, the painted gold scrollwork chipped where careless workers had run into it, the cracking Mexican tile beneath the staircases.

I could not help but think of the home in Belmont, once so grand, reduced to a pile of rubble.

One night as I ate my dinner outside, I observed a man and a woman sitting at a table off to the side of the stage. They appeared neither raucously drunk nor so old that they applauded the dancers in the way that grandparents did at dance recitals.

In fact, there were no drinks on the table in front of them at all. And though the man—I judged him to be in his thirties—looked perfectly at ease in his Billabong T-shirt and cargo shorts, and the woman was elegant in her beaded halter, they reminded me of the men at the mall, of the two women at the bar in the Four Seasons Hotel, so that I finished my dinner in a rush, wondering if I only imagined the weight of their gazes upon my back as I strode across the pool area toward my room.

The next night my room seemed too dark, the light of the lamps insufficient and sallow against the moonless night, the black of the ocean seeming to encroach upon the beach. I was edgy, irritated, checking the clock, the calendar on my laptop.

The wind shifted, and water pelted the casing of the sliding glass door. I got up to close it, and as I did, the phone rang. The sound, so electric, so mechanical against the backdrop of rain, of the waves I was able to hear from my bed at night, startled me. I had not heard the ringing of a phone in four days.

I frowned. The tour desk had tried relentlessly to sell me any number of day excursions, all of which I had declined— could they have taken to phoning my room? But it was well past ten o'clock, the time when most hotel guests were out dancing, drinking, or in town at the Cabo Wabo Cantina hoping for an appearance by Sammy Hagar.

When I answered, the voice on the other end of the phone was thick and so emotive that I barely made out the sound of my own name.

"Hello?"

"Clay? How did you do it?"

"Sheila?" I said, confused. I had left the number of my resort with her in case anything came up at work—or if the committee felt compelled to rush me any good news that couldn't wait until I returned. In fact, Sheila was the only one with my hotel number, as Mrs. Russo had not yet returned from Haverhill.

I thought again of Lucian's warning to keep away from Mrs. Russo.

"How—how did you do it? How do you get by?" Her voice

caught repeatedly as she spoke, making her sound like a child that had cried too hard to talk except in hiccupping gulps.

"Sheila, what's going on?" My alarm mingled with impatience. I was in Cabo. I had come here from the opposite coast on two long flights in a carefully researched package deal to get away from the office, from my single life in Boston, and from the winter.

I had come here to write.

"How did you do it?" she choked between staggering breaths.

"Do what, Sheila?"

"Get by. After Aubrey left." The last word was a sob.

"What do you mean, how did I do it? Sheila, what's going on?"

"I don't know if I can do it. I don't know how to do it."

My impatience sparked annoyance. The last thing I felt like dealing with was Sheila's self-inflicted turmoil. "I just did, Sheila."

"He just doesn't know. He just doesn't know." Her voice squeaked up an octave.

I'd never heard Sheila like this before—Sheila with her empathetic ear, who had never demanded much, if anything, of Dan, who turned the warm light of her love so readily on her family and children and friends.

"He doesn't know what? What's happened?"

"He's left. He left."

"I know, Sheila. But what happened tonight to cause this breakdown?" I hated the calm, measured sound of my own voice. It reminded me of the way Lucian talked to me that day in the bookstore.

"He—he doesn't know if he's coming back. Oh, Clay!" My name became a tight keen.

I sighed, tried to summon empathy. Had Aubrey cried like this when she left me? Had she ever shed a tear even? "Sheila, where are your children?"

"With Dan. They're with Dan. He took them. I don't mean he took them, but for the night."

"All right. And you're not worried about them, right?" I couldn't imagine either one of them doing anything stupid when it came to their children.

"No. I'm not. I'm all right." She inhaled sharply, her breath catching. "He doesn't know what he wants. It's all right. I'm not angry."

I stared at the receiver. She wasn't angry? She had cheated on him, and *she* wasn't angry? I had to work to suppress my rage, rising like tar on hot pavement. "I don't know what to tell you. It sounds like you have it figured—"

"You can't hate her," she said suddenly.

"Who?"

"Aubrey. She just didn't know what she wanted. It was a mistake. She knew it. She had to know it."

"Sheila, you're babbling," I said more firmly. I was trying to be diplomatic but found it more and more difficult. I was glad I wasn't in town where I might feel compelled to ask if I ought to check on her. I was sick of being a good guy. "You know what I think? I think *you* need to figure out what you want."

Silence. And then a sniffle. "You're right. You're right, Clay."

I didn't say anything.

"Thank you."

I nodded, though I knew she couldn't see it. I waited a moment more to hear the soft click of the line before hanging up the receiver.

25

O
n the morning I left Cabo, my plane sat on the tar-
mac for an hour. The storm had caused cancellations
and delays, and now that the sun was shining again,
planes were baking in line on the runway like fish laid out to
dry. I glanced repeatedly at my seatmate, trying to ascertain if
he was less human than he looked in his Bermudas and flip-
flops, until he dropped his head back, let his mouth fall open,
and started snoring.

Gazing out the window, I stared at the gray cement until
I, too, dozed. I woke, dry mouthed, just before the plane began
its descent into the Dallas-Fort Worth International Airport.
I wondered if I should have kept Sheila on the phone longer or
called Helen, wondered where Lucian had been these five days,
what the committee thought of my book.

My book. Sometime in the last few days it had evolved
from my manuscript to "my book." I had already decided that if
Brooks and Hanover didn't take it, I would submit it elsewhere.
Maybe I would ask Katrina to represent it, to take it to one of
the Titans—Random House, perhaps, or Hachette.

But I needed to know how it ended.

Sitting in a bank of seats at my gate in Dallas, I reached for my cell phone but hesitated before turning it on. Pushing that button carried so much finality; either there would be a message waiting from Helen, or there wouldn't. If there were, I might know now, before I even boarded my plane, the fate of my book. Or at least whether I should be calling Katrina.

What I would not know is how to finish it.

I didn't turn it on. I told myself that I should welcome this limbo. I had languished in purgatory through my separation, in between appointments with Lucian, nearly every moment of the last three months. Now, perhaps on the cusp of something— some new direction—I should sit here during this layover and savor the feeling of truly being in transit. In between.

I put the phone in my bag, shoved it toward the bottom, pulled out a pen and the last few pages of one of the manuscripts I had taken with me. My legs felt swollen again, the skin tight across my calves. I had meant to walk around for a little while, but they would only swell again on the next flight, and I had promised myself I would return home with every piece of work I had brought with me finished. Every piece except my own.

My pen hovered above the page as, with the same apprehension with which I noticed Aubrey's increasingly frequent absences in the months leading up to my discovery of her affair, I wondered where Lucian could be, where he went when he was not with me.

That's so pathetic.

Someone was staring at me—a woman, sitting in a row of boarding area seats across from mine and one row over. Her legs were crossed beneath a long, stretchy skirt. Her brown hair was slightly frizzy, pulled back into a ponytail that gave her a girlish appearance, though a closer look at the lines around her eyes and mouth put her, I guessed, in her forties. She wore one of those fabricated pieces of jewelry they sold at women's stores, the kind Aubrey used to disdain for looking like an antique or an art piece, though they were mass-produced and sold at exorbitant prices. Except for the jewelry, she would have fit in perfectly in Boston; she was wearing all black.

"Look at that sunburn," she said to me, the furrow above her lip marred by a thin scar. "The committee loved what we gave them, by the way."

I almost dropped the pages on my lap, so great was my relief. It was quickly followed by anger. "Where have you been?" I hated how transparent I was, how desperate I sounded.

"Roaming." She pursed her lips into a little kitten mouth. "I thought you deserved a vacation before things got busy."

"Busy? What do you mean busy? You said our time was short."

She came over to sit next to me. She was broad-hipped but not ungainly, her nails manicured with those square, white tips, the appeal of which I had never understood.

"They called it compelling, brilliant. They compared you to Poe, to Blake's *Urizen*."

I exhaled a silent exclamation, unable to speak.

"I'd ask for a slightly larger advance than what they're offering, but otherwise, I think we're almost set."

It was happening. It would happen. I fell back against the seat, papers sliding to the floor around me. And then I lowered my head to my hand. And laughed. It bubbled out of me, grew in volume until I was laughing so hard that the sound came out with the same near-hysteria I had noted in Lucian—and then I laughed harder.

Long moments later, that wild, roiling laugh still in my ears, Lucian regarded me with patronizing calm before reminding me that my story was not finished.

"You're right. And I have"—I checked my watch, which struck me as so ironic I almost laughed again—"a half hour before I board."

"Then calm down and listen."

I was going to publish. The advance didn't matter. But I would negotiate anyway.

"As you've noticed, I'm something of a philosopher. Now, after the ascension of the God-man and the conversion of these believers, I thought perhaps he was tired of being abandoned by the strongest of his creations, the most favored of his people. Who can guess the reasoning of El? I only know this: He is the author of the paradigm of the unlikely. Clay, listen!"

"I'm listening." I could buy a new table. I would get some new pants. I would go out on dates. Would Aubrey hear? Would she call to congratulate me?

"I've said Israel was special to El. But now something happened. Up until those days there was a great separation between the Jews and everyone else. The Jews were set apart by law and favor of El, and the rest of the world was on its own unless someone converted. El was a faithful lover of his people. But now these new believers were going out and giving this message indiscriminately to anyone they met, Jew and non-Jew alike. The rich man, the widow, the priest, the fishwife, the orphaned beggar on the street.

"Let me tell you something, these non-Jews, upon hearing and believing and accepting this new grace, this new gift, looked exactly the same as the other believers to my eye. All those shining stones like luminescent pearls in the muddied waters."

I recalled my vision on the beach. I had thought it a day-dream.

"I saw this with appalled fascination. I laughed like a fool, much like you just now, and heard something wild in my voice. Why not? Why not. Tell them all. How like El to be so extravagant and so longsuffering. Why limit his affection—and now it had grown to a great and totally undeserved gift—to any one race? Soon enough the entire ball of earth would be populated with pardoned, shining souls, a great deposit of glowing stones, imperfect yet brought into the fold of that relationship as only that first man and woman had experienced so long ago.

"I was manic, despairing. El had bestowed upon these believers the rights of his own children, authority over all fallen things, if they wanted it. Over me." She shoved a square-tipped fingernail into her sternum. "Imagine! And now I was being ordered about, told to leave, cast out of homes and presences by an authority belonging only to El himself."

I had never, in a thousand years, thought of this. And now my thoughts returned to Mrs. Russo, to the steeliness about her the day at the co-op, at the seeming sanctuary of our apartment building.

"I had found my place with Lucifer, and among you. How could I bear to be ordered about, ruled over by humans so frail and filthy and base?" At some point she had gripped my arm, and now those square nails dug into it. I remembered again the sight of her on the *T*, pulling at her skin as though it were covered with fungus.

"But I need not have worried. Lucifer, clever prince, had a plan. His efforts until then were paltry by comparison. We had been a haphazard force at best, only tenuously united—if you haven't noticed, loyalty and devotion are not our strong suits.

Now Lucifer unleashed a great storm of demons, myself among them, a battery of guerilla assaults, and attacked the children of El with every imaginable weapon." Her eyes were mad, her lips animated by a terrible smile.

"How he hated these new children of El! They might be assured of a future, but they were mortal yet."

"What did you do?" I sat very still.

"We killed many of them. A dead believer is a believer who cannot spread the word of redemption to any others. And I'm certain their ends made a good many humans think twice about making the same choice."

In my mind I saw the slain woman, the blood mottling her blonde hair on the pavement. My jubilation over my manuscript sobered.

"Lucifer conscripted us all. He would show the Almighty how quickly the redeemed would forget him, how little this covenant would change anything. The clay people were a miserable disappointment, and so they would continue to be, redeemed or not. They would scoff at El's great act of grace, and Lucifer would see to it. Lucifer, the accuser called Satan, declared war."

A rustle of gray passed in the periphery of my vision. Two nuns in orthopedic shoes and stockings were looking for seats. Lucian stood up and, with a gracious smile and flash of a white watch face on her wrist, indicated her seat and the empty one next to it. "Sisters, please."

The nuns thanked her, and Lucian, demurring, glared at me over a perfect smile.

 **26**

My burn had turned to a tan in some places—and a moist, bubbling peeling in others—the day Helen called me in to her office.

"Clay, you did something here. It's really amazing." She gestured to the pile of pages on her desk, my manuscript—my book. It seemed such a part of me, now severed and handed over, that it might as well have been my arm in front of her, my hand with the crooked pinky and calloused middle finger. And I felt both pride and bereavement, staring at it as she told me Anu would get me a contract to look over by Friday, that they'd like to release it in next year's second season if I thought I could finish it in the next two months. Unable to take my eyes off it, I asked for five thousand dollars more than what I knew they would offer me, and Helen shrugged, saying she didn't see why they couldn't make that happen.

"Marketing is excited about this one. I think they're going to have a heyday with it."

I smiled as one who comes out of a dream.

"Sheila wasn't at her desk," I said as I was about to leave. I had spent my short morning commute wondering what I would say to her, if I should even acknowledge our strange conversation or if she might be embarrassed by it, as I was by my lack of sensitivity. I had since realized that it wasn't just her call that had been so disturbing but her alarming emotional state. She had always been the one to listen with limpid gaze and sympathetic tilt of her head, the one who communicated as much by her silence as her simple words.

Of late those blue eyes, the girlish curves of her face and peak of her chin had struck me as somehow dangerous, a weapon wielded as recklessly as a sleepwalker with a gun. But after talking with her, I worried and wondered whether I ought to have invited her to call me back later, whether I should have called her the next morning to see how she was.

"She's taking a few days off for personal reasons," Helen said with a slight smile that seemed to say she knew exactly what those personal reasons were, that it was good of me to ask, though she had no intention of telling me.

As I turned at the door to thank her, I found the small floral back pillow abandoned on her chair and Helen coming toward me, her glasses swaying on their chain against her breasts. I could not remember when Helen had actually gotten up from her chair to hold the door for me and see me out. I could not remember the last time I had actually felt respected for my work as an editor or a writer.

But I liked it.

Inside the men's room, Phil stared bleakly into the mirror as he washed his hands. He looked beyond tired, which was strange. Always upbeat, even through his divorce and whirlwind wedding and birth of his son only a year and a half later, he had been the first—the only one, actually—to invite me out after my separation from Aubrey. We had drunk a few beers together at a couple of Red Sox games, but it had felt mechanical, our arranged camaraderie, and I had politely declined his invitations since.

"You all right?"

He nodded. "A lot happened while you were gone."

"Yeah?" I asked, trying to sound interested. "Helen said Sheila took a few days off. Is she doing all right?"

Phil sighed, tugged a paper towel from the dispenser. "She went to the hospital for alcohol poisoning a few nights ago."

I stared, my stomach contracting in on itself. "What?" In my mind I calculated the days, thinking back to the night she called. I felt guilty and not a little reprehensible.

"She's going to be all right, though I guess it was close. If Dan hadn't come back to pick up Amanda's epilepsy pills, who knows."

"I can't believe it. It's so uncharacteristic of her," I said woodenly. "It's the last thing Dan needs right now."

Phil looked at me strangely. "She's going through a tough time right now, Clay. People do stupid things at times like this." I didn't know whether he meant to insinuate it or not, but I remembered my own drinking after Aubrey left.

"I guess you're right." But I didn't believe our situations were similar at all.

"We've been helping with the kids so Dan can get some work done."

Now I understood the look of fatigue. Sheila's three children were, if I remembered correctly, between the ages of two and eight.

I almost said to let me know if I could do anything to help, but I stopped. "I'm sorry to hear all of this," I said instead.

"Hey, I meant to tell you, your manuscript is something. You need to get that thing finished, man, because I can't wait to see how it ends."

Me, too.

MY VISION SPECKLED AS I paused on the first floor, midway up from the basement laundry. My legs felt swollen, tight, and wooden. I caught my breath.

I need to get more exercise. And while that was true, I also knew I was neither overweight nor terribly out of shape. When I was done with this manuscript, when I finished and it was out the door, I would see a doctor.

As I let myself back into my apartment, I wondered again if Lucian, once he had accomplished his mission, would disappear from my life. Or would he loiter, watching me without my knowing it, as he had on the *T*? There was a time when I could not imagine enduring his intrusions. Now I found I could not imagine a life without them.

That night I stayed up well past two o'clock working on my book.

By the time I went to bed, I tallied more than 300 pages, over 85,000 words—a perfectly respectable length for a book. It needed nothing now but an ending. But my calendar remained empty.

Our time was getting shorter, he had said. Then where was he?

TWO DAYS LATER, SHEILA'S desk stood empty. Not only empty of Sheila herself and the perennial cardigan on the back of her chair but of the framed photos of her family, the pencil holder her son Justin made out of a frozen juice can, the painted rock frog paperweight with googly eyes and Caleb's name carefully painted on the side. Only her candy dish remained.

When I asked Phil what had happened, he said she had given her notice, that she was taking the kids and moving to South Carolina where her parents had retired to a golf course.

"Has anyone called Dan?" I felt vaguely like a schmuck. I should have done it myself, had thought I should many times.

"I've tried, but he won't answer. I don't think he wants to talk."

I knew that feeling. And I didn't blame him.

FOUR DAYS. IT HAD been four days.

That evening I tried to work in spite of my gnawing anxiety and annoyance, but there was nothing more to add to the manuscript. I felt powerless, creatively stunted, and my calendar remained empty.

I tried to finish editing jacket copy for next season's releases, to remember what I had loved about a new author's manuscript enough to go to bat for a larger advance . . . and then went back to my book, to tinker with grammar, rephrase sentences that had nothing wrong with them, check for overuse of hyphens—a writing tic I had only recently discovered that I possessed. I did all of this with growing disquiet, merely for the sake of doing it, unable to quell the unease snaking through my gut.

And then I remembered the e-mail.

I scrolled through my deleted folder and found it, the one about the temple curtain from "Light1." It did not give the full address—only the Light1 moniker—but on a whim I clicked Reply.

I wrote three words:

Where are you?

SOMETIME PAST 3:00 A.M. I fell asleep on my couch, dreaming of blood on doorways, wine in the Passover cup, of damnation like the closing of a vault, the tolling of a bell, of bells ringing over Arlington Street, bells slapping against the door of a café, bells . . .

My cell phone was ringing.

I rummaged through my pants and then fumbled through the pockets of the jacket I had left on the kitchen table. Finding the phone, I noted the caller: "Private." I thought of Sheila. I would be kinder, I thought. I had not realized how volatile, how precarious, her mind-set was.

"Hello?"

The voice, when it came, was gritty. "Hello, Clay." It might have been a man's or an older woman's. I did not recognize it.

"Lucian?"

Silence. I was impatient and anxious, ready to grab my coat now and meet him anywhere. "Is that you? Did you get my e-mail?"

Another pause. And then: "Were you expecting Lucian?"

A chill crawled from my shoulders to my nape.

"Is that you?" I whispered, my heart so loud in my ears I wondered if I'd be able to hear the reply. It came, with a soft rasp.

"No." And then, "No, *Clay.*"

I clapped the phone shut, my heart drumming against my ribs.

I sat very still. My door was locked. My computer had gone

into energy-save mode, and both living room lamps were on. I stared out past the window, at the black, predawn night.

I made myself stand and walk first to one lamp and then the other, turning each of them off with a quiet click. In the darkness I felt vulnerable, blind. I closed my eyes and slowly opened them, made out the shapes of my desk, my sofa, the television on its stand, the casement of the window. I made myself walk to the sill. I grasped it with one hand. The window looked out at the space between my apartment building and the house next door. I leaned against the frame and craned my neck, looking out toward the street.

At first I didn't see it—not until I swept my gaze away from the curb. There. A lone figure, leaning against the porch post of a house across the street, black against the darkness, looking up at me.

I knew, instinctively, that it was not Lucian. I jerked back from the window.

I hurried into my bedroom, shut and locked the door behind me, climbed beneath the covers on my bed, and listened to the percussion of my own heart.

WITH ONE GLANCE AT my clock, I shoved out of bed in a panic. It was Tuesday; I was missing my weekly editorial meeting. I stumbled into the bathroom and turned on the shower.

For a moment I stood dumb in the middle of my bathroom, remembering the phone call, the rasping voice.

The figure across the street.

It was daylight now. Emboldened, I walked straight to the window—not in my living room but in the spare room that faced the street. I pulled the shade.

There was the house, the apartment building next to it, and farther down, Saint Mary's, the liturgies of which I often heard drifting from the open windows of the church in summer. A mother and her young son passed along the sidewalk, bundled up in coats and scarves, toward Massachusetts Avenue. There was no one else.

I hurried to shower, shave, dress. I hesitated a moment before pocketing my cell phone and another moment upon stepping outside my door. Music was coming from Mrs. Russo's apartment, a soaring female voice that reminded me of Barbara Streisand. I couldn't make out the words, but the sound of it, like the daylight, heartened me.

On the single short ride from Central to Kendall Station, one of the train car's few passengers was holding onto the rail to my left and studying me. He looked at least fifty-five and wore a faded Carhartt jacket. His hair was orangish, in the way of men who colored their hair long after it was gray. His large, thick glasses took up the upper third of his face. An "I didn't vote for him" bumper sticker with a picture of the president was wrapped around his sleeve like an armband. As far as I could tell, he wore no watch.

"Can I ask you something?" He swayed with the car. Was he a tourist? No, generally they held maps folded open to red and green diagrams of the *T*, as though they were the complex capillaries of an organism and not five simple lines named after colors.

"Sure." I prepared to tell him he could switch to the Green Line two stops after Kendall.

"Has someone been talking to you? Contacting you?"

I froze. And then I studied the man more acutely: the faint age spots on his face and the edge of his upper lip, the flannel shirt under his jacket, the too-straight line of his hair across his forehead that indicated a comb-over.

"Don't be afraid." He regarded me through sagging eyelids magnified by those glasses. "Has someone been talking to you? Someone not like you?"

The chill and ensuing sweat of the night before returned to me—along with the same need to flee, to shut myself behind a door. The train slowed with a squeal of brakes, and I jumped up, grabbing for the rail near the door as it stopped completely. I squeezed past the doors as soon as they opened, hurried out into the station and up the stairs. Only on the street did I look behind me to confirm that he had not followed me.

I needed to talk to Lucian.

I went into the meeting late, flustered, unprepared. I contributed little, unable to think of anything but the man on the train, the voice on the phone. Were other members of the legion aware of what Lucian was up to, his ambition to have his story—and theirs—outed? Could they interfere?

Helen pulled me aside in the hallway after the meeting. "Clay, I know you're working on a brilliant piece of writing. And it is brilliant. But I can't have you doing it at the expense of your responsibilities. It's all right if it takes longer to finish. You and Anu are still working out the contract particulars, aren't you?"

"Yes." I'd forgotten the contract.

"Then give yourself the time you need to do your job in the meantime. Please."

I nodded, embarrassed and a little resentful at being openly chastised outside the conference room. I went into my office, shoved the door shut with more force than I meant to, dropped the stack of packets from the meeting onto my desk.

I went to the window and looked out at the people walking by, headed somewhere with a purpose I had once envied.

Returning to my desk, I unpacked my bag, pretending it was any usual day—not that I had had a usual day since early October—putting the packets on the corner of my desk, docking my laptop.

I signed in to the company server, opened my calendar, and faltered.

There. Five o'clock tonight: L. But that was not what caused me to hesitate. Below that, a line across the time block read:

Don't EVER try to contact me again.

I sagged into my office chair and rubbed at my face with trembling hands.

27

n the Marriott Starbucks across the street from my office, I
waited. For Lucian. For answers. For the end of the story.

Five o'clock arrived and passed. I sipped my coffee,
strained to see guests walking through the hotel lobby, studied
every patron that came into the coffee shop, most of whom left
again. Except for a businessman camped at a table with his laptop, I was the only one there.

I checked my watch. 5:07.

Was this his idea of getting back at me? For what—trying
to contact him?

5:11.

I thought through our last conversation that day in the airport before the nuns came along. They had thanked Lucian, not
in the way older women coo at the kindness of strangers but
in the regal way of those accustomed to respect. I had eaves-
dropped on their conversation, which consisted wholly of the
details of their trip, and had found myself disappointed not to
hear them debating Scripture or the devil.

5:19.

I thought about the man on the *T* and the figure in the darkness across the street from my apartment. They weren't the same person; the man on the *T* was short, slightly stooped. The figure across the street was taller, seemingly at ease in the darkness, apparently doing nothing but standing there.

Waiting to be seen. Watching me.

A man in cargo pants with zippered pockets and a "Carpe Brewem: Seize the Beer" sweatshirt strode into the coffee shop. He was tall, with straight features and a prominent nose. He wore thick socks inside his Birkenstocks, and I could see the gleam of a silver chain disappearing into the neck of his sweatshirt. He might have been a grad student at MIT.

He wasn't.

"I'm sorry, Clay." He sat down at my table. He did not smile.

"For being late?"

"Well, yes. But mostly for the situation we seem to be in."

"What situation is that? Did you call me last night? Was that you on the street outside my apartment?"

His bangs flopped over his forehead. He raked them back and then frowned. "Someone called you?"

I nodded. I had never considered that he might not know about the call. But he did not ask for details. Instead, he sighed. "I'm afraid I've pulled you into the middle of a conflict that existed long before you were aware of it, one that has been happening around you for . . . well, you know the story."

"There was a man on the *T*, asking if anyone had been talking to me."

"I've heard."

"He had auburn hair, bald on top—"

"It doesn't matter what he looked like. He could be one of millions."

"Of Legion?"

"I suspect he was with the Host."

"And last night?"

"I suspect the other."

I shivered, felt the sharp claws of anxiety inside my chest. In these meetings, these times together, we had existed in a world of story, separate from the spiritual and corporeal worlds we came from. Now, in the last twenty-four hours, I felt those three realms commingling in a volatile fusion of fiction, speculation, and every concrete thing that constituted life in this tangible world. And I felt it with a strange excitement mixed with grave fear.

"How can both want—or not want—the same thing?"

"The Host, because the truth is already available if you seek it. The Legion, because they don't want you finding it." He said this with too much calm, and that maddened me.

"Why then? Why have you done it?" My hands were trembling again, as they had after the phone call last night.

"I've told you that as well."

"What will happen to me because I did this? Will they put a hit out on me? Am I going to hell?"

Tires skidding on pavement . . .

He studied me. "You asked me once where you were going. I said I didn't know. Where do you think you're going, Clay?"

"I—I don't know! How am I supposed to know?" For the first time in weeks, months, I wanted my old life back, that pre-Oz gray I had known before the world was imbued with strange colors. I wanted back my simpleminded fixation on the marriage I'd ruined, the wife I'd been unable to keep. My

254 DEMON: A MEMOIR

failures as a husband and a man had been a comfort compared to these new terrors.

But I might as well have tried to crawl back into the womb. "How much time do we have?"

"Not much. Listen to me. The Host will not wait for you to talk but will speak first. A member of the Host doesn't come to you because you want it to or because you try to summon it. You might indeed summon an angel, but it'll likely be a fallen one. As I've said, even our master masquerades as an angel of light when it suits him."

I thought of my e-mail, of the call later that night. I had felt exposed, vulnerable, all day. "What will we do?"

"What do you mean what will we do?"

"What do we *do?*"

"We finish the story." As he leaned forward, elbows on the edge of the table, his fingers laced together, I saw the heavy stainless steel timepiece on his wrist. I did not consider then that I should have stopped him. That this answer should have been unsatisfactory. That to proceed in light of what was happening defied logic. I was focused on the singular point my universe had shrunk to: my book.

"One day, not so long after the crucifixion and resurrection and after the God-man departed, I awoke to a realization. It was as though I had been standing on the brittle edge of a melting lake. Looking down at the crumbling ice before me and the depths below it, a sense of exclusion settled upon me. I was aware that I stood on the fringe of damnation. This was far worse than my initial sense after the fall that something awaited me on the road ahead, because now here it was, a yawning pit." The bluntness of his stare was a touch psychotic.

"All that might have saved me, El had made available to you. You. You again. And because of it, you might never stand where I stood, on that brittle cusp. How deeply, how madly I *loathed* you.

"Now you know why fear and jealousy have become twin children to us: Something endeared you to him, something beyond the attachment of a creator for his creation—for we, too, were created. Something beyond what we were capable of, something beyond our control—and yours, too. For that alone, I hated you. For the love of God there was no word for the ill I bore you. That is when you truly became my enemy."

"You mean . . . when humans became the enemy of the Legion."

"No. I am both representative and individual. And this is the crux of it, Clay. I believe that if you were the only one, had been the only human *ever*—yes, just you—it would not have changed a thing. I would still be as I am, and he would love you so much."

I stared.

"That look on your face, that's how I feel. Baffled. Because what are you humans but insects? Holy blood for insects. It's as incongruous as diamonds in mud. It wasn't enough that he gave you his breath—he gave you his blood as well. Life physical and spiritual. He gave you everything. What makes you so special? Don't pull away! I ask again: Why you? You. You!" He banged a fist on the table. The businessman with his laptop glanced up. "It all comes down to you. Always, *you!*"

Leave. You need to leave.

I don't know where the thought came from, whether from fear or offense, self-preservation or another source altogether. I stood.

The demon watched me lazily. "You asked me where you were going. Do you think you should go to heaven, Clay?"

"I guess so," I said, warily, as though he were a wild animal.

"Why is that?"

"I've been a good person."

He said, without a trace of the escalating anger or hatred of a moment ago, "You haven't understood a thing I've said."

I left but was unable to erase the image of his parting smile from my mind. It followed me home, baleful, devoid of any attempt at congeniality. In the past he had been angry, capricious, even hostile.

But not quite like this.

Outside my building, I glanced at the house across the street where I had seen the stranger leaning against a post, but no one was there.

The music was still coming from behind Mrs. Russo's door, borne along now on the smell of baking desserts. Perhaps her small group was coming over tomorrow.

I wrote well into the night, chasing reason, exorcising insanity. With an editor's sense of rising narrative tension, I knew I was nearing the end, the climax when events converge to bring the story to a close. Knowing it, feeling it so near, was the one thing that gave me relief.

I worked past 4:00 a.m. and fell, exhausted, onto my couch.

 **28**

◆

I was sleeping on my sofa when laughter woke me. I had not experienced joviality, even vicariously, in longer than I could remember. Now I recognized Mrs. Russo's voice outside my door, wishing someone well. Apparently her group had already come and was taking their leave.

I bolted up with a curse, stumbled into the kitchen to see the time on the stove.

It was past noon.

I didn't even bother to shower, only changed my shirt and grabbed my coat, my laptop, my wallet. Outside my door, Mrs. Russo was still chatting with one of her group members, a man close to her age who held his jacket over his arm.

"Well, Clay! You're home on a weekday. Have you met Mr. Hollingswor— "

"I'm sorry, I can't talk." I brushed past the man and hurried down the stairs.

I could not remember the *T* ever operating so slowly. I was frustrated by the wait, by my inability to take the stairs out of the Kendall Station two at a time—I started to, but had to lean back against the railing to catch my breath and let my vision clear.

Inside the Brooks and Hanover offices I slipped past Sheila's desk, now occupied by a temp, a girl in her twenties who might have been pretty had she refrained from drawing her eyebrows on with a marker. If I could get inside my office without being seen, it was feasible that no one might know I had not been there all morning. I shut my door, docked my laptop, stared at the stack of office mail in yellow tie-top envelopes on the corner of my desk.

Exactly ten minutes later my phone rang. It was Helen. "Clay, can you come see me?"

"Helen, hi. I'm really behind—I was sick this morning. I'm trying to get going on my day. I know I haven't gotten the contract back to Anu—"

"Clay, can you just come in, please?"

I sighed. "Sure."

I scratched my unshaven face, combed my hair with my fingers. I didn't feel like another reprimand. I was soon to become a double asset to this house, and I needed some flexibility and respect.

Helen was wearing her usual cashmere turtleneck—nutmeg today—her glasses hanging on their beaded chain, her hair in a headband worn only by girls in high school and women in their fifties.

"Clay." She sighed as I sat down. "I don't know how to say this."

My first thought was of the book—she couldn't get the larger advance, or they'd have to defer its release by a season.

"We can't work this way. The marketing team is behind, you haven't had a single viable proposal accepted by the committee—not counting your own—in the last three months, and despite the fact that we just spoke yesterday, you still showed up well after noon today." She threw up her hands. "I mean, we just talked yesterday!"

I just sat there in my wrinkled slacks, mutely gazing at her.

"There's still a fine chance that we'll offer you a contract for your book, though I think we should give that a few weeks to re-evaluate how many projects we're going to be behind on and how quickly we can find an editor to take your place. It's a good book, Clay. This is not a statement on your work as a writer— only your work habits as an editor."

All of this came to me through a time warp, each of her words registering in slow, crawling baritone.

"Are you kidding me?" I said at last, incredulity slowly washing over me. "Are you kidding me?" I repeated when she said nothing. In one stroke she was relieving me of not only my job but also of the book that was, to my mind, all but published. How could this be possible?

I'm going to tell you my story, Lucian had said, *and you're going to write it down and publish it.* He had said it. And I had written it, and the committee had accepted it! Obviously this decision would be reversed. Something would happen to change Helen's mind.

Helen shook her head. "I'm afraid not."

"The contract is in my e-mail. It's been sent." Why hadn't I gone through it—or just signed it and sent it right back, never mind the details?

"It hasn't been signed, Clay," she said in that tone adults take with recalcitrant teens. "And this might be the best for both of us. We can both take some time to think. Maybe you should try your luck with a larger house. The book is certainly good enough."

"Are you patronizing me?" I realized my voice had risen. "And we didn't talk yesterday, Helen. You pulled me aside like a wayward student in the middle of the hall."

"Clay, I'm sorry about that, but the fact is—"

"The fact is you have no idea what my life has been like. What I've been going through these last few months. You have no clue, Helen." I was shaking, venting my anger as I waited, waited for the reversal that I knew must happen.

"Clay"— her voice steeled—"You're not the only one with problems."

"Exactly. And when Sheila put herself in the hospital after drinking herself half to death, did you fire her? No. I don't think you did. You gave her time to get her act together. That's some kind of double standard, Helen."

I was on fire, all the tension of the last week, of the last three-and-a-half months, spewing from me as if from a cannon.

"Clay"—she rose and extended her hand—"I wish you luck."

I stared at her hand for an instant before turning on my heel and striding out, slamming her door behind me.

In the hallway, the temp waited with a box. "I'm supposed to help you get your things." What was she, twenty-two? Fresh out of college, maybe, if she had gone at all? Sheila had gone to community college at least. What did this temp straight from— wherever—know? What gave her the right to follow me into my office with a box?

I shoved items off my desk and into the box, threw in the contents of drawers: pictures and books, most of them signed by authors I had acquired, greeting cards accumulated through the years. I sorted through my card file, pulled a few to keep, Katrina Dunn Lampe's among them. I threw in coffee mugs, a Cross pen set, a quote-a-day calendar from the year before

opened to July 7. I left the rest—the manuscript pages, the proposals, the galleys, the covers—where they lay on my desk and
then, on impulse, knocked the stack to the floor.

I undocked my computer and put it into the box. The temp
chewed her lip. "That's a company laptop, right?"

I stopped cold. My story was on that laptop. Almost as
important, my calendar was on it too. It was the only one I
kept, and every one of Lucian's mysterious appointments had
appeared on it.

I forgot the demon's horrible smile, the dire awareness so
similar to that first night in the café, the voice within me compelling me to leave the Starbucks. He had frightened me before,
I had walked out before, and always there had been another
meeting. But without my computer, what would happen to the
appointments? How would I know if he made one?

I had no way to contact him. No way to tell him. He had
told me never to attempt it again, and after what had happened
the last time, I was too afraid to try. Would he know? Would his
buzzing network tell him?

I rummaged around in the box, found a cheap flash drive,
and copied my book onto it. Then I deleted my manuscript on
the hard drive along with my sent and deleted e-mails and, face-
tiously, several drafts of edited copy.

No one stopped me. As I left, no one rushed out after me.
I had arrived at work an editor, writer, and soon-to-be-published
author and left the proud owner of a box full of junk. As I walked
to the station, I noticed a dumpster outside a neighboring building. I set down the box, threw open the lid, and dumped the
entire box, contents and all inside. It was all junk. The only thing
of value, the flash drive with my manuscript on it, was already
tucked into my coat pocket.

TURNING IN MY LAPTOP meant I had no computer. Despite the fact that I now had no idea how I would pay for my trip to Cabo, let alone a new computer, I walked the several blocks to the Galleria. Had I my own laptop, or had Helen given me any warning, I could have ordered one online. As it was, I was at the mercy of whatever the computer store had in stock.

After enlisting the help of a kid half my age, I chose the most affordable, basic model I could find and charged it to my credit card. I took a cab home via the local liquor store, my new computer resting on my knees in its small, white carrying box, a paper bag on the seat beside me.

FOR THE NEXT TWO days I drank, slept, and somehow set up my new computer, which came complete with its own schedule, contact, and mail software. I set up the calendar, which now had nothing on it, and opened a new e-mail account through a free online service. And then I waited.

How strange it was to see that expanse of pristine days, each of them legal-pad yellow, unmarred by meetings or deadlines.

I have no life. I found this insanely funny.

It wasn't, really, but I had just finished the second bottle of boutique merlot on an empty stomach, and terrifically funny seemed better than horribly sad.

THE NEXT DAY, AMID a pounding headache and tripping heart, my entire body sore and swollen, I called my family doctor and set up an appointment for the following week.

I checked my calendar, my e-mail. Nothing.

Perhaps with the status of my manuscript uncertain, he had no more use for me.

I ate and slept at odd hours. Helen's new henchwoman called to request the last of the manuscripts on my desk at home. She would send a FedEx box for them—boxes again—no need to come in. Not that I had any intention of taking them in.

I almost asked about the contract but thought it best to wait. Meanwhile, the only thing that mattered to me was Lucian and finding an end to my book.

So I left my new laptop running, the calendar alive in the corner, waiting, the volume turned up so that I might hear that ping from any place in my apartment if I were away from my desk. But I was never away from my desk for long. I returned to my manuscript, combed through it, rewrote sentences and then entire passages that did not need it. My back hurt, and my eyes strained from looking at it in the half light of day and early afternoon twilight. When the screen and the lamp gave off the only light in my apartment, I got up, turned on another lamp, wondered when it had gotten so dark, and returned to my desk to check my calendar again.

Days passed.

I realized I was growing an inadvertent beard. I wondered if I was slipping into some stereotypical decline, if I was, as people said, hitting bottom.

You're losing it, man.

No, I'm waiting.

But my calendar remained empty, a vacant face staring back at me every time I opened it. I came to regard it with contempt, swearing at it for yielding nothing, calling it names and slamming my desk drawers.

On the eighth day, I sat on my sofa, staring at the laptop across the living room, the glow of it like an oversized LCD nightlight. I found myself thinking of Sheila and wondering how she was, wishing I had her phone number so I could call her and apologize for my callousness. She might have made a mistake, but she had obviously suffered for it in ways Aubrey never had.

I thought also about how centerless and adrift I had been after Aubrey's leaving—until I found a new, more compelling body by which to fix my existence: Lucian. But now I wondered if he would leave me, too, and what could possibly take his place as he had taken Aubrey's. Even in losing Aubrey, I had not felt this level of anxiety, these jolts of panic, had not gone to these mental lengths. I felt sad about that, in retrospect, sad and regretful. While I might never have measured up, might not have prevented her leaving, I saw so many things now that I could have done—if not to keep her, then at least to have allowed myself more closure.

The monitor started to go into hibernation. As I got up to tap it awake, it blinked to life. I sucked in a breath.

4:30: Hurry.

It was 4:28. I stuffed my feet into my shoes, grabbed a jacket, and left.

I WALKED ON SHAKY legs to the closest restaurant, a wrap-sandwich-and-soup joint on the corner of Norfolk and Massachusetts Avenue. I had never eaten here; I had always thought it looked dingy. Scanning the sparse, stained tables, I saw I was right. A college student talked on the phone behind the counter. A couple ate in chilly silence on a pair of bentwood chairs. A blonde woman, the only other patron, waved impatiently to me.

Her eyebrows were too dark for her sallow complexion, the wavy blonde hair bleached too light. She did not smile at me as I sat down.

A wrap sandwich lay on a plate between us. She pushed it toward me. I didn't want it.

"I lost my job."

"I know." She sat back, regarded me with a dispassion I found amazing and infuriating. I had been sick with waiting, with the need for explanations, and now she sat, looking at me like a babysitter biding her time until my parents returned.

"But they're still considering the contract, Helen says. I hadn't signed it yet—"

"I'd be surprised if they take it."

My mouth opened, but no sound came out.

"You ruined it, Clay."

I blanched. "But you said they'd publish it."

"No, I said *you* would publish my story."

"Do we have to argue semantics? You said—"

"Just because I say something doesn't mean it will happen, Clay." She crossed her arms, regarded me over high cheekbones that seemed too patrician for the bad bleach job and cheap makeup. And I saw my hoped-for payoff in all of this, the reward I felt I had coming to me, begin to trickle away.

"Then—then I'll submit it elsewhere. It's bigger than Brooks and Hanover anyway."

She seemed to consider this, a ring-laden hand toying with a strand of pale hair, her gaze returning to me, searching mine. "All right. Then let's get to it."

And then I noticed her eyes. They were the least human I had ever seen them, glittering in a ménage of mercurial colors beneath a brown veneer. I sat, transfixed, not knowing what to do, hearing again the voice in my head: *Leave!*

"How does it end?"

"With you," she said simply. "As I said, it has always been about you."

"You say that, but what do you mean?" My every question seemed laced with desperation, every answer not enough.

"My story has given way to yours. Don't you see? No, of course you don't. Listen to me. It was all done. These children of God were bursting to life like kernels of corn popping into bloom. Suddenly, El was everywhere, manifest by the sheer act of belief in this Messiah, this gift of spilled blood drunk from the cup of acceptance. We were forgotten, disinherited in favor of the mud race.

"I saw that black lake yawning beneath me, a little bit wider with each passing day. We all did. And we could have given up, lain down. Instead, we struck out more vehemently than before, assuaging pain with more pain. Our hearts turned numb, and our fear became the more palatable mission of hatred. We felt better because we felt less. We were bent on only one purpose: the destruction of El's believers."

"But you played havoc with them before."

"Not like this. Now, with the bellow of Satan loud in our ears, we went to war. As in any campaign, any ethnic cleansing, we struck out at their members, their leaders, their generals. They're not who you think."

"What do you mean?"

"There's a reason Jake Salter is dead, Clay."

The flesh rose on my arms. Jake Salter, the punk kid who,

I had learned that day in the Commons, died just years ago. "He drowned," I whispered.

She looked at me as though I were an insect flailing in a web.

"As for the pretty jogger—"

I sat back in my chair, pushing away the pastiche of death: cracked windshields, an orphaned sneaker, and always, always, the shattered pink iPod.

"There's an interesting story to that one. Her husband left his wife for her last year. This year he decided to have a crisis of conscience. He was on the cusp of becoming one of them, those blooming souls. We couldn't have that. He's an influential man."

"So you killed *his wife*?"

"Despite your American beliefs, there are no rules in war."

"How is killing her supposed to stop him?"

"He's bitter, throwing the blame at El's feet." She shrugged. Her voice was flat, devoid of emotion. She reached up, slid her fingers through her hair, her back arching slightly.

"Do you—does this happen often?"

"I told you. This is a war."

"Can't people see through that? Don't people know?"

"Have you seen through it?" She leaned forward, the *V* of her sweater gaping. "We have other methods of distraction as well, palatable, innocuous distractions condoned by your social mores. Gratification. Success. The striving for everything your culture says is important and worthwhile: the trips to Mexico, the brandy in the Four Seasons. The Audi, the private Belmont school."

She stared at me as she pulled them from my brain like folded lottery numbers from a fishbowl. I felt my face redden. "And it works. Everyone thinks they deserve happiness, after all. It's practically written into your Constitution. What a great country." She smirked.

I thought of the day in Belmont, my aspirations and vision of a house there. "And for every human you distract, deceive, or kill . . . what do you get?"

She shrugged. "Nothing."

"What do you mean, *nothing?*"

"This isn't an incentive program, Clay. It's the principle of the matter. Haven't you understood anything? It is all about you. How carefully he formed you in your fragile mud glory. How long-suffering he has been with you, how willingly he labored with you, ultimately offering you the once-for-all atonement when you deserve it so little. No, when you deserve it not at all!"

With every sentence her palm beat the top of the table. Now it slammed down, the salt and pepper shakers rattling atop the smudged surface like loose teeth. "You again!"

Leave.

But I stared, transfixed by her anger, by the blazing black light of her eyes.

By her hatred of me.

She leaned back, instantly composed. "But not every-one wants El's great gift. It hasn't turned out as badly as I thought."

"What do you mean?" It came out barely above a whisper. Too soft, I was sure, for any human to hear.

"Because people are good. Just like you, Clay. You're a good guy. You've lived a good life. And just like you, humans aren't in the habit of accepting charity. They'd rather work for redemption. But I ask you, what is good, really, Clay? Decency? A relative state of not-so-bad? Having good intentions? Well, you know what they say about the road to hell. And if intentions and states of relative goodness were good enough, do you think El would have gone to the trouble? You think you've suffered. What do you know of suffering?"

I wanted to strike her. Suffering! She dared speak to me of suffering? But even as I formed the thought, self-righteous and indignant, I saw the corners of her mouth turn up, and I knew that my suffering, such as it was, was pathetic to her.

"But who am I to challenge you?" Her arms crossed. Fury seemed to rise from the surface of her skin, like heat off a stove. "If you insist on being judged by the merit of your works, El will honor that. I've seen it many times. But what I haven't seen is anyone who measured up. Maybe you'll be the first, hmm?"

"Tell me about Mrs. Russo."

Lucian stared at me as though a snake had slithered out of my ear.

"She's religious."

"I don't mind religious." But she looked as though she had bitten into a bug.

"She goes to church."

"That's fine with me."

"What?"

She shrugged but appeared unsettled. "Churches are inbred, if you ask me, worshipping a radical god with conventional methods. So traditional. And so *comfortable*. Mind you, the church community is no paradise. Image takes effort. And one has to appear to have things in order, or else how can they judge anyone else? I see more judgment from churchgoers than any-one. In fact, I have a theory."

She practically pounced on the table's edge. Her eyes were wild, storming. "I think they secretly delight in the shortfall of others. It relieves the pressure of having to be so holy. For a body of people who have received so much grace, they exhibit a stingy amount in return."

Her eyes flickered toward the window behind me. I turned to see what had caught her attention. "I'm bored with this. With you."

My head snapped back around. "What?"

"Go away. Go live out your gnat's existence."

"But we're not done!"

Her eyes lolled back to me. "Yes, we are."

"But—I don't know how it ends!" And now I remembered something else. "Or what it has to do with me—you said this story was ultimately about me. What does this have to do with me?"

"What does this have to do with me?" she mimicked. "Can't you do anything but think of yourself? Go home."

"But how can I—"

"Go."

"I don't know—"

"GO!" She screamed it, lunging across the table at me.

I bolted up, stumbled back, knocking over my chair.

She screamed again. "GO!"

I never saw the couple's reaction, what must have been the gaping mouth of the student behind the counter. I pushed out the door and ran to the corner of Norfolk, down the street toward my apartment, the dizziness closing over me like a hood. As I scrambled up the stairs, through the door I had forgotten to close, let alone lock, darkness overtook me like a pursuer in a black alley. I fell without feeling toward the floor, realizing as I did that something had been very wrong in this last meeting.

She hadn't been wearing a watch.

29

White Shoulders. It was the same perfume my grandmother had worn. I knew this only because I had once chased the cat across her backyard with that glass bottle as a boy, spraying it in the animal's eyes—a feat that had landed me a sound spanking.

Something brushed my face, soft and furry. For a moment I thought it was the cat, back from boyhood, its tail teasing my nose.

"I think I'd better call an ambulance, dear."

Mrs. Russo knelt next to me in her wool coat and gloves, her scarf brushing my cheek as she felt my head.

"You didn't bump it too badly, at least, as far as I can tell."

"I'm fine," I said, only now understanding that I was laid out on my floor, the front door hanging wide.

She reached back for a chair, slid onto the seat with a creak of her knees. "I still think we'd best call 9-1-1."

"Please, no." I made myself sit up, slowly, mortified. "I'm fine. My blood sugar dropped—I came running up the stairs."

And then I remembered why.

I had never seen Lucian like that. And I had run home, like a child back to his mother's skirts, to the protection of a building inhabited by religious Mrs. Russo.

No, it wasn't the religion that made her so fearsome to them. I knew that now. I thought of the day in the church.

It was the prayer.

I sat up, wiped blood from my chin onto the back of my hand. At least my growing beard would hide the scab.

"I'm going to get you something to eat. I want you to leave the door open while I fix it."

I nodded and moved onto the sofa.

WHEN SHE RETURNED, I made my way through a bowl of homemade noodle soup—"It's from the freezer, but it's homemade," Mrs. Russo said—a sandwich, and three cookies. She watched me eat, telling me about her grandson's part in the school play, the Debussy he had recently learned to play on the piano. "Oh no, dear"—she didn't miss a beat—"finish that sandwich."

I finished, and I had to admit I felt better. Better, and tired.

As she studied me with kind but troubled hazel eyes, I thought the wrinkles around them seemed more prominent, somehow more human than ever. She looked like she wanted to say something, but I assured her that I was fine, that I was just extremely worn down.

I promised to come knocking if I needed anything. I started to pick up the dishes, but she swatted my hand and carried them to her apartment.

She returned for a moment to tell me to come get her if I needed anything, and then left, closing the door behind her.

As I got up to lock it, I wished I could close out the memory of the demon's scream, the pernicious smile. For the first time in months I wished I could delete the memory of Lucian altogether, erasing him from the story of my life.

I SLEPT AND DREAMED of sandwich wraps, of blonde, wavy hair, of that smile, that terrible smile, of the jogger and her faceless husband.

I woke with a start. It was well past 3:00 a.m. I walked on steady legs into my living room to fumble with the lamp, wanting to banish the dark.

At my desk I woke the laptop, bypassed my calendar, and began my search for Jake Salter. It took me a while to find him, finally, on my high school alumni page under Passings. Deaths were listed by year.

"*Jake Salter '86. Youth pastor, Our Savior's Church, Independence, MO.*"

I STAYED UP UNTIL dawn exorcising the conversation in the sandwich store onto the page. When it was done, I determined I would not add it to my account. It was out of my system and that was all that mattered. I could sleep now—for days, if I wished. I could find a new job. But I was determined that I would not go back to the story. That I would leave it like a poisonous thing, a horror story come to life, a demon game that kills its human players like a bad B movie.

But by six that morning I was writing, adding my reactions to the belated revelations about Jake Salter and the jogger in the Garden, the shape of Lucian's mouth as she screamed at me

. . . waking up under the scarf and care of Mrs. Russo, White Shoulders and angora fuzz in my nostrils.

Some time after ten o'clock, I pushed back from my desk. I went to the kitchen for a snack and one of the bottles of juice Mrs. Russo had left in my refrigerator along with sliced turkey, provolone cheese, and a quart of milk. Cans of vegetable soup, a loaf of bread, and an assortment of fresh fruit sat on my counter. She had done it in spite of my protests, saying it was a privilege to serve me, that she had been "burdened" for me, as she put it, for months now.

I was just returning to my desk with a partially eaten apple when I stopped and stared at the screen.

It was the *Is* that jumped out at me. The first-person narrative. The story encasing the story.

I sat down slowly, my fingers sticky, the chunk of apple like Styrofoam in my mouth.

And I saw, as I had that day in Belmont, the deconstruction of everything on that page—not as a pile of wood and metal rubble, of furniture legs and earth—but of two stories: Lucian's . . .

And mine.

My story is very closely connected to yours, he had said. *My story is ultimately about you.*

And then, just yesterday: *My story has given way to yours.*

As I stared at the narrative *I* on the screen, at my every fear, incredulous amazement, and myriad questions, I realized that indeed, it had.

I had written a tale, the main character of which was not Lucian, the demon, but I.

İ SPEⁿT ALL DAY rereading it, the entire thing, with new eyes. Each word from Lucian's mouth imbued with new and sinister meaning. I saw myself no longer floating along the eddies of Lucian's story as I had thought, but caught now, dead center in the current.

Between two firing armies.

I reconsidered the phone call in the middle of the night. The pair of women at the Bristol Lounge. The man on the train. I had thought myself the observer in all of this but found now that I had been the one being observed and that this conflict had come to include me.

A war, Lucian called it. A satanic grudge match against an omniscient God who loved his human creation. A God I did not know.

I wanted to rail as he had railed, to accuse him, but I knew without checking that my calendar remained untouched.

The demon had left me.

He had accomplished his purpose. He had put up his story like so much window dressing, spinning his tale as deftly as a spider, and it had been a distraction to me, as solid and real as the stately houses in Belmont. And just as the mansions were that day before my eyes—crumbled to the ground, ruined— I now stood stripped of all things I once was: husband, editor, would-be writer. An honest man. A "good man."

Worst of all, I was alone. Who could I talk to? Who could I tell who would not consider me a madman? I had lost Aubrey and alienated Sheila. I had not seen any of my supposed friends for months. I could call my sister, but where would I start, and if I did, how would she ever believe me?

I thought of Mrs. Russo, the kind, praying warrior who kept even the brash Lucian at bay. How could I tell even her?

I cancelled my doctor's appointment. I vacillated between desperation and fear. I could not spend my life like this, but if I had inadvertently wandered into a battlefield of opposing spiritual forces, neither did I want to become yet another piece of collateral damage.

I returned to the online Bible, compared it again with my account—and I saw now that it was truly my account—of our every interaction. But while Lucian had finished his tale of jealousy, revenge, and his probable end, I knew—with the sense of one who has spent his entire life reading stories—that mine was not finished.

TWO DAYS LATER, I knocked on Mrs. Russo's door. I had no idea what I would say, what to even ask for. But I knew she could help me find it.

When she pulled it open, she did not greet me with her characteristic smile and "Hello, dear!" but told me to come in even as she hurried into the kitchen.

She was breathing quickly, her hands hesitating in the air before her as though they had forgotten what they were about.

I had expected to come in, to search for words, to be afraid to look into those aging hazel eyes. That she seemed flustered was even more unsettling.

"Open that refrigerator, Clay, and take out the perishables. You need to take them."

"Mrs. Russo, you've given me enough food to last for days. Is everything all right?"

She went into the bedroom and came back, a sweater over one arm, a book in another. A homemade sandwich was wrapped on her kitchen counter next to an apple, a bottle of water. She packed them into a carry-on bag on her kitchen table.

"Clay, would you set those flowering pots in the sink and run some water into them? Run it good, dear, until it comes out the bottom."

"Are you leaving town?" I asked with growing alarm.

"My son had an accident this morning on his way to work. I need to go help take care of my grandchildren."

"I'm so sorry. Is he all right?"

"He's in the hospital, and I need to get to their house so Beth, my daughter-in-law, can be with him. On second thought, can you just take those plants with you? And will it be much trouble for you to collect the paper and mail for me while I'm gone? I don't know how long it will be, but I'll let you know if I'll be more than a few weeks. I might have to trouble you to send me my bills."

I assured her that it was no problem, that I was glad to help. And while I tried to be as helpful as possible, I felt desperately alone at the thought of her impending departure.

"Why don't you just call me when you know more? And if you think of anything else, I have my key."

"Thank you, dear. I meant to knock on your door earlier, but then I realized if I hurried, I could catch a train tonight, and I got distracted." She looked around, lost, but then fixed her eyes on something—a worn Bible on her coffee table, which she added to her bag.

I loitered, like a child watching a parent pack for a business trip. "I meant to ask if you'd been to that little church down the street, the Gospel Room."

"No, I haven't, which is a shame since it's so close." She looked around as though searching for anything she might have forgotten.

"Maybe," I said awkwardly, "we could go there together after you get back."

She paused to give me a wondering smile. "Why, I'd like that very much, Clay. I would like very much to visit that little church."

Somehow, in that moment, I knew that what I'd thought was true, that within her lay wisdom to counter Lucian's knowledge and answers I had been afraid to ask for.

"I'll enjoy our Sunday outing when I'm back. Especially if those grandkids of mine don't do me in before then." She chuckled.

THAT NIGHT I ATE a sandwich with some of the lettuce and tomato from Mrs. Russo's stash of "perishables."

I found myself thinking of Aubrey more and more, practically by the hour, as I once had. And I felt inexplicably guilty for the days I had forgotten her, for my mental absence, as if I had been taken in by someone new, like an interesting new friend in school who makes our old loyal standbys fade in comparison. Or a new fling, next to whom old relationships seem stale, familiarity having bred its inevitable contempt—only to discover that the luster of the new face had grown thin or, worse, that I had become the one passed over in favor of a new infatuation.

Never mind that she had been the one to leave. When I was truthful about it, when I was honest with myself, I could admit that I had left her first—in spirit if not in deed.

Now, abandoned by Lucian, I found my thoughts returning to her in lieu of any other crutch on which to lean. My selfishness filled me with self-contempt, even as I wondered if she was happy or if she might be tiring even now of Richard, of his habit of playing the radio too loud, of chasing his food around on his plate with his fork as if it were a hockey puck, of predictably retreating from certain topics or conversations, of repeating the catchphrases that had once seemed funny but had grown as tedious as a pull toy. For the first time since the day in the museum, I considered calling her.

But I returned to my manuscript instead, adding to it my conversation with Mrs. Russo, my thoughts of Aubrey, my dread of the monster at the end of the book.

With Mrs. Russo gone, I felt exposed, vulnerable, fearful. And hopeful.

Would Lucian come back to me now that she was gone and the "spiritual static" was no longer present? And if he did, would I welcome him? I could not shake the memory of our last encounter—hearing that screaming, even in my mind, sent chilly spikes through my gut.

I told myself I should get back to my life. There was still a life waiting for me as far as I knew, and I needed, if nothing else, to find a job.

One night I lay in bed trying to picture my future. It was filled with insomnia and demons. I stared at the ceiling and thought of Mrs. Russo.

"El?" I spoke, softly, feeling foolish. And then, "Elohim?" The night answered with silence.

I missed Mrs. Russo. I hoped for selfish reasons that her son would recover quickly. Lucian was right: I was not such a good man.

I WAS GATHERING MAIL—mine and Mrs. Russo's—the next day when I saw it, peeking out from between a bill and her *Cooking Light* magazine. I knew the letterhead by the large *B* showing on the corner. I pulled it out of the stack and, by the feel of the single page inside it, knew I didn't even need to read it.

But I did anyway.

> *Dear Clay:*
>
> *In light of our recent separation, we feel it best to pass on* Demon: A Memoir *at this time. Please feel free to pursue publication with another house.*
>
> *Best of luck,*
> *Helen Gennaro*
> *Editorial Director*
> *Brooks and Hanover*

My manuscript, my story—and now I knew that it was indeed my story—was my truth broadcast to the world. It was my voice.

But now that, too, was gone.

THE NEXT MORNING CAME upon me in a panic. I dressed in the same clothes I had worn the day before, hurried to my computer, and slammed my fist down on the keyboard when my calendar yielded, as I knew it would, nothing.

Outside on the street I turned away from Massachusetts Avenue and walked toward Saint Mary's. But I wasn't going to Saint Mary's. I stopped half a block shy of the cathedral, in front of the diminutive Gospel Room, a converted house that could not hold more than fifty people, if that. I stood there for a long moment before opening the tiny chain-link front gate and trying the door.

Locked.

Why were houses of God always locked?

As I turned away, I caught sight of someone standing on the corner of Inman, watching me. It frightened me at first, and then I became indignant.

"*What?* Who are you with?"

The figure, a man in a short jacket, just stood there.

"Is that you?" I asked it with a spark of I knew not what— hope, anger, desperation, recklessness. I started across the street, but the figure turned and sauntered away. Something about that posture—the man leaning against the post of the house! Could it be him? Willing the glowing spots from my vision, I started after him again, but when I gained the corner, he was gone.

I SCROLLED THROUGH THE directory on my phone and dialed a number I had not called in months—had only saved, in fact, in order to identify the caller and avoid answering if I didn't feel up to talking to her.

After five rings of waiting, for once, to actually get her on the phone, I resigned myself to leaving a message. But then someone picked up, and I thought I must have had the wrong number; the voice sounded nothing like the woman I knew.

"Is Katrina there?" Perhaps she had changed her number.

"This is she."

"Katrina," I said, caught off guard. And I knew why I had not recognized her at first: She sounded *tired*.

"Clay?"

"Yes, sorry. This is Clay." I said, fumbling.

"I heard you left Brooks and Hanover."

"I guess you could say that. Did I wake you up?"

"No, no. I'm just worn out."

Katrina Dunn Lampe? Worn out? I was speechless. "You sound so different."

"Yeah, well, I'm going through treatment for a small tumor."

I hesitated, having never considered that Katrina might be subject to the same whims of nature as other mortals. "I had no idea. I'm so sorry." And I meant it. *Why do bad things happen to good people?*

There are no good people.

"I'm glad you called. I'm sorry I haven't been in touch. I've cut back to just a few days here and there." A dog barked in the background. After someone shushed it, she added, "I'm considering leaving the business, actually."

I stared, unsure what to say, what to ask. This was the most I'd ever known about her beyond the artifice of name-brand purses and manicured nails. And there was something remarkably attractive about the moment, and about her in it, despite the circumstances. Something remarkably human.

We talked for the better part of a half hour. I listened as she said she had gone to Connecticut for a few months to stay with her sister during treatment, that she had taken some time off to heal, to reevaluate.

"You'll think it's wild, Clay, but this experience has really made me think about things like spirituality."

She was the last person from whom I ever expected to hear anything of this sort.

Of course, anyone might have said the same of me.

I almost said something. I almost told her. But instead I said, lamely, "That's really great, Katrina."

"My friends call me Kat."

"Kat. That's really great."

I left the conversation without mentioning my manuscript, but saying I would call her again next week.

THAT NIGHT, AS I drafted letters of application to a few local publishers, I glanced toward the window. Was he there? Was anyone? For all I knew, with Mrs. Russo gone, Lucian himself might show up at my door at any time.

But my calendar remained staunchly empty, as bright and impersonal as the face of the moon.

31

◆

I went out for coffee every morning. And every morning I looked for the figure on the corner. For people loitering in pairs. For humans with fine watches and glittering intellect in their eyes. Three days after the morning I stood in front of the Gospel Room, I swore I saw a blonde soccer mom walk around the corner of the local Starbucks. Remembering Lucian the day at Vittorio's, I hurried to get a glimpse of her, but she disappeared a block ahead of me as I tried to catch up to her.

Two days later I thought I saw the black man who had met me in church the day we saw the Halloween masks. But I lost him when he crossed the street just before an onslaught of cars.

A week and a half had passed since the day Mrs. Russo left to stay with her grandkids. She didn't call, and though I might have been able to look them up in Long Island, I took it to mean that she was busy and so left her alone. Meanwhile, I continued to water her plants and collect her mail. I had eaten all of her perishables and regularly went to the co-op for soup and the daily special. My life, my mind, might be falling apart, but I was determined to get my body back together. I rescheduled my appointment with my doctor, the dizziness continuing to plague me despite my improved habits.

Though I recovered some semblance of routine, I knew other vestiges of my former life had left me forever. Every expensive car that passed me on the street, every new display in the window of Bowl and Board summoned to mind a pile of debris. I found I craved none of these things, all of them equally unpalatable to me.

I spoke with Katrina a second time, just briefly. She was ill that day, and we had had to keep it short. I told her I had something to show her when she felt up to it, though I knew she had plenty of clients she was already unable to give her time to. She was gracious enough to say she would discuss it with me later.

Thinking of her health, I felt like a clod. But I needed to sell the book if I could—not for the hope of interviews in the Bristol Lounge, or for the *Paris Review*, but because I had received my last paycheck from Brooks and Hanover and had yet to hear back on any of my application letters.

Meanwhile, I continued to stare at the blinking cursor at the end of the story that had once been Lucian's but was now solely mine.

RETURNING FROM MY MORNING coffee run four days later, I thought I saw the punk kid from the Commons coming out of a shop. He was half a block down from where I was crossing the street when I saw him. But as with the soccer mom and the black man—and the taxi driver I thought I'd seen just yesterday dropping a passenger at a corner before speeding off, deaf to my hailing—he never turned when I shouted. And

I wondered if I was not really the author *of Dreaming: A Memoir,* having hallucinated this entire series of encounters.

Still, I looked every day for that cast of guises, for the figure sauntering onto Inman, or leaning against the post of the house across the street.

That day I arrived back at my apartment to find Mrs. Russo's door standing open. For the first time in longer than I could remember, my heart lifted with a jittery start induced by hope rather than fear.

"Mrs. Russo?" I stepped inside. Sounds issued from farther in, shuffling, the crinkling of something being rolled in paper. "Mrs. Russo?"

Her daughter, Jeanette, who often came to visit with her children, came out of the bedroom. Her face was haggard, her eyes swollen and red-rimmed.

I halted.

"Clay." Jeanette offered a slight smile, and then her mouth crumpled. She lifted her hand to her eyes, and then pushed her hair back from them.

I stared at her. I could hear someone working in the bedroom and assumed it was her husband, Kevin. My heart took on a ragged rhythm.

"Mom had a stroke." It came out in a tight squeak. Behind her Kevin emerged from the bedroom.

"No. No." I was unsure if I said it for her or for myself or out of some strange guilt that I felt settling like a load of boulders upon me. Kevin laid an arm around his wife's shoulders and reached out with his other to clasp my cold hand in greeting.

"But she went to New York." I gave Kevin's hand an absent shake. None of this made sense.

290 DEMON: A MEMOIR

"They took her to the hospital, but she never regained consciousness," Kevin said.

"What does that mean? What happened?" My hands began to shake. Had I contributed to this in some way? Had I brought undue attention to her by the simple fact of hiding in her prayerful shadow, albeit unwittingly, all these months?

Jeanette laid her hand along my arm, as if she was the one comforting me. "It means God called her," she said with a tiny smile.

"Why?" I felt like a child.

Her smile, just then, was too much like her mother's, with that hint of serenity amid obvious pain. "Would you want Mom far from you?"

But I need her here! I wanted to shout. The apartment was collapsing around me, the plants, my new computer, the stairs, into a heap of rubble, of meaninglessness.

Jeanette squeezed my shoulder. "Mom sure loved you, Clay. On her last visit she brought your name up in church, asking for prayer for you. You were on her heart." Tears rolled down her cheeks. She eventually turned away, her hand over her face.

I fell back a step, unable to take it all in. Unable to believe Mrs. Russo would not be back, could not go with me to the tiny Gospel Room, tell me the things I needed to know.

"I have her plants," I said faintly, stupidly.

"I don't know what we're going to do with all her things. Rob, my brother, is still recovering from his accident. If you wouldn't mind keeping them—"

"No, no, I don't mind." I looked around her apartment. She had packed her carry-on bag there on the table, had given me her perishables standing here in the kitchen, had told me to water the plants until water came out the bottom.

"I'm sorry. If I can do anything to help . . ." I don't know if I said it more for them or for me.

Inside my apartment, I reeled, grabbed at the back of a dining room chair, the table, the wall. I rushed to my desk. I grabbed the top of that stack of mismatched manuscript pages now numbering in the hundreds and, with a long, full motion, ripped them apart. I dropped the fraying halves, caught some of them as they fell from my hands, and tore them in half again. I grabbed another stack and ripped them, too, catching at the pieces, tearing them and then tearing them again.

"You wanted your memoirs published. I did everything I could, I sacrificed everything! Killer! Murderer!" It occurred to me that anyone hearing me—Jeanette and Kevin, most likely— might think I was crazed. Good. I was.

I grabbed another stack of pages, but before I could rip them into pieces, palsy stilled my arms. The words jumped off the page at me, the forest of Is, and then the question on the very page in my hand: *"What does this have to do with me?"*

I fell onto the floor against the desk and sobbed, torn half pages and quarter pages slipping over the edge and falling around me like ashes drifting from the sky after a fire. I covered my eyes, great heaves shaking my shoulders. If there was a God, I cried out to him, thinking that only he could understand my keen over the deep that had once been my world.

I stayed like that for a long time. Even once my weeping subsided, I was too exhausted to rub at eyes that had nearly swollen shut.

I had been unable to escape Lucian before. I could not escape him now, even when he had abandoned me. This was purgatory.

No, this was hell.

32

The apartment building I had once considered homey seemed, overnight, dormlike and shoddy. The industrial carpet on the landings was cold and dirty, the mailboxes impersonal despite the nameplates stamped out on a label-maker.

I forgot my morning coffee. I stared at Mrs. Russo's door, now devoid of coffee cake and chocolate-chip cookie smells, of inspirational music and the sound of visitors. I thought of finding the old e-mail, of risking another message to **Light1**, of calling him out despite the consequences. Of posting a message on a blog site: "Demon encounter? Ever talked to one? Was his name Lucian?"

But I did none of these things. I decided that when I saw the doctor in three days I would ask for a psychiatric referral, even if I suspected that I was psychologically sound.

I would also ask for an antianxiety prescription.

My sleep was harassed by a cast of human faces, each of them jeering in turn, by masks with black rubber horns, the eyes of which were no longer vacant but fixed solidly on me, by watches with faces inside faces in an infinity of time like an image eternally reflected by two mirrors, by the ticking of the second hands, loud as bells tolling in my ear.

WHEN I AWOKE, THE bells, ringing like those from the steeple on Park Street, had passed. I had been in bed nearly three days. I made my way to my desk, turned on the computer.

I stared at the file of my manuscript, my unfinished story. The memoir into which I had funneled every bit of my energy, my life.

I selected it.

Just before I hit the command to delete it, a notice appeared in the corner of my screen.

> 5:00 p.m.
>
> L.

THAT AFTERNOON I PLACED a call to a number I had not expected to dial—not today, perhaps not any day ever.

The voice on the other end was surprised but not hostile. "This is so unexpected."

"I just called to see how you are."

"I'm fine. I'm very fine. I'm surprised to hear from you. Is everything all right? Are you all right? You sound tired."

"So do you."

"I suppose that's the truth. Are you still seeing that woman we met at the museum?"

I hesitated. "No. Not really."

"You know you're allowed to, Clay. You deserve that. To be happy." Her statement reminded me too well of Lucian's words in the sandwich shop.

Everyone thinks they deserve happiness.

"I was wondering: Have you talked to Sheila?"

"Only once since she moved home. She's withdrawn. Rather the way you did, I suppose."

"She called me before she left. I'm afraid I wasn't very sensitive. Actually, I was rude."

"She told me. She thought you'd be able to help her. More than I could." She gave a slight, mirthless sound that wasn't really a laugh.

"Why would she think I could help her?" I thought of the day in my office, the call to my hotel in Cabo San Lucas.

"Didn't she tell you why they're separated?"

"Not—no. Not in so many words."

"Dan left her, Clay."

I stared off toward the bedroom without seeing it or anything but the look of Sheila in my office that day, asking if I would speak to him, wringing her hands and looking like a bird about to pull her own feathers out. I felt ill.

"Yes, but—"

"She came by the house several evenings, worried that he might be seeing someone. I wasn't the best friend to her, Clay. I was too ashamed to tell her that everything she said made sense. And he was, too—he was seeing someone from work. One of the women in the office e-mailed her and asked to talk to her. She told her everything."

The night she returned my text message from a friend's house. The "have to see you" e-mail on her computer. Lucian had alluded to her affair without saying it, and once I believed it, he had not dissuaded me.

Fiend! I felt worse than horrible. I felt responsible. "I need to call her, Aubrey. Can you give me her number?"

I took it down, not sure when I would call or what I would say.

"Aubrey?" I said, at the end of the call. "What was it that was never enough for you? Was it money? What I did for a living?"

"Don't." I heard a tremor in her voice. "Don't do that. You did everything right."

"I don't think I did."

"Yes, you did. You're a good man."

I hated those words. I hated hearing them. Being a good man had won me nothing. Lucian's words echoed somewhere between my brain and the phone line.

I ask you, what is good, really, Clay?

And I knew the answer: not good enough.

But I thanked her anyway, knowing she meant well, and asked her again if she was well.

"I am. I'm pregnant."

And with those words, I felt her fall irrevocably away from me. All the hope I had harbored, but had been afraid to admit even to myself, slipped away like coins through a grate.

"That's wonderful, Aubrey. That's really something." My voice was hollow. I wished her well again and we hung up.

It seemed so unfair. She would have the house, the children, the life I had wanted with her. She would never endure what I had, would never know what those months had been for me.

It was unfair, but it had tethered me too long. And despite our reasons and expectations—realistic or not—I had surely let her down as much as she had betrayed and abandoned me. I was a good man, but I was no better than she.

I forgave her.

İ HAD ΠOŤ BEEΠ to Esad's since that first night. The strap of bells against the glass sounded sharp and metallic, too loud. The smell of the grill, the chicken and burgers and gyros, flooded my nostrils and I was there again, that night in October.

But tonight I was a different man.

The Mediterranean stranger was there, sitting at the same table. This time I did not wait for him to summon me but walked directly to his table and sat down.

"You let me believe lies."

His hair curled over his forehead as it had before, though this time I did not find his looks enviable. His wool trousers did not summon to mind cognac, yachts, or Cohíbas.

His watch, stainless, heavy, and surely expensive, did not interest me.

He studied me, his eyes darting across my face as though he were reading a book. He smiled slightly. "But I never lied." He picked at his slacks, at the cuff of his cashmere sweater. It reminded me of Richard, struck me as fastidious and affected.

"And Mrs. Russo?"

"What business is it to you?"

He was right. I supposed that was between her and her God. I did not expect to get a straight answer from Lucian now, anyway. Besides, asking would not return her to me, grant me retribution, or help me now.

The demon looked away, deflecting my gaze.

"The story isn't finished," I said.

"Ah, the story," he said coldly. He tapped his chin in a mockery of thinking and sat back, regarding me over his slightly hooked nose. "How about this. I had a dream—if demons truly dream—the other night. I dreamed I stood before a great mirror—one that distorted all the things I once thought beautiful, recasting them in ghoulish images, casting me into an ugly mold I have known only in my own mind. And it threw Lucifer into such grotesque state that I barely recognized him except by his eyes and that presence I know to be his. And when I shook free of it, my strange waking dream, it occurred to me that I was not looking at a mirror at all but into the reflection of all things as they are, for all things must be seen in their true light when held up to the mirror of Truth."

"What does that have to do with anything?" My anger, my grief, my outrage bubbled up all at once.

His mouth formed a tight line. "I saw Lucifer the other day. Still brilliant, my Prince. Still beautiful. Perhaps not quite as stunning as before—it may be that the millennia are finally working their wear upon him, as the shining cloth wears at last upon the finish of an antique, as even kisses wear down the gold leaf of an icon. But he's lovely yet." His eyes shone with terrible light. "It's almost more than I can stand, remembering him in the long idyll of first Eden, before, though I have long since come to terms with all that has happened since. To look upon him now is still amazing, though he is not—will never again be—the perfect creature he once was. But then, none of us are what we were. Even you, Clay." He looked at me, clearly expectant.

"Do you feel better saying that? Ruminating about your life, though your future is set and there's nothing you can do about it—living in the past, as we say? I don't care that you saw Lucifer! How does it finish? The story isn't finished!"

The dark smile changed, transformed itself into a terrible glare. "But mine is. And that is all I am concerned about. I'm tired, Clay. I came back to you, not because I wanted to, but because I was compelled to. I played a game with you, and for the game to end I must finish it. So here I am. And this is all I have for you and all you will get from me, for I know very well how my own story shall end. Oh, there's more for you, a bit more, but this is the end as it pertains to you and me. My tale has given way to yours. Don't you see it, or are you still blind, you idiotic human? In the end, as I have said, it has always been about you."

"No." I said, my emotions heating to a roiling rage. "I don't see at all what this has to do with me. And without that, it has no ending. And without an ending, it can't ever be published. So there's some truth for you!"

"That doesn't matter."

"What do you mean it doesn't matter? That was your aim all along!"

"No." His mouth curved, revealing white teeth. "It wasn't. I told you I needed to tell you my story. Yes, I knew you would write it. I knew your ego would find the opportunity irresistible. But my goal all along has been to tell you my story."

"Just to be heard? Just to ruin my life?" I was shaking now.

"How long do you expect to live, Clay?"

"What?"

"I hope not very long."

My heart was beating erratically. He glanced at my chest, as though he could see it through my flesh.

"That heart of yours has outgrown its casing. It happened a long time ago. You'll go to the doctor in a couple of days, and he probably won't even properly diagnose it. But here, what's a trifle to me? I give you a parting gift: restrictive cardiomyopathy."

I blanched. "What? What is that?"

"Look it up. You're handy that way. Be sure to inform your doctor, or he might well miss it or, more likely, dismiss it as an anxiety disorder. It doesn't really matter if he does. The only thing that could possibly save you by now is a transplant."

Sweat trickled down my sides inside my sweater. "Why? Why did you do this?"

"Because this is your life, Clay: fleeting, ephemeral, and insignificant except for one thing, that El loved you. And you have missed it. Missed it all, completely. And now, look at you. Sweating, worried about your life, your story. Did you expect to live forever? Did you think this day would not come? It had to, if not in this way then in some other. I've done you a favor!"

"*What* favor?"

"Still blind!" His eyes flashed with an evil I found both horrible and horribly mesmerizing. "Look around you! Open your eyes! In telling you the truth about yourself more clearly than anyone ever hears it, I have shown you a choice that was before you all along. But no, even now you cannot see it."

"What choice?"

In the sandwich shop the demon had been incensed, but here before me now, I knew the purest hate in the universe was leveled, in this moment, at me.

"The truth, Clay! In the end I have told you the truth—a truth that, having heard, you are now doubly accountable for. Yes, if you become one of them, those shining souls, what can I do about it? But reject the truth even by refusing to decide, and reap the consequence you rightfully deserve. Do you hear that? That is accountability. It is the sound of hell, calling for you! Having had such an extravagant gift offered you, your rejection can only result in damnation far greater than that of those to whom it was never offered."

His lips pulled back from his teeth. "This then, shall be my singular consolation, my bitter solace: that when you die—and the time will be soon—there will be at least one of El's precious clay humans more damned to hell than I!"

I gaped as he got up. This time it was I who grabbed his wrist. But he shook me off as though I were an insect.

I fell back. "Where are you going?"

"I have an appointment," he growled. And he strode out into the black night, the light of the moon blue in his hair.

I STAGGERED HOME, HEARTSICK—literally—knowing he was right. But knowing, also, what I needed to do.

I had come to the end of the story only to find that it was no story at all. That my childhood training in the stuff of myth was a living and breathing reality.

That indeed, there was a monster.

Just not the one I thought.

EPILOGUE

Kat,

Here it is, in its entirety. I need you to believe me when I tell you this story is true—true, and double-edged. As you read these pages, do so knowing they will force a decision from you, one that was in front of you even before you held them in your hands.

I want to talk when you are done. If, by chance, something has happened to me by then, bury the pages, burn them, publish them—it doesn't matter. As I said, the choice is there whether the others read it or not.

In the end I don't know what was more poisonous—his story and my obsession with it, my vacillating belief, or Lucian himself.

He's gone. He's accomplished what he came for. As for me, I need time to think and to make my own decision. Unfortunately for me, time is the one thing I do not have.

Take care, Kat. I would have liked to have known you better.

Clay

Author's Notes

I have based Lucian's account of prefall bliss on a widely but by no means universally held understanding of Ezekiel 28:11–19. Some commentators view this passage as a literal lament or prophecy against the ruler of Tyre, a wealthy Phoenician city in what is now Lebanon. Others believe the prophet addresses the power energizing the throne of Tyre—Lucifer himself. Advocates of this second interpretation cite the fact that the king is referred to as having dwelt in Eden, been an anointed cherub, been created (rather than propagated), and been blameless since his creation. This is the interpretation I chose to underpin my fictional imagining of Lucifer's prefall existence.

I have supplemented my imagining of Lucifer's fall with a similar interpretation of Isaiah 14:12–14, wherein the "son of the morning" states his intention to ascend to heaven with five famous "I wills." Again, this is a widely known but not universally held understanding of this passage, which on the surface laments the prophetic fall of the pagan king of Babylon, a contemporary of the prophet.

In the ancient Near East, cherubs were depicted as beings with an animal body (usually a lion or bull), wings, and a human head. Large cherub statues often guarded the gates of ancient pagan temples. Biblically speaking, cherubs may be found guarding the gates of Eden (Genesis 3:24) adorning the lid of the ark of the covenant as golden statues (Exodus 25:17–22) and holding up God's throne (Ezekiel 1:4–28; 10:1–22).

I've only referenced cherubim, seraphim, and angels (including archangels) in this story, but the Bible notes other significant rankings of spiritual forces: thrones (Colossians 1:16), dominions (Ephesians 1:21; Colossians 1:16), principalities (Ephesians 1:21; 3:16; 6:12; Colossians 1:16) and powers (Ephesians 1:21; 3:10; 6:12; Colossians 1:16). The only authority over the upper (cherubic) rank is Elohim; even the well-known archangel Michael must employ God's authority against Lucifer as in Jude 9.

I have assumed that the rock garden in Eden of Ezekiel 28:13 where Lucifer resided before his rebellion physically preexisted the Eden of Genesis and that it was the (unspoiled) earth mentioned in Genesis 1:1. For the sake of story, I've theorized a chaotic ruin of Lucifer's first garden in Eden before the formless and dark Eden of Genesis 1:2.

Ezekiel says the object of his lament dwelled in "the holy mount of God" (Ezekiel 28:14, 16). The exact phrase, "the holy mount of God" occurs nowhere else in Scripture though Jerusalem is sometimes called "the holy mount" where God dwells in His temple (Psalm 99:9; Isaiah 56:7). For this telling, I have imagined God's heavenly dwelling as a spectacular spiritual mountain—that is to say, something both and either physical and figurative simply because I cannot think that our concrete world would rely on the same physical laws and logic as one inhabited by spiritual beings in a perfect Eden before even the creation of the sun or moon. Other references to a mountain of God indicating government are: Isaiah 2:2 and Daniel 2:34–35, 44–45.

The Bible distinguishes between angels fallen and unfallen/ elect (1 Timothy 5:21), and is specific about the judgment and fate of the lost (2 Peter 2:4; Jude 6). Therefore, I have based Lucian's odium on the fact that the Bible makes no mention of a messianic provision for fallen angels, no matter how they curiously long to look into the mysteries of salvation (1 Peter 1:12).

Lucifer derives his name from several sources. In Isaiah 14:12 the Hebrew is *helel*, meaning "shining" (in the way of celestial bodies)—hence, the interpretation "son of the morning," or "morning star." As the morning star (Venus) is considered the brightest of "stars"—and some hold that God referred to angels in Job 38:7 as "stars"—Lucifer was to have been the brightest of all creation. Throughout the New Testament angels are referred to as shining beings (Matthew 28:2–3; Revelation 10:1), and Lucifer is said to pass himself off as an angel of light. Satan is associated with Lucifer as having fallen like lightning from heaven (Luke 10:18, as associated with Ezekiel 28:17), and having fallen because of his pride (1 Timothy 3:6, as associated with Isaiah 14).

The name *Satan*, at its most basic, denoted an adversary or enemy of human or spiritual origin. In the lives of Job and Joshua, Lucifer embodied the role of antagonistic accuser and adversary of the faithful. Throughout the Bible Satan is given many other names including God of This Age (2 Corinthians 4:4), Prince of the Power of the Air (Ephesians 2:2), and Prince of This World (Matthew 4:8; Luke 4:5–7; John 14:30).

Lucian's human guises are based on the abundance of angels that appear as humans throughout the Bible. The book of Job indicates that Satan has the power to inflict sickness

(Job 2:7), control elements (Job 1:16–19), and inflict discourage-
ment, doubt and disappointment (Job 3:1–10; 7:11; 10:1–18).
Job is explicit that Satan has no power to harm those protected
by God. Ephesians 6:10–18 indicates that children of God pos-
sess the means to withstand Satanic attack.

I need to cite my great reliance on H. LaVern Schafer's work,
Satan: The Enemy Without (Schafer, 1996) in addition to the
usual commentaries and indexes, as well as books such as Billy
Graham's *Angels*.

Last, I should say that despite my research I have never come
to the point that I feel I completely understand the implications
of God's relationship with spiritual beings or the nuances of
passages like the ones found in Ezekiel and Isaiah. I chose the
interpretations I did for the sense they make to me and also for
their storytelling merit. I encourage you to pass my views and
these notes through the sieve of your own discernment and to
use them as a springboard for your own investigation.

Why I Wrote
Demon: A Memoir

One day, as I drove the stretch of Nebraska road that leads to my acreage, I found myself wondering what it would be like to be angelic and fallen. Would I go around tempting people to lust, covet, envy . . . just for kicks? It seemed too shallow a motivation for any complex, spiritual creature. There had to be more to it.

Suddenly, I realized that being angelic and fallen was similar to being human and fallen—except for one major difference: the provision of a Messiah.

I immediately wondered what it must feel like to be unquestionably damned—and worse, to watch humans luxuriate in and take for granted the grace made available to them from a doting God. And I thought: *Why wouldn't an angelic creation resent a human recipient of God's grace? And why wouldn't a demon want to prove that creature unworthy again and again as a result?* Now I knew what it must feel like to be an angelic outsider looking in with jealous eyes and razored heart.

And so let me ask you: What if you made one mistake?

One.

What if one moment you were worshipping the Mighty God and Creator that brought you into existence . . . and the next you were damned for eternity?

You had never seen sin, you had no experience with death, you had never felt separation from your God. But you had turned your worship to the greatest being under God in an impulsive moment that seemed to make sense at the time. You only belatedly realized that something had changed. You just weren't sure what.

What if you watched as that same God replaced you in his affections with a baser, uglier, mortal breed—a creature made of clay. And what if you watched in horror as he breathed into their mud bodies the essence of his own spirit—a gift you had never received?

And what if they took every God-given thing considered precious by you for granted as they failed again and again . . . and then turned away from God altogether?

Would you feel some satisfaction when God, unable to allow them to continue, decided to destroy their world and all of the clay people along with it? And would that satisfaction be lost when you learned he couldn't bear to kill them all but had decided to spare a family—a seed group of those mud people to repopulate the earth?

What if you watched as God patiently taught them laws so they could stay in relationship with him . . . and they continued to do the same things that had ruined their relationship with him in the first place—over and over again?

Remember: You only did one thing.

And what would you think if that same God decided, in a radical move, to become one of them, to take on that mud flesh forever, and to let them kill him, and to die for them, so they could be reconciled with him and with him again . . . forever?

You were supposed to be with him forever. You only did one thing.

And how would you feel upon knowing that not every mud person jumped at the chance to have that great gift you feel so much more deserving of—only one thing—that the majority of the mud people decided they didn't want or need?

Would you be jealous? Would you hate the mud people?

Would you want them to die?

Of course you would.

And so I reread the story of God's love affair with humans through this new lens, and *Demon: A Memoir* was born.

Interesting Facts about Demon

- The quote by Isak Dinesen is from the book *Out of Africa*, which is also the author's favorite movie.
- The liquor stores mentioned in the book were originally written as "package stores," a New England term.
- The Borders store in chapter 2 was the location of the author's first book signing of *Demon*.
- Esad is based loosely on the story of a local Bosnian tailor in the author's home city.
- Sheila's two boys, Justin and Caleb, are the two sons of the author's friend since first grade, Julie.
- The star-shaped perfume bottle that used to sit on Aubrey's bathroom counter is "Angel" by Thierry Mugler.
- Lucian's "Carpe Brewem" sweatshirt in the coffee shop chapter came from Lazlo's brewery in Lincoln, Nebraska.
- Lucian in the coffee shop (wearing the brewery sweatshirt) is the author's friend, Scott.
- The Asian man on the plan with the receding hairline is the author's father.
- Lucian's "Animals Taste Good" T-shirt in the Commons chapter is made by David and Goliath.

- The author and her sister have a cameo at the bar at the Four Seasons Hotel.
- Every piece of art mentioned in the museum chapter was on display at the time of the chapter's writing in 2005.
- The house in Haverhill is based on one owned by the author's college friend, Heather.
- Clay's small apartment building on Norfolk is based on one exactly like it in real life.
- The Gospel Room is a real church the size of a house across the street on Norfolk.
- The tea shop in Cambridge is called Tea Luxe in real life.
- All of the Bible searches conducted in *Demon* (based on BibleGateway.com) yielded the same results that Clay found at the time of *Demon's* writing.
- Clay's office exists as described in Cambridge, across from the former Quantum Books.
- The author is named for a Puccini opera. The operas mentioned in *Demon* are Puccini operas.
- The dim sum restaurant is the China Pearl, in Chinatown.
- The Four Seasons Bristol room was indeed refurbished just before the rewriting of *Demon*.
- The Grover book is a real book acquired by the author in the manner described by Clay.
- Clay's Cabo getaway took place at the Riu resort.

You really do have a choice to make.

You can find more expanded materials on *Demon: A Memoir* at www.Pureenjoyment.com!

Acknowledgments

When *Demon* was first published in 2007, I had no idea what lay before me. I knew it would be a great journey, but what I did not know is how many amazing people would come alongside me, or the chord that this story would strike in the hearts of others.

I have the best readers in the world. Thank you—for your letters, your prayers, your support and encouragement. You are with me each time I sit down to write; you are constantly on my mind.

Thank you to the champions: my agent, Steve Laube, and my editor, Karen Ball. Words are feeble tools; they cannot do my gratitude to either of you justice.

Julie Gwinn, I am so grateful for you. Everyone at B&H, it is a privilege to work with you. Kris and Jeff Beckenbach, Chad Bring, Katie Weaver, Kristin Nelson: thank you for keeping me relevant and (relatively) sane. And thank you: my friends, my sister Amy, my heart-sister Meredith, and Rick, my beloved, for loving me even when I'm not (sane—which is most of the time).

I owe a great debt of gratitude to those who enabled my obsession and made this book possible: Joyce Hart, Jeff Gerke, Karen Lee-Thorp, Reagen Reed, Dan Mueller, Conan Schafer, Peggy Malzacher, Don Hawkins, Greg Stier, Tim Hodges, Scott Boles, Alice Yoon, Angie Bentley, and my parents (all of them).

Thank you most eminently to my God, Elohim, for your relentless pursuit of this girl's heart.

PROLOGUE

I have seen paradise and ruin. I have known bliss and terror. I have walked with God.

And I know that God made the heart the most fragile and resilient of organs, that a lifetime of joy and pain might be encased in one mortal chamber.

I still recall my first moment of consciousness—an awareness I've never seen in the eyes of any of my own children at birth: the sheer ignorance and genius of consciousness, when we know nothing and accept everything.

Of course, the memory of that waking moment is fainter now, like the smell of the soil of that garden, like the leaves of the fig tree in Eden after dawn—dew and leaf green. It fades with that sense of something once tasted on the tip of the tongue, savored now in memory, replaced by the taste of something similar but never quite the same.

His breath a lost sough, the scent of earth and leaf mold that was his sweaty skin has faded too quickly. So like an Eden dawn—dew on fig leaves.

His eyes were blue, my Adam's.

How I celebrated that color, shrouded now in shriveled eyelids—he who was never intended to have even a wrinkle!

But even as I bend to smooth his cheek, my hair has become a white waterfall upon his Eden—flesh and loins that gave life to so many.

I think for a moment that I hear the One and that he is weeping. It is the first time I have heard him in so long, and my heart cries out: He is dead! My father, my brother, my love!

I envy the earth that envelopes him. I envy the dust that comes of him and my children who sow and eat of it.

This language of Adam's—the word that meant merely "man" before it was his name—given him by God himself, is now mine. And this is my love song: I will craft these words into the likeness of the man before I, too, return to the earth of Adam's bosom.

My story has been told in only the barest of terms. It is time you heard it all. It is my testament to the strength of the heart, which has such capacity for joy, such space for sorrow, like a vessel that fills and fills without bursting.

My seasons are nearly as many as a thousand. So now listen, sons, and hear me, daughters. I, Havah, fashioned by God of Adam, say this:

In the beginning, there was God . . .

But for me, there was Adam.

I

A whisper in my ear: *Wake!*

Blue. A sea awash with nothing but a drifting bit of down, flotsam on an invisible current. I closed my eyes. Light illuminated the thin tissues of my eyelids.

A bird trilled. Near my ear: the percussive buzz of an insect. Overhead, tree boughs stirred in the warming air.

I lay on a soft bed of herbs and grass that tickled my cheek, my shoulders, and the arch of my foot, whispering sibilant secrets up to the trees.

From here, I felt the thrum of the sap in the stem, the pulsing veins of the vine, the beat of my heart in euphony with hundreds more around me, the movement of the earth a thousand miles beneath.

I sighed as one returning to sleep, to retreat to the place I had been before, the realm of silence and bliss—wherever that is.

Wake!

I opened my eyes again upon the milling blue, saw it spliced by the flight of a bird, chevron in the sky.

This time, the voice came not to my ear, but directly to my stirring mind: *Wake!*

There was amusement in it.

I knew nothing of where or what I was, did not understand the polyphony around me or the wide expanse like a blue eternity before me.

But I woke and knew I was alive.

A rustle, a groan practically in my ear. I twitched at a stirring against my hip. A moment later, a touch drifted across a belly I did not yet know I owned, soft as a leaf skittering along the ground.

A face obscured my vision. I screamed. Not with fear—I had no acquaintance with fear—nor with startlement, because I had been aware of the presence already, but because it was the only statement that came to lips as artless as mine.

The face disappeared and returned, blinking into my own, the blue above captured in twin pools. Then, like a gush of water from a rock, gladness thrilled my heart. But its source was not me.

At last! It came, unspoken—a different source than the voice before—the words thrust jubilantly to the sky: "At last!"

He was up on legs like the trunks of sturdy saplings, beating at the earth with his feet. He thumped his chest and shouted to the sun and clapped his hands. "At last!" He cried, his laughter like warm clay between the toes. He shook his shoulders and stomped the grass, slapping his chest as he shouted again and again. Though I did not understand the utterance, I knew its meaning at once: joy and exultation at something longed for suddenly found.

I tried to mimic his sound; it came out as a squawk and then a panting laugh. Overhead, a lark chattered an extravagant address. I squeaked a shrill reply. The face lowered to mine and the man's arms wrapped, womb-tight, around me.

"Flesh of my flesh," he whispered, his breath warm against my ear. His fingers drifted from my hair to my body, roaming like the goat on the hills of the sacred mount. I sighed, expelling the last remnants of that first air from my lungs—the last of the breath in them not drawn by me alone.

He was high-cheeked, this Adam, his lower lip dipping down like a folded leaf that drops sweet water to thirsty mouths. His brow was a hawk, soaring above the high cliffs, his eyes blue lusters beneath the fan of his lashes. But it was his mouth that I always came back to, where my eyes liked best to fasten after taking in the shock of those eyes. Shadow ran along his jaw, like obsidian dust clinging to the curve of it, drawing my eye to the plush flesh of his lips, again, again, again.

He touched my face and traced my mouth. I bit his finger. He gathered my hands and studied them, turning them over and back. He smelled my hair and lingered at my neck and gazed curiously at the rest of me. When he was finished, he began all over again, tasting my cheek and the salt of my neck, tracing the instep of my foot with a fingertip.

Finally, he gathered me up, and my vision tilted to involve an altogether new realm: the earth and my brown legs upon it. I clutched at him. I seemed a giant, towering above the earth—a giant as tall as he. My first steps stuttered across the ground as the deer in the hour of its birth, but then I pushed his hands away. My legs, coltish and lean, found their vigor as he urged me, walking far too fast, to keep up. He made for the orchard, and I bolted after him with a surge of strength and another of my squawking sounds. Then we were running—through grasses and over fledgling sloes, the dark wool of my hair flying behind me.

We raced across the valley floor, and my new world blurred around me: hyssop and poppy, anemone, narcissus, and lily. Roses grew on the foothills amidst the caper and myrtle.

A flash beside me: the long-bodied great cat. I slowed, distracted by her fluidity, the smooth curve of her head as she tilted it to my outstretched hand. I fell to the ground, twining my arms around her, fingers sliding along her coat. Her tongue was rough—unlike the adam's—and she rumbled as she rolled against me.

Far ahead, the adam called. Overhead, a hawk circled for a closer look. The fallow deer at a nearby stream lifted her head.

The adam called again, wordlessly, longing and exuberant. I got up and began to run, the lioness at my heels. I was fast— nearly as fast as she. Exhilaration rose from my lungs in quick pants—in laughter. Then, with a burst, she was beyond me.

She was gone by the time the adam caught me up in his arms. His hands stroked my back, my hips, my shoulder. I marveled at his skin—how smooth, how very warm it was.

"You are magnificent," He said, burying his face against me. "Ah, Isha—woman, taken from man!"

I said nothing; although I understood his meaning, I did not know his words. I knew with certainty and no notion of conceit, though, that he was right.

AT THE RIVER HE showed me how he cupped his hands to drink, and then cupped them again for me. I lowered my head and drank as a carp peered baldy from the shallows up at me.

We entered the water. I gasped as it tickled the backs of my knees and hot hairs under my arms, swirling about my waist as though around a staunch rock as our toes skimmed a multitude of pebbles. I wrapped my arms around his shoulders.

"All of this: water." He grunted a little bit as he swam toward the middle of the river where it widened into a broad swath across the valley floor. "Here—the current."

"Water." I understood, in the moment I spoke it, the element in all its forms—from the lake fed by the river to the high springs that flow from the abyss of the mount. I felt the pull of it as though it had a gravity all its own—as though it could sweep me out to the cold depths of the lake and lull me by the tides of the moon.

From the river I could see the high walls of our cradle: the great southern mount rising to heaven and, to the north, the foothills that became the long spine of a range that arched toward the great lake to the west.

I knew even then that this was a place set apart from the unseen lands to the north, the alluvial plain to the south, the great waters to the east and far to the west.

It was set apart solely because we dwelt in it.

But we were not alone. I could see *them*, after a time, even as we left the river and lay upon its banks. I saw them in sidelong glances when I looked at something else: a sunspot caught in the eye, a ripple in the air, a shock of light where there should be only shadow. And so I knew there were other beings, too.

The adam, who studied me, said nothing. We did not know their names.

THE FIRST VOICE I heard urging me to wake had not been the man's. Now I felt the presence of it near me, closer than the air, than even the adam's arms around me.

I returned the man's strange amazement, taken by his smooth, dark skin, the narrowness of his hips, his strange sex. He was warmer than I, as though he had absorbed the heat of the sun, and I laid my cheek against his flat breasts and listened to the changeling beat of his heart. My limbs, so fresh to me, grew heavy. As languor overtook me, I retreated from the sight of my lovely, alien world.

Perhaps in closing my eyes, I would return to the place I had been before.

For the first time since waking, I hoped not.

I slept to the familiar thrum of his heart as insects made sounds like sleepy twitches through the waning day.

When I woke, his cheek was resting against the top of my head. Emotion streamed from his heart, though his lips were silent.

Gratitude.

> I am the treasure mined from the rock, the gem
> prized from the mount.

He stirred only when I did and released me with great reluctance. By then the sun had moved along the length of our valley. My stomach murmured.

He led me to the orchard and fed me the firm flesh of plums, biting carefully around the pits and feeding the pieces to me until juice ran down our chins and bees came to sample it. He kissed my fingers and hands and laid his cheek against my palms.

That evening we lay in a bower of hyssop and rushes—a bower, I realized, that he must have made on a day before this one.

A day before I existed.

We observed together the changing sky as it cooled gold and russet and purple, finally anointing the clay earth red.

Taken from me. Flesh of my flesh. At last. I heard the timbre of his voice in my head in my last waking moment. Marvel and wonder were upon his lips as he kissed my closing eyes.

I knew then he would do anything for me.

THAT NIGHT I DREAMED of blackness. Black, greater than the depths of the river or the great abyss beneath the lake.

From within that nothingness there came a voice that was not a voice, that was neither sound nor word, but volition and command and genesis. And from the voice, a word that was no word, but the language of power and fruition.

There! A mote spark—a light first so small as the tip of a pine needle. It exploded past the periphery of my dreaming vision, obliterating the dark. The heavens were vast in an instant, stretching without cease to the edges of eternity.

I careened past new bodies that tugged me in every direction; even the tiniest particles possessed their own gravity. From each of them came the same concert, that symphony of energy and light.

I came to stand upon the earth. It was a great welter of water, the surface of it ablaze with the refracted light of heavens upon heavens. It shook my every fiber, like a string that is plucked and allowed to resonate forever.

I was galvanized, made anew, thrumming that inaugural sound: the yawning of eternity.

Amidst it all came the unmistakable command:

Wake!